STEADFAST

Also by Claudia Gray

EVERNIGHT
STARGAZER
HOURGLASS
AFTERLIFE
BALTHAZAR

FATEFUL

SPELLCASTER

STEADFAST

~ A SPELLCASTER NOVEL ~

CLAUDIA GRAY

HARPER TEEN
An Imprint of HarperCollinsPublishers

HarperTeen is an imprint of HarperCollins Publishers.

Steadfast
www.epicreads.com

Library of Congress Cataloging-in-Publication Data
Gray, Claudia.
    Steadfast : a Spellcaster novel / Claudia Gray. — First edition.
    pages cm
    Sequel to: Spellcaster.
    Summary: "Nadia must stop the evil sorceress Elizabeth before
she lures the One Beneath to Captive's Sound, destroying the town
and everyone Nadia holds dear at the same time"— Provided by
publisher.
    ISBN 978-0-06-196122-9 (hardcover bdg.)
    [1. Witches—Fiction. 2. Magic—Fiction. 3. Blessing and cursing—
Fiction. 4. High schools—Fiction. 5. Schools—Fiction. 6. Family
life—Rhode Island—Fiction. 7. Rhode Island—Fiction. 8. Horror
stories.] I. Title.
PZ7.G77625Su 2014   2013015445
[Fic]—dc23   CIP
                                                                  AC

Typography by Torborg Davern

14 15 16 17 18   LP/RRDH   10 9 8 7 6 5 4 3 2 1
❖
First Edition

1

NEARLY EVERY GRAVESTONE IN THE CEMETERY OF Captive's Sound made a promise about forever.

The tombstones said things like *Remembered Evermore* or *Always In Our Hearts*. But for all those promises of unending devotion, nobody seemed to visit very often.

Today, though, three people had arrived.

Nadia Caldani stood directly under the cast-iron gate, which bent into curves to imitate leaves, roses, and thorns. Nothing about her wine-red sweater or dark jeans betrayed the most important secret Nadia had: that she was a witch— young and only half-trained, but more powerful than she'd once believed.

Her thick black hair was gathered back into a ponytail, which revealed the bruise on her temple and the small cuts along one cheek. Less than thirty-six hours before, she'd fought the darkest magic she knew of—wielded by Elizabeth, a sorceress, a servant of the One Beneath. Somehow, against all odds, Nadia had won. She knew she should feel elated. And yet fear still flickered inside her, a fire that wouldn't quite go out.

I got lucky, she thought. *But at least Elizabeth's gone, and we can start picking up the pieces.*

Next to her stood Mateo Perez, letter jacket slung over the black T-shirt and jeans he'd have to wear for his shift at the restaurant later. Nadia knew he'd always thought of himself as an outsider in Captive's Sound, isolated by the curse that followed his family. For a long time, he'd believed he had only one true friend—but that had only been Elizabeth playing games with his mind. Elizabeth had used him, and the curse, for her own purposes.

Nadia had been able to show Mateo what Elizabeth really was. More important, she'd discovered who he really was: someone strong enough to bear the curse. Someone who could serve as her Steadfast, the person who could amplify the strength of her witchcraft. Someone who now could *see* magic at work in the world, both light and dark. She had known within weeks that she needed him beside her, always. They'd kissed for the first time only days before; she felt like she could taste that kiss, feel his lips against hers, every moment.

We have time now, she thought as he looked sideways at Nadia. *All the time in the world. So today isn't about us. It's about Verlaine.*

Verlaine Laughton leaned against the gate, trying to catch her breath. Her pale hand clung to the cast-iron leaves; around her wrist dangled the white plastic bracelet she'd worn in the hospital and hadn't cut off yet. Though her dads had protested her going out with her friends so soon after being discharged, she'd convinced them she needed it. "Sunshine," she'd said. "Fresh air." That sounded healthy, right?

Now she was about to walk to her parents' graves for the first time in far too long. Through Nadia's magic, and maybe Mateo's abilities as her Steadfast, Verlaine would learn whether their deaths had been caused by dark magic—whether every sorrow in her lonely life, all the way from being orphaned as a baby to having silver-gray hair at age seventeen, was a result of a spell Elizabeth had cast.

Elizabeth's gone forever, Verlaine told herself. *I can't get back at her now no matter what. There's nothing we can do to reverse the spell now that Elizabeth's dead. So what good does it do to find out?*

Nadia put her hand on Verlaine's shoulder. "Are you okay?"

"Yeah." Verlaine straightened to her full height—several inches taller than Nadia, even a couple above Mateo. "I'm fine."

"We don't have to do this now," Mateo said. "We could come back in a few days. There's no rush."

"I know we don't have to do it now." The words rattled out of Verlaine, too fast and too shaky, but determined. "We don't *have* to do it ever. But I want to know. Let's just get it over with."

"All right. Come on." Nadia put her arm around Verlaine, and that human contact helped her feel better.

Nadia had said that the magical resonance around Verlaine was old, going back very nearly to the beginning of her life. If Elizabeth had been responsible for the spell, they would be unable to break it—now that Elizabeth was dead.

But the magic around Verlaine was an especially cruel one. It kept her from being fully noticed or appreciated. The magic kept her from being loved.

It wasn't an absolute barrier. Her family, who had loved her from infancy and thus before the spell, still cared deeply for her. And there had been moments during the past few weeks when other, stronger magical forces had temporarily canceled out the effect of whatever it was that had been done to Verlaine—when she felt like her friends truly cared for her.

Those moments were fleeting, however. Even now, Verlaine knew Nadia was here mostly out of a sense of obligation; when her eyes met Mateo's, she saw the same sense of guilt. It wasn't their fault any more than it was Verlaine's. The magic was to blame.

Even if the curse is forever, I want the truth. Just so I know what I'm dealing with, instead of always wondering why.

They walked slowly along the rocky path that outlined the graveyard. Captive's Sound had clung to this craggy, joyless bit of the Rhode Island coastline since colonial times; several of the tombstones were centuries old, blackened with age, the once-deep carved letters worn to mere scratches by rain and time. The chill of the November wind was sharpened by the salt air as it sent gold leaves skittering past their feet and caught at Verlaine's long, gray hair.

Captive's Sound was somehow fundamentally sick. Rotten at the core, Nadia thought, from all the dark magic that had been worked here over the centuries by Elizabeth Pike. She'd hoped Elizabeth's death might have begun to heal the town. But the trees were still stark and too small, the light more watery and less bright.

Then again, it was only November 2. *Give it time to heal,* Nadia reminded herself.

Verlaine stopped short, her Converse sneakers kicking up dust on the path. "There. My parents are over there."

She pointed at a still-smooth granite block, one of the long tombstones that bracketed dual graves. Nadia helped lead her toward them. She noticed Mateo taking care not to step on any place where a dead person might lie. From some people that would only have been superstition; from Mateo, she knew, it was a sign of respect.

Finally they were at the foot of the graves, looking at an epitaph that read: *Richard and Maisie Laughton, beloved children, loving parents.*

Gone from us too soon.

"They don't have any flowers." Verlaine's voice was small. "I used to want to bring them when I was little, but it always made Uncle Dave cry. He was close to my mom; he said she was his best friend, always. Coming here hurt him so much that I quit asking. But now they haven't had flowers for years and years."

"It's okay," Mateo said. "They know you still love them."

"Do they? We proved magic exists, and witches exist, and also crazy-ass sorceresses who sit near you in chemistry class, but we don't know anything about heaven, last I checked." Verlaine wiped at her face, though she wasn't crying; it was as though she was trying to focus herself, Nadia thought. "Or is that in your Book of Shadows, Nadia? Proof that there's an afterlife?"

"Nope. That's as mysterious to you as it is to me." Nadia decided the best way to comfort Verlaine at this point was to stay focused on the task at hand. "Verlaine, I want you to go stand between the two graves."

The effect was immediate. Verlaine steadied just at the thought of having something constructive to do. "Up by the gravestone? Or does it matter?"

"It doesn't, but there might be some, uh, physical impact. So standing farther back is good." She glanced over her shoulder. "Getting a little distance is a good idea for you, too, Mateo."

He smiled at her, and it was one of those moments where it hit her all over again—how somehow this wonderful guy had come into her life exactly when she was trying to shut everyone out. Mateo had beaten down the doors. Burned the fences. Picked the lock on the gate. "Distance," he said. "Got it. You don't need a Steadfast for this?"

"I always need my Steadfast," Nadia said softly. "But you'll be more than close enough."

Verlaine positioned herself between her parents' graves, a strange look on her face as she gazed down at the place where her mother lay. Her usual vintage look was less polished today, but she'd put on acid-washed jeans and a poufy white sweater for an eighties vibe. All Nadia could think was how pale and thin she looked. Like a ghost among the graves. "Here?"

"That works." Nadia lifted her hand and took hold of her wrist—specifically, the quartz charm that dangled from her bracelet. The bracelet wasn't just a piece of jewelry; it was her way of keeping the primal elements she needed for her witchcraft close at every moment.

But the elements alone weren't the magic. They only grounded Nadia, made her ready. For magic, she needed the spell.

For revealing magic done long ago:

Fear conquered.
Love betrayed.
Secrets laid bare.

Those were the ingredients. Now, to give them power. Nadia closed her eyes and thought of the deepest, most emotionally resonant memories that fulfilled each—

Standing with Mateo in the Halloween carnival fire, aware the house was about to collapse around them, facing Elizabeth's magic and fighting back with her own.

"It's better this way," Mom said at the doorway, suitcase in hand, not even looking Nadia directly in the face before she left her daughter behind forever.

Meeting Elizabeth's eyes across the chemistry lab as one of Nadia's spells went haywire, and Elizabeth's mocking smile, her utter lack of surprise, revealing that she was another witch—but horribly, undoubtedly, a Sorceress.

Nadia opened her eyes to see a bottle-green mist drifting around them—centered on the graves, and on Verlaine. A soft sound rustled through the air, like silk on silk. Verlaine's long, silver hair began to drift around her, as though she were underwater.

"It's cold," Verlaine whispered.

"Stay very still." Nadia held up one hand as a warning. Verlaine's eyes went wide, but she didn't move.

The mist swirled a little faster, then froze in place—literally. One moment it was vapor; the next moment, greenish crystals of ice sleeted down around them. Verlaine winced and covered her head as the ice rattled on her parents' gravestones. It instantly melted, running through the carved letters to drip down onto the brownish grass below.

Verlaine peeked through her fingers. ". . . That's it?"

Nadia nodded. Mateo stepped closer to them, and when she turned toward him, what she already suspected was confirmed in his eyes.

"What did it look like to you?" she asked. Mateo, as her Steadfast, possessed a window into magic that even she could never match.

"Dark red metallic . . . streaks, I guess." He struggled, obviously trying to find the right words. "Like they were raining down in this greenish mist."

"We saw the mist, too. That was a freebie." Verlaine

walked toward them, her steps unsteady. Nadia wasn't sure whether that was from the lingering effects of what Elizabeth had done to her last week or the emotions she had to be feeling. "So. Dark red. That's old magic, right? What did the spell tell you, Nadia?"

Best to say it as quickly and cleanly as possible, Nadia decided. "It's not just an echo of an old spell. Whatever spell this was—it was cast a long time ago, but it's still at work. It's linked to your parents' deaths. It's unquestionably dark magic. And"—the next was just Nadia's judgment call, but she was certain—"yes, Elizabeth was the one responsible."

Verlaine didn't react at first. Her pale face remained almost expressionless, and except for her wind-tossed hair, she didn't move.

Mateo took a step closer to her. "Verlaine? Are you okay?"

"I could at least have brought some flowers." With that, Verlaine crossed her arms and let her head droop, drawing into herself.

Verlaine had told them the story of how her parents had died—and even to her it was only a story, one she'd been told, because she was still a baby when it happened. She'd been found wailing in her crib; her parents' dead bodies lay in their bedroom, both apparently so severely and suddenly ill that they'd been unable even to call for help before they perished. Now they knew Elizabeth was the one responsible. Elizabeth would have been there that day, ignoring baby Verlaine's cries as she looked down on her two victims.

But why? Had Verlaine's mother been a witch, too,

someone Elizabeth destroyed for opposing her? If Elizabeth had killed the father out of spite, why leave Verlaine alive? Had Elizabeth kept people from caring about Verlaine so that, perhaps, nobody would investigate her parents' deaths?

None of it made sense. Next Nadia would try spells to find out what had been done—that much, maybe, she could manage. However, she'd never be able to tell Verlaine why Elizabeth did it. That had died with Elizabeth.

She thought again of Mom walking out the door, leaving her family for good. Sometimes Nadia thought the worst part of it all was not knowing why.

Mateo took her hand as they both stepped closer to Verlaine. The touch was still new enough to send a thrill along Nadia's skin. "Hey," Mateo said quietly to Verlaine. "Are you okay?"

"Next time I'll run by Jasmine's first." Verlaine brushed back her silvery hair; her hand was still bruised from the hospital IV. "That's the florist in town, Nadia. I forgot you were new here and you might not know. I can run by there and pick up a dozen roses. Two dozen. Or—how many roses do you think they might have at any one time?"

Nadia wanted to tell Verlaine that everything would be okay, but she didn't want to give her friend false hope. "Listen. I want to try something."

"Another spell?"

"Yeah. I want to find out exactly what was done to you, and whether there's some way to reverse it."

Verlaine glanced up at that. "*Can* you reverse it?"

"Maybe. We won't know until we try." Nadia gave her an encouraging smile. As long as they remained near the bodies of her parents—the first victims of the spell, and thus the ones who bore the deepest marks of magic—Nadia thought they had a shot.

She raised her hand to her bracelet, ready to begin her next spell—

Verlaine screamed. Mateo grabbed Nadia and pulled her back—only moments before her hair stood on end. It was as if lightning struck, but instead of a second's flash of lightning, a column of fire swirled up in front of them, twisting and writhing with its heat. The roar of it deafened Nadia, and she staggered into Mateo's arms.

"My parents!" Verlaine cried. The flames danced on their graves. No, not danced—*consumed*. As Nadia watched in horror, the graves caved in, as though the coffins and bodies within them had instantly disappeared.

The fire vanished as quickly as it had come. For a few moments they all stood there, staring at the scorched earth, their quickened breathing the only break from the silence.

"What—" Verlaine had to stop and take a deeper breath before she could finish. "Nadia, what did you do?"

"That wasn't me," Nadia said.

From behind them came a voice: "No. It was me."

They all turned as one. Standing beneath a stone angel was Elizabeth.

Alive and well.

Elizabeth smiled. "Just who I was looking for."

2

THEY ALL SEEMED SO SURPRISED TO SEE HER. ELIZABETH
would have assumed they understood the full dimensions of
her power by now, but apparently not.

"You're dead." Mateo's eyes narrowed; every word he
spoke was rougher than the last. "You died in the carnival
fire. You were trapped there; I saw you."

"I saw you in the carnival fire, too," Elizabeth pointed
out. "You seem to be alive and well. Why not me? And
Nadia also, I see."

Important though Mateo had been to her in the past,
Elizabeth had come here for one reason only. Nadia Caldani
was the one who interested her now.

Nadia found her voice. "We stopped you. I know we did.
Halloween was the only night you could have pulled it off.
That means you failed."

How naive they were. "Did you think my plan was to

12

destroy Captive's Sound? That was only collateral damage. You were clever to find a way around it, Nadia."

And I remain alive to help the One Beneath on His great journey into the mortal realm, to bridge the gulf between His world and this one, not just for a moment, but for all time.

"The deaths of all those hundreds of people—maybe thousands—was only *collateral damage*?" Nadia's expression was disbelieving, though Elizabeth wasn't sure why. It hardly signified.

"I'm sincerely grateful." Elizabeth saw no reason not to be honest. "You're a gifted witch. But you're untrained in the higher forms of the Craft, and without a teacher."

Nadia's head jerked back, as though she had been struck. Reminding her of her mother's abandonment hit a nerve.

Elizabeth continued, "You need someone to guide you as you complete your training. Without instruction, you'll never fulfill your potential, which would be a crime. Don't you agree?"

"It's none of your business," Mateo said, stepping between her and Nadia.

"It is," Elizabeth said, "if I become her teacher."

The effect of this was what Elizabeth had anticipated: flat disbelief. Several moments passed before Nadia managed to say, "You're not serious."

"Is it not one of the guiding principles of the Craft? To offer instruction and assistance to one another?"

"You're not a member of the Craft—not any longer!" Nadia retorted. The bruises on her face must have hurt terribly; they made her anger look ugly, almost desperate. "You're sworn to the One Beneath!"

"You mean I broke one of the First Laws?" Elizabeth cast a meaningful look at Mateo. "Like speaking of magic to a male?"

Nadia shook her head. "That's different."

"Is it? A coven wouldn't think so. They'd throw both of us out, not just me. We're outsiders together, you and I. You just haven't realized it yet." The wind pulled at Elizabeth's curls, made her skin prickle into goose bumps beneath her thin cotton dress. Now that she was no longer immortal, she could feel the cold. It was a curious sensation, new enough not to be unwelcome despite the discomfort.

The world was fresh to her again. After centuries of boredom, Elizabeth found this an almost boundless delight.

"Think of it," she said to Nadia. "I've lived longer than any other witch. I know magic nobody else can ever touch. I'm willing to teach you everything. What have you got to lose?"

"My soul, for one." Nadia wrapped her arms around herself as she stepped closer to Mateo, who embraced her. "Serving the One Beneath is evil. I'll never do that. *Never.*"

People who had never been immortal had some strange ideas about *never*. Elizabeth considered pointing this out, but at that moment, the gray-haired girl spoke.

"You destroyed my parents," she said, voice trembling. "Even their bodies. That was all I had left."

"Blame your friend for that," Elizabeth replied. "I can't have you undoing all my hard work."

"This isn't happening." The gray-haired girl's words were

hardly more than a whisper, as though she lacked the breath to put any force behind them. And she was breathing fast—far too fast. "I'm not seeing you. This is a dream I'm having. A nightmare. That's all. It isn't real."

Elizabeth cocked her head. "Why would you think nightmares aren't real?"

The girl fainted, collapsing on the ground, her gray hair stark against the dark earth.

"Verlaine!" Nadia immediately kneeled by Verlaine's side, followed by Mateo. "What did you do to her?"

"Nothing. It's the shock, I suppose."

"Get away from us." Mateo looked as though he wanted to get up and punch her in the face, as foolish as it would have been to try. "You're pure evil."

Elizabeth shrugged and left. As she walked away, she heard them trying to rouse their fallen friend, their words caught in the rustling of the autumn leaves. It didn't matter what they were saying, just as it didn't matter that Nadia had refused her. Elizabeth had anticipated no other answer to this first invitation.

But the One Beneath had seen Nadia. Valued her potential.

And what the One Beneath wanted would be His.

Elizabeth would see to it.

"What the hell is Elizabeth doing alive?" Mateo said as he drove, occasionally glancing into the backseat, where Nadia had Verlaine's head pillowed on her shoulder. "That should be impossible."

"Not impossible." Nadia kept fanning Verlaine's face; although Verlaine was awake now, she was in a sort of daze. *I should have known she was too fragile for this!* Nadia thought. "Everything I thought Elizabeth was trying to achieve—that wasn't even her plan. Just the shadow of her plan. Obviously I didn't understand what she was up to at all."

Mateo peered around again. "But you stopped her."

"I stopped her from destroying the town. I didn't stop her from doing whatever she actually wanted to do." Her ignorance stung as badly as her failure. But Nadia refused to give in to it. Okay, fine, Elizabeth escaped this time. Not next time.

"So how do we figure out what she's really up to?" Mateo said.

"I go through every resource I've got, starting tonight—and oh, my God, Mateo, look at the road! We nearly hit that truck."

"Okay, okay." Mateo turned to the front again. Nadia imagined driving Verlaine's enormous clunker of a car was a far cry from steering his motorcycle around, and the last thing any of them needed was another accident.

Particularly Verlaine.

"Verlaine?" She patted the side of her friend's face. "Are you okay?"

Wearily Verlaine nodded. "Sure. Fine. Except for the suicidal ideation, I'm dandy."

"Don't joke about that," Mateo said. He sounded harsh; no doubt he meant to. His mother had killed herself while

16

in the throes of the family curse.

"I'm sorry," Verlaine said. "Really. I mean it. I just—seeing Elizabeth, and knowing she killed my parents—I wanted it to be a bad dream. I kept thinking if I wanted it enough I could just make her *not be there.* Which doesn't make any sense, but my brain wasn't exactly in good working order at the time. I'm not sure it is now, either. By the way, I might throw up."

"It's your car. Hurl away." But Nadia scooted her legs away just in case.

Her mind raced the entire time they got Verlaine back to her dads' house, apologized profusely for overtaxing her, and helped her uncle Gary get her tucked in. Nadia had hardly had a chance to catch her breath since the Halloween carnival, or any time to analyze what had happened there. It had never occurred to her that Elizabeth might have another agenda besides causing death and destruction.

She glanced over at Mateo as they walked away from Verlaine's house. The two of them had saved countless people in town, even if nobody else ever knew it. That mattered more than anything else.

Their last victory had only been a partial victory. Fine. Nadia decided it was also only her first victory. One way or another, Elizabeth was going down.

"I want to go straight to Elizabeth's house with an ax," Mateo confessed. "That's a bad idea, right?"

"Very bad." Nadia shuddered as she remembered the one time she'd broken into Elizabeth's home. Elizabeth hadn't been there; she hadn't needed to be. Because her Book of Shadows was there—the spell book each witch created throughout her lifetime. With every spell added, a Book of Shadows would gain magical power until it could become a vital source of energy. Elizabeth had been around for about four centuries, which meant her Book of Shadows was so powerful it was nearly sentient. The book itself had trapped Nadia in cobwebs, attempting to keep her until Elizabeth could return to deal with her personally. Her skin began to itch as she remembered the spiders, and she swatted once at her jean legs. "Ax murder? Bad idea, the vast majority of the time."

"Okay, fine, no ax murdering—but what *are* we doing? We can't just let Elizabeth get away with it!" Mateo looked furious as he turned to her, but when their eyes met, his expression softened. He slid his arms around her waist and drew her near.

The touch surprised Nadia more than it should have. But they were still so new. She had to remind herself that he loved her *back*, and they actually had a chance to make this work. After everything they'd been through, this sense of possibility was completely unfamiliar. Something had gone right in her messed-up life, just this once. Love was dizzying, wonderful, even a little bit scary—

"I'm sorry," he said. "Elizabeth makes me crazy."

"Who could blame you?" Perhaps the cruelest part of Elizabeth's manipulations was the way she had convinced Mateo that she was his best friend, even his only friend.

He had loved Elizabeth like a sister until the moment he learned that every fond memory he had of them growing up together was false, a lie implanted to win his trust and make him easier to use. "Of course you hate her. You have the right. But we shouldn't confront her until we know what we're doing."

"I know. I get that. It's just hard to think about anything else, you know?" Mateo brushed a lock of hair away from her forehead; though he was careful, and his touch soft, he came too close to one of her cuts. The sensitivity crackled across her nerve endings. Nadia sucked in a breath; Mateo's eyes darkened and he brought her closer. "Hey, Dad's at La Catrina for another couple hours. You want to come by the house?" His smile was teasing, warm, hopeful. "Give us both something else to think about?"

"I can't. Dad and Cole's flight got in a little while ago. They'll be here within the hour."

The thought of going back to Mateo's for a while—lying in his arms, kissing her fears away—warmed her from the inside.

But right now Nadia wanted to see her father and brother even more. After all, when they'd left for New York the day before Halloween, she hadn't known whether she would ever see them again.

When Mateo nodded and smiled, she knew he understood without her even having to explain. He whispered, "Then give me a good-bye kiss."

Their lips met gently at first, but then their mouths parted slightly and the warmth and taste of his mouth seemed to be the only thing in the world. Nadia leaned into his embrace, clutching him closer. The kiss deepened—but then a rush of cold wind raked across them, rattling tree branches and chilling them to the quick. Leaves swirled up around them so fast and thick that for a moment Nadia thought they were being rushed at by a flock of birds. She and Mateo stepped back from each other in their surprise, then laughed at how weird that had been.

And I thought Chicago winters were bizarre, Nadia thought.

Mateo kissed her again, sweet and swift. "Okay. Come on, let's get you home."

"We went to Chelsea Piers!" Cole said as he towed his little backpack upstairs, Nadia by his side. "We got to go wall climbing *and* ice skating both!"

"Awesome!" She ruffled his hair. "You had a good time, huh?"

"Definitely."

Her father called from the hallway, where he was hefting the suitcase to his room. "Velma's totally all right?"

He could never recall Verlaine's name correctly. Dad wasn't very absentminded; in fact, he was pretty sharp. Nadia wondered if his inability to remember his daughter's best friend was part of the strange spell that surrounded Verlaine.

She said only, "Apparently Verlaine's fine. The hospital says there's no permanent damage. She's still kind of weak, though."

"Well, thank goodness she woke up. Scary stuff." He appeared in the doorway of Cole's room, where Cole was "unpacking" by taking his stuff from his backpack and throwing it on the floor.

Nadia thought her dad looked completely wrung out; a few straight days of handling Cole on your own could do that to you. She laughed. "Did you get a moment to yourself the whole time?"

"Oh. Well." His face colored slightly. "Remember how the Paulsons moved to New York just before we moved here? I, ah, called Ethan's mom while we were in town, so he and Cole could get together and play. Thought it would be fun for him to see one of his old friends, you know?"

Never pausing as the mess around him increased, Cole said, "We all went and got pizza."

Nadia wasn't quite seeing the reason for her father's awkwardness until, with a start, she remembered that Mrs. Paulson had been widowed a couple of years ago. "Wait. You went on a date?"

Dad gave her a look that clearly meant *Not in front of Cole!* but her baby brother was oblivious. In a low voice he said, "No, it wasn't a date, but—once we got there, I realized Gretchen maybe thought it was, and . . . I think she felt rejected, and it kind of put a damper on the evening." He frowned. "That's too much information, isn't it?"

"No," Nadia replied in a small voice, though she profoundly wished she'd never heard a word of it. Okay, Dad hadn't been MILF-hunting in New York, but how long would it be before he started dating?

Even though Mom was long gone, even though she'd made her desire for the divorce emphatically clear, Nadia couldn't imagine seeing her father with someone else.

Obviously Dad had picked up on her mood, and blessedly changed the subject. "How was the Halloween carnival? You made it, right? Not snowed under by homework?"

"Oh, did you not hear?" Nadia had thought it might make the news, but that had been stupid of her. Like anywhere else in the whole world would pay attention to Captive's Sound. "The haunted house burned down."

"What?"

"To the ground. Nobody knows what happened." Which was putting it lightly. "There's some big town meeting about it soon."

Simon Caldani shook his head in disbelief. "Well, thank God we didn't go. Wow. You were right about that being unsafe."

"Mmm-hmmm." Nadia nodded. Before they'd gotten home, she'd loosened her ponytail so that her thick, black hair fell around her face and hid the small cuts and bruises. "Good thing Cole was nowhere near it."

"At least nobody died," Dad said as he went to stand by Cole and the pile of dirty clothes he'd created. "Hey, buddy, remember how we talked about the laundry hamper?"

She hugged herself as she turned away. Someone *had* died—not as a result of the carnival fire, but by Elizabeth's hand. A guy from her class, Jeremy Prasad, had been murdered; Mateo had been there, enchanted by Elizabeth and unable to stop her. It was weird that she hadn't heard any town gossip about it; even the somnolent newspaper, the *Guardian*, had roused itself enough to cover the haunted-house disaster, but had reported nothing about the suspicious death of a seventeen-year-old.

Maybe the body hadn't been found yet. They'd been on the beach; maybe Jeremy's corpse had been carried away by the tides.

Nadia closed her eyes, overcome for a moment by the horror of it. She hadn't liked Jeremy Prasad much. Nobody could. He'd been a snob, a sexist, and a bully. But in the end, he'd been cut down for no reason at all.

Mateo had said Elizabeth gouged out Jeremy's eyes.

Why the eyes? What magic is that a part of? Was it part of what she was really up to on Halloween, or something else?

She didn't know, couldn't guess. Once again she had to deal with the fact that she'd never completed her training— and with her mother gone, totally incommunicado, her chances to learn anything more about witchcraft were severely limited. The secrecy surrounding witchcraft meant she didn't even know another adult witch who was willing to train her.

Except Elizabeth herself.

If I had one more chance to talk to Mom, what would I say? Ask her why she left? Bitch her out for abandoning us? Make her find me another teacher? Find out why she doesn't love Dad anymore? Get her to explain Elizabeth's real plan? Tell her Cole's had nightmares ever since she walked away?

I want to ask it all. I'll never get to ask any of it.

Nadia rubbed her temples. Her head was starting to hurt.

But that night, once her dad and brother had fallen asleep, she crept up into her attic workspace. There, beneath her painted blue ceiling, fortified by a couple of Hershey's Miniatures, Nadia began the work of scouring through her resources again. Right now that was just her Book of Shadows and one that had belonged to a Captive's Sound witch from centuries before, Prudence Hale. Still, that gave her a place to begin.

Before Halloween, Nadia's energies had naturally been devoted to stopping Elizabeth's destruction of Captive's Sound. She intended to change her focus; from now on, it was going to be all about stopping Elizabeth, period.

If only there were a spell to just de-magic another witch, or remove evil intent, or—but she stopped herself. The highest level of witching magic was spell creation; that was when a witch invented her own spells instead of relying on those handed down through the centuries. Most witches never ascended to those heights. Mom had said that only a couple of witches in a century mastered magic so completely.

(When she was little, Nadia had protested that if it *could* be done, then she should try to do it. Mom had laughed and told her to worry about that when she was big enough to brush her teeth without being reminded.)

There was no point in dreaming of something that could probably never be. Nadia needed to find a weapon against Elizabeth here and now.

And when she found that weapon, she intended to use it.

❧ ❧

School had been canceled on Monday due to the carnival fire. It made no sense, but Nadia figured in Captive's Sound, people made the most out of every bit of excitement they got. Now, though, Rodman High's students had returned, and the rumors could really get going.

"So, I heard that some guys were smoking in there," said Kendall Bender as she walked down the hallway, holding court, trailed by rapt listeners. "And also, like, apparently they're worried about arson, and maybe there was some faulty wiring, too. Plus some people said they saw lightning? Which, you know, it wasn't raining, like, at all, but maybe it was heat lightning, if heat lightning can start fires."

Well, at least people didn't have any idea what was really going on.

What with all the chaos and chatter in the hallway, she found Mateo only a few moments before class began, and Verlaine just after that. Mateo held out his arm for Verlaine to take hold of, an old-fashioned gentleman's move that made Nadia smile.

"I can't believe I'm actually happy to see Rodman High," Verlaine said. Today her clothes were from the 1940s—a dark brown skirt with a silky, red shirt that tied in a bow at the neck. "Maybe at this point I'm just glad for a little bit of normal, you know?"

They turned the corner—and nearly ran into Jeremy Prasad.

"Long time no see," said the dead guy with a smile, before heading off to class.

3

VERLAINE MANAGED TO WEDGE HER PHONE BETWEEN HER copy of *Great Expectations* and the end of the desk. Sound to silent—okay—let the texting begin. *How is Jeremy alive?*

Maybe it didn't really happen, Nadia texted back. *Mateo might have seen some . . . nightmare vision, because of being my Steadfast. Elizabeth was doing some intense magic that night. Who knows?*

That made sense. Relaxing slightly, Verlaine peered over the cover of her book at Jeremy, who sat in front of her, one row over.

She'd spent a lot of time in Novels class watching Jeremy Prasad. This was partly because Novels class was a no-brainer to anyone who actually read for fun; Verlaine had usually gone through the assigned book three or four times before the rest of the class had found its way to Chapter Two.

But it was mostly because she liked looking at him.

It was one of the things she hated most about herself—the

involuntary attraction she'd always had to Jeremy Prasad, one so strong that even his obnoxious personality couldn't overcome it. Her mind was well aware that he was arrogant, entitled, mean-spirited and more than a bit slutty, and despised him for all of it. (Except the slutty bit, because slut-shaming was a tool of the patriarchy, even when applied to guys.) Her mind definitely had all Jeremy's flaws down pat.

However, her body only knew that he was completely scorching hot. Whatever it was about him—whether it was his angular cheekbones, his dark skin, that thick, shining, curly black hair he wore just the tiniest bit long, his lean, wiry body—well, there was something about him that got to Verlaine on a level she couldn't entirely control.

She justified this the same way she usually did. *I'm not responsible for . . . involuntary hormonal tsunamis. Besides, given all the crap Jeremy dishes out, especially at me? He owes me a nice view.*

Today he was living up to his end of the bargain in a black sweater cut close to his body. . . .

"So, here we meet Miss Havisham," said Mrs. Bristow. "What's the first thing that strikes you about her?"

"Um, she's crazy?" someone said in the back, and most of the class snickered.

"Fair enough." Mrs. Bristow wrote *Insanity* on the board. "But she's not out of control, or even delusional, is she?"

"I'd argue that she's delusional," Jeremy said.

Verlaine sat up straighter. Jeremy had never volunteered

to speak in class before. Not in Novels, not in any other subject.

Mrs. Bristow looked as surprised as Verlaine felt, but she recovered quickly. "Okay, Jeremy, why would you say that?"

He doubled down on the surprise factor by not giving a smart-ass answer. "Well, she blames the man who jilted her for ruining her life. He hurt her, of course, but he didn't ruin her life. She could easily have found someone else or done something productive with her time. Instead she locks out the world and surrounds herself with memories of how someone wronged her. Miss Havisham didn't give herself any more chances for happiness. So I think she's delusional for blaming anybody else. She ruined her own life."

"That's—very good." Mrs. Bristow blinked. "Excellent insight."

It was the first evidence Verlaine had ever had that Jeremy might have a brain in his head. She had a lot of evidence to the contrary. And he'd been polite, even pleasant, when he spoke—

Quickly she snatched her phone again and texted, *There's NO WAY this is really Jeremy Prasad.*

"Verlaine's right," Mateo said as he and Nadia headed toward chemistry class. "I know what I saw, Nadia. It wasn't a dream, a vision, anything like that. It was the most real thing ever. Jeremy Prasad is dead."

"And he's also walking straight toward us," Nadia said.

Mateo glanced up to see she was right; Jeremy seemed

totally unbothered as he sauntered toward class, just like always, except for the disappearance of his usual smug expression.

Still, when Mateo looked at him, all he could envision was the way Jeremy had fallen into the wet sand, utterly lifeless. As he passed them, Jeremy just nodded like any other guy would—any other guy but Jeremy, who seemed to come up with snide comments for every occasion.

Mateo pulled Nadia close; it wasn't like Jeremy-or-whatever would try anything right here, but he felt better trying to keep her safe. It had only been a few nights ago that she'd been lying unconscious at his feet. He'd thought she was dead. He'd been given a glimpse of his world without Nadia, and he didn't ever want to see it again.

"Raising the dead," he said. "Can witchcraft do that?"

"No. At least not any way you'd ever want them to be raised. I'm going over the alternatives, and all the ones I know are . . . extremely, extremely bad." Nadia went pale; her arms tightened around Mateo. "And it just got worse."

Mateo glanced over his shoulder and saw Elizabeth walking into class.

Nobody else looked remotely surprised to see her; why would they? She attended school as though she were any other student. Granted, she was out a lot of the time, because she could make the teachers and other students forget her absences completely—but that only made it weirder that she chose to come at all.

And of course, Elizabeth was still his lab partner.

"Ah, young love," said Mrs. Purdhy, who had walked up while they were distracted. Mateo and Nadia pulled apart slightly. "What a beautiful sight. Also, what a stupid reason for a tardy. You two want to get into class?"

"Oh, yeah, right." Nadia shared a glance with Mateo. They were stuck.

As they walked in, Jeremy was arranging the stuff for today's experiment neatly on the lab table he shared with Nadia. *(Oh, crap, how did I forget that he's teamed with Nadia?)* Elizabeth went calmly to her own table to wait for Mateo, staring at him the whole time he approached. She didn't so much as glance at Jeremy.

Memories flickered through his mind: the two of them as eight-year-olds, making cookies and giggling. Swimming together in the surf on a blazing-hot summer afternoon. Hiking around Breakheart Pond two years ago, on a cool, bright autumn day much like this one.

Those were some of the happiest memories of Mateo's life—and each and every one was fake.

"What the hell are you doing here?" he muttered as he came to the table.

"Learning about—" She squinted at the board. "Combustion, apparently."

"Stop lying to me!" That came out too loudly; a few people turned their heads in his direction.

Elizabeth just smiled and pushed up the sleeves of her cardigan. Her hair was a little disheveled, her cardigan not quite on straight. Had she always been like this? Slightly askew?

"I doubt you'd like the truth any better. But don't worry, Mateo. I'm not here for you today; I'm not even here for her." She nodded over at Nadia, who was currently watching the un-Jeremy obediently start filling out today's worksheet. "I have my own reasons."

From the front of the room, Mrs. Purdhy started lecturing. "Okay, everyone. We got an inadvertent lesson about combustion over the weekend—" People groaned at the bad joke, and she nodded. "Yeah, yeah, I know. Work with me here. Today's lesson is going to be a lot more controlled than that, and hopefully a lot more fun."

Between Elizabeth standing there next to him like nothing was going on and the *dead guy* right by Nadia, Mateo could hardly pay attention to what else the teacher was saying . . . but then he realized she'd stopped talking.

He looked toward the front. Mrs. Purdhy was standing very still, her eyes wide with what he knew was fright. She wasn't looking at Elizabeth or Not-Jeremy, not at anything in particular. Her eyes seemed glazed with fear.

People started glancing at one another, looking for confirmation that this was definitely weird. After a moment, Kendall Bender raised her hand and said, "Um, Mrs. Purdhy, do you know you're, like, acting all weird?"

There was no answer. Slowly Mrs. Purdhy lifted one hand to her throat, like she might be about to cough.

"Ma'am?" Kendall's voice was a little quieter. "Are you okay?"

Mrs. Purdhy opened her mouth. A drop of liquid appeared

at the corner of her lips and trickled down her chin—black as tar.

People started to swear. A few students in the front row shoved their desks backward or hurried to the rear of the classroom. One guy started filming it on his phone. Someone else dashed into the hallway and started yelling for the school nurse. Nadia pushed toward the front, to Mrs. Purdhy's side. "Are you all right? Can you talk?"

Mrs. Purdhy showed no sign she could hear, or see, or take in anything besides whatever was happening to her. The liquid coming out of her mouth increased—a slow pour, thick as chocolate syrup, and getting thicker by the moment. Black streaks were beginning to rain down her shirt. When droplets hit the floor, the linoleum made a horrible sizzling sound.

Mateo turned to Elizabeth. "What the hell are you doing?"

Elizabeth never even glanced sideways at him. "I told you I wasn't here for you."

With a gurgling cry, Mrs. Purdhy clutched at her throat and passed out. Nadia caught her and eased her to the floor.

To hell with Elizabeth. Mateo ran to Nadia's side; somebody else had to help. As he knelt beside them, careful not to touch whatever that gunk was, he saw that Nadia had pillowed Mrs. Purdhy's head on her knees—the better to take hold of her bracelet and cast some kind of spell. Mateo wrapped his arms around Nadia's waist, knowing that the closer they were, the more she would be able to draw upon the increased power he gave her as her Steadfast.

But after a moment, Nadia whispered, "I can't get at it. Whatever it is—it's too strong."

Mateo looked down at Mrs. Purdhy, who was beginning to convulse on the floor. As he pressed down her arms to keep her from hurting herself, he thought for a moment that the tarry stuff coming out of her had streaked all along her face and hands. Then he realized that the black streaks were beneath her skin, widening and darkening like grotesque veins.

What's happening to her? He looked at Nadia, who shook her head in despair.

Then the school nurse came in, and she shooed them off, and it turned out Kendall had called 9-1-1 because the paramedics showed up about ninety seconds after that. Within a few minutes, they were running down the hallway with Mrs. Purdhy on their gurney, and in the panic nobody had thought to send in a substitute or anything else. People huddled in the room, crying, talking, or posting details on Facebook.

Nadia curled into Mateo's embrace. "I feel so helpless."

"If anyone can help her, it's you." He stroked his hands through Nadia's black hair. "Don't blame yourself. We know who's really to blame."

As Mateo turned his head to glare at Elizabeth, he saw her walk through the other students to the black puddle on the floor where Mrs. Purdhy had fallen. Everyone else was leaving that gunk severely alone; no doubt a custodian would show up any second to mop the floor clean, but Mateo wondered if it would disintegrate the mop or something. Whatever that crap was, it wasn't good.

Elizabeth went to her knees beside it and pulled her cardigan half-down, exposing her shoulders. Then she dipped two fingers into the stuff. Smoke rose from her nails as she raised her hand and painted two stripes on the very top of her arm. The skin there burned so quickly that he could smell it—the disgusting odor that came from cooking meat that had gone bad.

Nobody else paid attention. Nobody else could even see what Elizabeth was doing; she had willed them not to see. Her power was so vast that she could do her worst right in front of people, without them ever knowing a thing.

But once you knew the truth, Elizabeth's power became easier to see. Mateo and Nadia both stared, and Nadia whispered, "She's burned."

The red streaks on Elizabeth's arm bubbled, immediately blistering. A surge of sympathetic pain lanced across Mateo's shoulder; his nerve endings didn't understand that she didn't deserve sympathy.

And the light that shimmered around her as she did it—the glow of it was febrile and sick. Mateo understood instinctively that this was something only he could see with his Steadfast power. So he stared at it long and hard, this orange halo that melted around her for a moment and was gone. *Tell Nadia this. Tell Nadia everything.*

Elizabeth simply pulled her cardigan back on and walked

out of class. As usual, nobody noticed.

For a few moments, Mateo and Nadia could only look at the doorway she'd walked through. Mateo's mind kept replaying that horrible gurgle Mrs. Purdhy had made—like she was both trying to breathe and trying to scream.

Whatever had happened to her was Elizabeth's fault. Just like the curse, and Mom's death, and everything else in Captive's Sound. All because of Elizabeth.

Then Jeremy came up beside them, gesturing in the direction Elizabeth had gone. "What a bitch, huh?"

4

ABSOLUTELY EVERYONE ELSE IN VERLAINE'S PSYCHOLOGY class had been texted about Mrs. Purdhy's sudden collapse . . . everyone, that was, besides Verlaine.

Not that she was upset about being left out. Between Nadia's magical powers and Mateo's hero complex, no doubt her friends were right in the thick of it. Like usual.

Now she intended to get in the thick of it, too. Yes, the world of witchcraft was dangerous and terrifying, but it was also about a thousand times more interesting than anything else Verlaine had going on.

So Verlaine darted through the hallways with her books clutched to her chest, not even bothering to go to her locker, ducking and weaving around other students to reach the chem lab before Nadia and Mateo left. As she got near, she saw that the guidance counselor, Faye Walsh, was closing the room, using duct tape the way police might have used yellow crime-scene banners. Standing nearby were Nadia and Mateo, clinging to each other like . . . socks out of the dryer.

Oh, stop it. Just because you haven't got anybody is no reason to resent Nadia and Mateo for falling in love.

But then she noticed guy who was *not Jeremy Prasad* standing right next to them.

"What happened?" she said as she ran up, trying to keep an eye on the not-Jeremy while not being obvious about it. Crowds of students kept hurrying past, trying to get a look at the scene. She kept hearing murmurs like *seizure* and *overdose.* "Is Mrs. Purdhy dead?"

"She wasn't when the ambulance left," Mateo said. His arm was around Nadia's shoulder, and neither of them was bothering to hide the fact that they were staring at the dead person; Not-Jeremy seemed to be smiling, as though amused by their attention. "Beyond that, we don't know."

Nadia said, "Elizabeth did it. We know that much. I have no idea what kind of spell that was—or what the burning was about—but I doubt she did it alone."

Verlaine gave in and stared at Not-Jeremy, too. He sighed, for a moment so put upon and annoyed that he seemed like his old self again. "You know, I should probably make you guys guess a while longer, but what the hell."

With a grin, he brought his hands together, as if to clap—

—but the moment Verlaine heard the sound, all the other noise around her stopped.

So did all the movement. Everybody around her froze

in place, midstep, midword. One girl's blond ponytail levitated in air, midbounce. Ms. Walsh held the silver duct tape slightly above her head, like she was studying it in the light. Verlaine kept turning from one direction to another, trying to make herself believe what she was seeing. Nadia and Mateo were doing the same.

And the guy who was now definitely, positively *not Jeremy* leaned against the wall and folded his arms against his chest.

"There's not that much I can do on my own," he said. "But I can do this. Nice trick, hmm? You'd be surprised how often it comes in handy."

"Who are you?" Verlaine demanded. "No. *What* are you?"

"You may call me—" His voice choked off for a moment, but then he smiled, casual again. "Asa."

Nadia jerked backward, out of Mateo's embrace, so far that she knocked into a frozen-in-place cheerleader. Her pom-pom rustled, but otherwise the cheerleader remained still. "You can't say your true name."

"Asa" sighed. "Elizabeth thought your training might not have gotten far enough for you to recognize my nature. I'll enjoy telling her she's mistaken."

"What does that mean?" Verlaine demanded, looking from Nadia to Asa to Mateo to the weird stopped-time scene around them. Not even the hands of the wall clock were moving. "Why can't he say his name?"

"Because he's a demon," Nadia whispered.

For a few moments, nobody spoke. Asa just shrugged,

like, *Yeah, you got me.* Then Mateo said, "Since when did demons come into this? There are *demons*?"

"A *demon* demon?" Verlaine couldn't stop staring at him. "From hell?"

"We call it hell sometimes," Asa said. "Just a figure of speech, though I promise you, it's appropriate. Where I'm from isn't a collection of evil dead people, if that's what you're thinking. I've been down there for centuries—haven't run into Hitler once."

"Demons come from the realm of the One Beneath." Nadia's eyes were narrowed now, like she was mad as hell but still hadn't decided what to do about it. "They're souls bound to serve Him."

Oh, okay. This was starting to make a little bit of sense. "You mean, he's like Elizabeth," Verlaine said, relieved to have put some of this together.

But Nadia shook her head, never taking her gaze from Asa. "No. Elizabeth chose her path; no one controls her but the One Beneath himself. A demon was either captured by the One Beneath or one of His servants, or brought into being by one of their spells. They don't have a lot of power on their own, but once they're summoned into service, they can perform levels of dark magic no human being ever could."

"Like a Steadfast for a Sorceress?" Mateo said.

"Not exactly." Nadia gave Asa a thin, mirthless smile. "More like a Sorceress's slave."

As weird, screwed-up, and freakish as this whole scene was, Verlaine couldn't help thinking Nadia had skated over a pretty critical point. "But—if they got captured—if they didn't choose to be bad—then they're the victims of the One Beneath. Slaves, you said. That's wrong, isn't it?"

Asa turned his head toward her as though he'd never seen her before. And then, in his dark eyes, she glimpsed something that had never been there when this was Jeremy Prasad.

No. Something that had never been there when anyone looked at her, ever. It was as though—as though he could *see* her, but he didn't mind what he saw—

"Don't waste your pity," Nadia said. "Asa can only be here because Elizabeth brought him to do her bidding. I never thought they could walk in our world like this, but apparently there's some kind of spell to put a demon inside a dead body."

"A spell that involves digging out the eyes." Mateo's face was ashen, and Verlaine remembered the horrifying story he'd told them about having to stand there motionless, bound by Elizabeth's magic, watching her slice into Jeremy with the serrated edge of a seashell. "The big question is why you're telling us all this."

Verlaine half raised her hand. "Actually, I think the big question is how he *stopped time*. And also why."

Asa stepped closer to them, and Verlaine imagined that she could feel a kind of heat radiating from him . . . but it wasn't her imagination. It was as though he were running a fever, one so high no human could ever have survived it. "I stopped time and told you who and what I am because I thought it would be much less annoying than listening to you whispering and guessing and carrying on. I only get so long here on Earth. I intend to enjoy it."

That wasn't all. It couldn't be all. Verlaine sensed that much.

Apparently there was also something about saying his real name, whatever it was. He found it difficult.

"We know one thing," Mateo said, folding his arms. "You don't like Elizabeth much more than we do."

"Are you honestly surprised? With that charming personality of hers." Asa just smiled. "Still, I never forget: She's the boss."

With that, he clapped his hands together—and time began again, everyone rushing past them in the hallway like before. Nadia had stepped right into that cheerleader's path, and she huffed and said, "Excuse you" before sweeping by the three of them.

The assistant principal glanced over her shoulder at them. "Move along. There's nothing to see."

"How wrong she is," Asa whispered in Verlaine's ear. His breath was so hot—like steam against her skin.

He walked away, quickly blending into the crowd.

Mateo turned to Nadia. "Demons?"

"What do they do?" Verlaine asked. "What is Elizabeth going to use him for?"

Nadia shook her head. "I—I don't know. There's too much I don't know." She bit her lower lip, so obviously troubled that Verlaine didn't have the heart to ask her any more questions. "I'll dig into Goodwife Hale's Book of Shadows

41

tonight. Go over my own materials. See if I can find anything else. But demons . . . that's arcane magic. High-level magic. The kind of stuff I don't know nearly enough about."

Well, that wasn't encouraging. Mateo responded to Nadia's disquiet the way he responded to her happiness, or her absentmindedness, or anything else these days—by hugging her tightly.

Verlaine was sure of only one thing: The situation had just gotten worse.

Elizabeth opened the door to her back room. She had not entered it in years, but knew that until very recently, it had not looked like this.

Spiderwebs shivered as the wind blew through the room behind her, ruffling her chestnut curls. The room was thick with them, corner to corner, floor to ceiling. The one chair in the corner was nothing but silver white now, as though it were made of wool instead of rotting wood. Some chips of the remaining paint dangled in the webs, wrapped in cocoons as though they were prey. Elizabeth stretched her hand forward, her long fingers breaking web after web; spiders skittered along her skin, and she paid them no mind.

Here her Book of Shadows had attempted to trap Nadia Caldani—and had failed.

The webs thickened, breaking across her face, sticking to her hair. Elizabeth bent to kneel on the floor; through the misty grayness of the webs she could see the Book of Shadows. She smiled, almost fond. If Elizabeth had ever had a friend, she had long since forgotten what that felt like. The affection she felt for this book, and the primal, unthinking loyalty it gave her in return, were the closest Elizabeth would ever come to friendship again.

"I would have thought you could hold her," Elizabeth murmured. She knew the book did not hear, but she spoke gently all the same. "There is something uncanny about her power. Something I must understand."

Her fingers closed around the Book of Shadows. Its leather was dark with age, but not brittle in the way any ordinary binding would have been after nearly four hundred years. Instead it felt rough, too thick—like scar tissue that had never quite healed. When she lifted it from the floor, she could see the rectangular space where it had long been, free of dust or cobwebs. But one long-legged spider, as large as her palm, scurried into the spot as though to fill it up.

Elizabeth folded the book close to her chest. For so many years she had not consulted it, only drawn on its power.

But this close to the completion of her great work, she could not allow anything to go wrong. She would have to draw on every resource she had. Permit no interruptions. No mistakes.

She walked back into the area of the house where she spent most of her time. For a moment, Elizabeth saw it as a human would have seen it, were they free of her glamours: a derelict place, furnished with only a few threadbare chairs and a sofa that had not been sat in for decades and probably would no longer bear weight. Faded walls. Water bottles left over from the terrible thirst that had so long racked her but had now departed along with her immortality. (Elizabeth found that she still drank from them often, but it was now merely a matter of habit.) Her old stove, the same one that had once burned wood in the nineteenth century, which now glowed with a very different kind of flame. Broken glass strewn along her blue floor, the shards so familiar to her that she stepped through them easily, without hesitation.

Nadia would have had to wind her way through all this to reach the back room.

Elizabeth sat cross-legged in the middle of her floor, book in front of her, then unbuttoned her dress far enough to allow the shoulders to slip down her arms. The burned flesh there stuck to the fabric, and she had to tug it away; the pain was as meaningless as the stray spider at the hem of her skirt.

Without her having to speak, or even consciously think of what she wanted, the Book of Shadows fell open to a symbol she had drawn there long ago. The One Beneath had showed her this more than a century past, pooling a victim's blood into the precise markings He needed. She had pressed this page against the symbol, and the maroon stains still held every line perfectly.

She held two fingers to the symbol, checking the sweep of those two lines—then lifted her hand to her upper arm. Yes, the arc and angle were correct. Although Elizabeth knew this by heart, when it came to this, she wanted to make utterly, completely certain.

The front door opened.

Elizabeth was only startled that so much time had passed without her realizing it, but communing with her Book of Shadows could have that effect. "Enter, beast."

"You know, if Asa doesn't work for you, you could just call me Jeremy." The demon sauntered in as if she were to do his bidding, instead of the reverse. "*Beast* is rude."

She flicked her hand toward him, calling up spell ingredients without even having to ask, the malachite ring around her finger automatically providing the grounding. Asa staggered backward, gripped by pain of some nature she didn't bother to recall. As he slumped against the wall, she said, "You let your human guise deceive you. Don't believe that you have their freedoms. Their souls. It will hinder me and hurt you, when once again you face the truth of what you are."

"How kind—of you—to remind me," he gasped. But already he was straightening; the pain had been vicious but had not lasted long. She had gauged it well. "Name your task."

"For now I only want you to stay close to Nadia Caldani and her friends."

"Difficult, seeing as how Mateo remembers Jeremy Prasad's death. And Nadia's more than far enough along in her training to know a demon when she sees one." Asa lifted his chin, attempting to display a bit of his earlier nonchalance; it would have been more convincing if his skin weren't still shiny with the cold sweat of pain.

"Do what you can," she said. "I still don't understand

how Nadia made him her Steadfast. No man should be able to hold that power. They're trying to learn more about the fate of the Laughtons, which is meaningless on its own, but could lead them too close to things they cannot discover."

Asa's eyes darted over to the stove, to the unearthly glow that flickered through the narrow slits of its door. He understood. Good.

"Eventually they'll think they can use you to get to me." Elizabeth slid her dress back on her shoulders, once again felt the distant sting of pain on her arm. Probably she should bandage that. Though her earthly body only needed to serve a brief time longer, there was no point in being weakened by illness or injury when the One Beneath's work had to be done. "Maybe you'll think so, too. But we both know how this ends."

"Yes. We do." Asa looked down on the symbol in blood; the two lines she'd already drawn on her flesh had begun to glow slightly. Elizabeth felt the answering heat on her skin.

5

THE TOWN HALL FOR CAPTIVE'S SOUND WAS IMPRESSIVE, for a small town—almost too impressive—so much so that the contrast drew comic attention to itself, like a balding, middle-aged man with a red sports car. In the middle of this small, dreary town was an enormous, white Palladian creation with pillars and a dome. Nadia thought it looked more like the Supreme Court than the venue for a community chat about how the Halloween carnival had gone wrong.

"Thanks for coming to this with me." Verlaine was scowling down at her phone as they walked through the square, trying to get her Voice Memo app to work. "Not even a paper as lazy as the *Guardian* can ignore the haunted house burning down in the middle of town. And of course, the *Lightning Rod* will be the source for real news, if anybody ever reads it."

"Oh, come on. *Someone* has to read it."

"The week before I went into the hospital? We got fifteen hits, not counting my own log-ins. Eight of those clicked straight through to find out when Shangri-La was having two-for-one drink specials."

"Shangri-La?"

"The local nightclub."

Nadia was still new to town, but she would have thought she'd have heard of this place, if only because sources of fun here were so rare. "I can't believe Captive's Sound has an actual nightclub."

"You can't believe it because we don't. You have understood our Podunk nature perfectly. But Shangri-La's just in the next town over. They don't card." Verlaine paused. "At least, I hear they don't card. I never had anybody to go with, so I don't actually know for myself."

"We'll go," Nadia promised, really without thinking about it. But when she saw how Verlaine lit up, she felt guilty for how much Verlaine needed to hear that.

Remembering the dark magic that screened Verlaine away from the rest of the world was a constant challenge, and tonight it had been one of the last things on Nadia's mind. Mostly she had come to the meeting to learn precisely what people had seen the night of the Halloween carnival— whether they would mention details that just seemed odd to them but might, for Nadia, be recognizable as signs of magic. Those signs could give her some clue as to what Elizabeth's master plan really was.

But I have to remember Verlaine, Nadia thought as they went up the steps, falling in with other people coming to the meeting. Verlaine's gray hair was now in a sloppy bun held back by two cloisonné chopsticks; the hairstyle revealed her neck, and showed just how thin she was, how fragile. *She needs me and Mateo. She doesn't have anyone else.*

The meeting hall had rows of seats not unlike those of a theater, the fabric a little shabby in comparison with the high ceilings and big paintings of what Nadia assumed were famous people from Rhode Island history, though none of them was famous enough for her to recognize. For Verlaine's audio to work, they had to sit in the very front row, dead center. Nadia felt a little self-conscious and glanced around—just in time to see the Prasads come in, Asa behind them.

"Demon in the house," Verlaine said. "Crap. What is he doing here?"

"Right now he might just be pretending to be Jeremy," Nadia said. The Prasads obviously hadn't realized anything was wrong. Mrs. Prasad was even now affectionately pushing Asa's hair out of his eyes. "But Elizabeth brought him here to help her. So we can't ever trust him or anything he does. Remember that. Demons can make it hard to deny them."

Verlaine just kept looking down at her podcast equipment; apparently the phone app was just for backup. "Is his body dead or alive? Like, after a couple of weeks, will he get sort of—zombie-esque?"

"I don't know. But I doubt it." Nadia watched the way

49

the Prasads kept talking to the thing they thought was their son. She was repulsed to see the evident love his mother felt being poured out to a demon, a servant of the One Beneath, who was actually using her child's corpse to do Elizabeth's bidding. "It's sick. It's wrong. I can't even stand it."

"Uh-oh—that sounds bad," said Faye Walsh as she took her seat a few chairs down in the front row; she was chic as ever in a white trench coat and large hoop earrings. Nadia realized she must have looked stricken, because Ms. Walsh held up her hands. "Sorry. Didn't mean to eavesdrop."

Which was probably the truth. But Faye Walsh was one of those guidance counselors who expected to actually counsel, who wanted you to pour out your soul before you took the college brochures. She was already "concerned" about Nadia because of Mom's vanishing act; the last thing Nadia wanted to do was attract even more of her attention. And while Ms. Walsh might not be trying to pry, she was sitting so close that there was no way she couldn't hear.

Flustered, Verlaine said, "I, uh, what was that? Sorry. AV equipment gets all, um, tangled, with the cords, and then I lose track of things." Her eyes widened as if to say, *Sorry that wasn't more believable.*

Of the ninety thousand things Nadia had to worry about, was even one of them completely normal? There had to be something she could say that would sound like a completely ordinary problem. She blurted out, "I can't believe my dad's already thinking about dating again."

"*Ewww.*" Verlaine wrinkled her nose. "Really?"

"Yeah, really. Well, maybe really. Apparently an old friend of his in New York—female friend—tried to ask him out while they were there. Nothing happened, but still, he must be thinking about it."

"Even if he's not, they'll be after him soon." Verlaine nodded, like she'd seen it coming all along. "Every single, divorced, or widowed woman in Captive's Sound between the ages of twenty-five and fifty probably already has him in her sights. They're just trying to figure out the line between 'too soon' and 'too late.'"

"But why? There have to be other single men in town."

"First of all, not so much, seeing how small Captive's Sound is. And second, your dad's hot."

Nadia made a face. "Oh, gross, Verlaine."

"I don't mean *hot* hot. I mean dad hot. Listen." Verlaine started counting off points on her fingers. "He hasn't gotten fat, he still has his hair, he has a job, and it seems like he looks in the mirror when he gets dressed in the morning. After forty, that's all hot is."

Okay, that was disturbing. Before Nadia could think any more about it, mercifully, the meeting began with the banging of a gavel. A half dozen people seemed to make up the city council—including Mr. Prasad, which was probably why his family was here. All of them seemed grumpy in the extreme, though Nadia couldn't blame them once the questions got going.

"Why wasn't there a fire extinguisher in the haunted house?"

"Well, if there was an extinguisher, why didn't anyone use it? Isn't that someone's job?"

"First the roads start collapsing from the sinkholes, and now this? What exactly is the city council spending the infrastructure funds on? We demand an audit!"

"All I know is my salary pays for the fire department of this city, and if the fire department can't find a damn three-story house ablaze in the middle of town in less than twenty minutes, they've got a problem!"

"For once," Verlaine whispered, "this is almost interesting."

Almost—but the novelty wore off fast. Within a few minutes, Nadia was back to staring over her shoulder at Asa—at the demon—with the woman who believed she was his mother.

She was just so *loving.* So much so that any real kid of hers would have been annoyed. Mrs. Prasad kept petting his arm, glancing over at him, smiling . . .

Mom had acted that way with Nadia and Cole sometimes—when Cole had gotten done singing a song with the rest of his kindergarten class at their "graduation" ceremony, or when Nadia had managed to cast a really tough spell that day but Mom couldn't say anything directly because Dad and Cole were around. Instead she just did that thing Mrs. Prasad was doing now, radiating pride, so much that you almost hated it but didn't really.

All at once Nadia couldn't stand it any longer. It was wrong—beyond wrong—for Asa to sit there soaking up love he didn't deserve. He was working for Jeremy's murderer. This was sickening, and it couldn't go on any longer.

She has to know, Nadia thought, looking at Mrs. Prasad. *She has to at least understand that something's seriously wrong with her son. I want her to look at him and see that something's not right.*

So. A spell of revelation.

Never taking her eyes from Mrs. Prasad, Nadia's fingers found the pearl charm on her bracelet. For a moment she wished Mateo were here with her instead of on shift at La Catrina; still, she shouldn't need a Steadfast's power for this. It was a stronger revelation spell than she'd ever used before. She'd never had the emotional ingredients for it until now.

Laughter at a time of sorrow.
Bloodshed at a time of joy.
Salvation at the moment of despair.

Nadia kept her gaze on Mrs. Prasad as she lived each emotion in turn:

Packing to leave Chicago forever, going through the dressier clothing Mom had left behind, watching her dad's face fall with every nice gown or glittery shoe Nadia pulled from the closet to reluctantly throw away, until he said, "I guess I could perform a drag show," and then the two of them rolled on the floor laughing until they cried.

The laughter at the Halloween carnival, popcorn and cotton candy in everyone's hands, all the little kids running around in their costumes, never realizing what was about to unfold within the haunted house.

Being trapped underwater in the sound, seaweed tangling around her ankles, binding her with the force of a magic so old she couldn't fight it, desperate to breathe and sure she was about to die—until Mateo found her there in the cold and dark, pressed his mouth to hers, his breath to hers—

Mrs. Prasad screamed.

Everyone in the room turned to stare—except Nadia, who had been staring already. But she hadn't expected a reaction like this. Suspicion, maybe. Trepidation. Caution, which would be a good thing around a demon from hell.

Instead Mrs. Prasad had gone straight to full-blown panic.

"Get away!" she cried, plowing over a few other people as she tried to back away from Asa. For his part, though he must have sensed what was going on, he looked nearly as shocked as everyone else. "Get away from me!"

Mr. Prasad's voice came over the microphone from the city-council podium. "Honey? Honey, calm down. Nobody's making this personal."

But Mrs. Prasad had completely lost it. Her screams kept rising in pitch, and when Asa rose as if to go to her, she staggered back like she might pass out.

It's too much, Nadia realized in horror. *This spell's too powerful. She's seeing the demon within in a way that I can't—a way even Mateo can't. That's going to drive her crazy, if it hasn't already. I have to take it back!*

Quickly she grabbed her quartz charm and called up the first useful spell she could think of: a spell of equation, one that witches sometimes used to cover up evidence of their magic, to convince people that the phenomenon they'd just seen was something totally regular—that the thing that had seemed so different to them a moment before was in fact just like everything else around them. This, too, was one Nadia had never cast before, but this seemed like the time to try it.

Snow turning into rain.
A fear suddenly realized to be false.
The interruption of the extraordinary by the ordinary.

Nadia closed her eyes, the better to concentrate:

Mom saying, "Oh, shoot," as she stood on the balcony of their Chicago condo one unexpectedly warm Christmas, as the snow that would have made the day perfect vanished into rain, turning the whitening scene below almost instantly gray.

That time on the bus when she'd been sure this weird guy was following her, and it was only the second week her parents had let her take the bus on her own, and her heart had been pounding as he got off the bus behind her, but then he'd walked right past her into the Billy Goat Tavern and she'd laughed at her own stupidity.

The moment in her attic when she'd just finished cutting Mateo's hair, and they'd never been so close for so long before, and they leaned into each other for what would have been their first kiss—except that Cole came in, and they'd laughed and pulled apart even though she still yearned for him so badly it hurt—

"Oh, my God!" Mrs. Prasad screamed. She didn't sound better. She sounded a whole lot worse.

Nadia opened her eyes—just in time to see a crazed Mrs.

Prasad run straight to the emergency fire ax and break the glass with her elbow.

"She isn't—" Verlaine gasped. "Oh, crap, she is!"

Mrs. Prasad swung the ax at the people nearest her; everyone started to run and shriek. Horrified, Nadia realized that the spell of equation hadn't made her see Asa as normal again; instead Mrs. Prasad thought everyone in the room was a demon.

And she was now trying to kill them.

What was she going to do? She had no idea. What spell could she cast for this? Even if she could think of one, which she couldn't, Nadia knew she'd just screwed up her last two spells in ways she didn't even fully understand. It wasn't like she hadn't known before this that her training was incomplete, that she didn't know everything she needed to know, but never before had she done anything that went so incredibly, dangerously wrong.

"Somebody stop her!" one guy yelled, and a few people tried to get nearer, but Mrs. Prasad seemed like a woman possessed. She kept swinging, kept advancing, eyes wide with terror but never flinching from her homicidal determination. Wildly Nadia thought that if she ever were surrounded by demons, she'd want Mrs. Prasad by her side.

Then Asa was next to her, his breath warm against her ear as he stepped behind her. "I think someone's gotten a little ahead of herself."

Snap! The entire room went motionless again—even Verlaine this time, who was frozen in place with her phone held up to get video of the entire incident. Mrs. Prasad had halted midslash, someone who'd been trying to leap away suspended in midair in front of her. People's hair and dresses and coats were spiraled out around them from their attempts to flee. Only Nadia and Asa were able to move.

Nadia turned toward him; he was standing too close for comfort, so close he was only inches away. "What are you doing?"

"What are you doing, more like. Let me guess. You meant to kindly inform Jeremy's mother that her son was, perhaps, no longer with the living. Why you thought she'd enjoy that knowledge is beyond me, but it's the only sensible possibility." Asa raised an eyebrow as he glanced at Faye Walsh next to them, paused in place as she attempted to crouch and take cover behind her seat. "If 'sensible' comes into this. Which I doubt."

She wasn't taking lectures from a demon. "You don't think it's sick, walking around in his skin, not letting her know her own child is dead?"

"What I think is irrelevant. I didn't ask for a role in Elizabeth's little dramatic production, but I play it as best I can. Let the Prasads live without grief while they can. I promise you, it can't be for long." His expression had been unreadable for a moment there—almost angry—but a mocking smile spread over his face. "I bet you're weaving more memories of Mateo in with your spell ingredients. Aren't you? Love is powerful, Nadia. Maybe more powerful than you realize. Certainly more than you can control."

This chaos—this was because she loved Mateo so much? Nadia felt a sick sort of shiver inside. "Why are you talking to me now?"

"So angry. So rude. And here I am, helping you out."

"Helping?"

Asa held out his hands, gesturing at the entire frozen-in-place scene around them. "Giving you a moment to get your bearings, to think how you might undo the worst of what you've done? Very useful, if you'll take advantage of it. But I'd hurry up, if I were you. My existence is eternal, but my patience isn't."

Nadia knew better than to trust a demon's word. "Why would you help me?"

"You know, just because Elizabeth brought me here doesn't make me her servant," he said, very quietly. He stepped even closer, tilted his head, as if studying her expression; she could feel the heat radiating from his body, even through her clothes. "I serve the One Beneath, not her. Yes, if she commands me to do something that helps them both, I have to do it. But that doesn't mean I'm incapable of acting on my own. Serving my own purposes. Even working against her, if it doesn't betray my unholy lord and master. You think I'm your enemy, but there are ways I could be a very powerful ally, Nadia."

For a moment she paused. Could Asa be telling some sliver of the truth?

But she said only, "You need Mrs. Prasad to believe in you again, or else you'll have blown your cover. You'll be punished."

He smiled mirthlessly. His black eyes seemed to look through her—as though he knew what she looked like without her clothes. "You say it so easily. What do you think the punishments of hell are like? Have you ever considered that?"

Her heart thumped wildly in her chest. "It doesn't matter. I have to make Mrs. Prasad forget it for her own sake. So I guess it's your lucky day."

"Only if you think fast." Asa held up his hands, obviously about to allow time to resume.

Nadia went for her bracelet again, this time reaching for the aquamarine charm. A spell of forgetting was simple, really. Basic. And one of the first lessons she'd learned, one she ought to have remembered before now, was that the simplest way out was almost always the best.

Snap! People were screaming again, and she heard the *chunk* of the ax against wooden seats, but Nadia kept concentrating on the spell.

Letting go of what was once irreplaceable.
Smiling through pain.
Making right a wrong.

"Are you seeing this?" Verlaine yelled, backing away from the fast-approaching Mrs. Prasad. She was still filming. "Nadia, *move!*"

Packing a box for Goodwill full of Mom's stuff, and dropping in the heart-shaped locket she'd given Nadia on her thirteenth birthday, the one Nadia had thought was so beautiful that she'd wear it forever.

Joking about her broken arm after coming home from the hospital, and letting Cole be the first to sign her cast, in green crayon.

Coming to see Verlaine in the hospital, finally acting like the friends they would've been all along but for the dark magic, and seeing Verlaine's face light up.

Mrs. Prasad stopped. Slowly she lowered the ax. Nobody moved, or spoke, or even seemed to breathe. Then Mrs. Prasad said, "Where am I?"

"You're okay, Mom." Asa went to her immediately, putting one arm around her shoulders while with the other he took the ax. People sighed in relief as he handed it to someone nearby. "It's okay. I think those new meds of yours aren't good. You just need to lie down."

A wave of voices rose—people either expressing sympathy or anger or bewilderment. Really, though, Nadia could tell most people were just relieved it was over. Nobody seemed to be asking any more questions about the Halloween carnival. Asa shepherded Mrs. Prasad toward the door, Mr. Prasad falling into step alongside them.

Nadia looked down at the aquamarine charm, still held between two of her fingers. She didn't think Mrs. Prasad had full amnesia, though she'd have to check later. Her spells had been so powerful before—

—could Asa be right? Could her love for Mateo be throwing her off balance?

"Nadia?" Ms. Walsh stepped closer. "What are you doing?"

She was staring down at the bracelet, the one with all the

charms Nadia required to practice witchcraft.

"Holy Christmas, what was that?" Verlaine came up, already looking at the playback of the video on her phone. "This town is getting even weirder. Now we have possessed PTA moms wielding axes."

Nadia let her hands fall to her side. To Ms. Walsh she said only, "We should get out of here. Let them sort things out."

Which didn't make much sense, but Ms. Walsh simply nodded. She backed away slowly, never taking her eyes off Nadia. The bracelet of charms around Nadia's wrist had never felt so conspicuous before; she always thought of it as looking like just another piece of jewelry, but now she felt as though she were wearing a flashing sign that proclaimed her a witch.

That was ridiculous, of course. But as she watched Ms. Walsh go, one thought flashed through Nadia's mind: *She knows.*

6

"FREE CHIPS," GAGE SAID THROUGH A CRUNCHY MOUTH-
ful. "Free salsa. To what do I owe the honor?"

"To Tuesday nights usually being the slowest of the week
at La Catrina." Mateo was wiping down the next table, getting it ready to turn over—though from the looks of things,
it would be a while before it was filled. The red leather
booths were mostly empty; the brilliantly colored skeletons
on the walls almost had the place to themselves. Gage was
the only person in Mateo's section at the moment. "Also to
my girlfriend being at the town hall meeting with Verlaine."

"Verlaine—that's the girl with gray hair, right?" Like
most people, Gage didn't seem to be able to remember
Verlaine for very long. "Girlfriend, huh? You and Nadia
sound serious."

"Definitely." Mateo knew he was starting to grin, and
that he was probably going to get teased about it, but he

didn't care. "As serious as it gets."

"Whoa, whoa. Check yourself. 'As serious as it gets' is my grandparents, who just had their fifty-third anniversary."

"Okay. As serious as it gets before that."

Gage shook his head. "Listen, don't bite my head off for this, but it wasn't that long ago that you and Elizabeth Pike were acting like you were way more than friends."

The memory made Mateo's gut turn over. At Gage's party, he'd passionately kissed Nadia . . . at least, someone he'd believed to be Nadia. But Gage and everyone else there had seen the truth: Mateo had been in Elizabeth's arms the whole time. Elizabeth had cloaked herself in magic and tricked him into thinking she was Nadia.

"That was a one-time deal," Mateo said. "One time only. The biggest mistake ever."

"So Elizabeth's available again?" Gage looked hopeful.

"Seriously, don't go there." Although Mateo seriously doubted Gage would ever get up the courage to so much as talk to Elizabeth, or that Elizabeth would pay him any attention if he did, his friend's old crush on her was so powerful that he felt like he should warn him off just in case. "Trust me on this."

"You aren't talking like you're totally over Elizabeth. Or even slightly over her."

"There's nothing to get over," Mateo said, temper rising— but he bit it back just in time. Gage Calloway was the closest thing he had to a best friend besides Nadia, and it wasn't Gage's fault he could never know the truth about what had

63

happened with Elizabeth, or what she really was. "I promise."

Gage shrugged as he dug another chip into the salsa. "All I know is, Elizabeth better be on the same page about you guys being 'over,' or you're setting yourself up to be the guy in a Taylor Swift song."

"She's on the same page. That much I know for sure." At least he didn't have to worry about her touching him ever again.

Mateo's phone buzzed in the pocket of his black apron. He lifted it to see a text from Nadia. As the messages kept coming, line after misspelled, rushed line, his eyes widened.

"Uh-oh," Gage said. "Girlfriend drama?"

Now Verlaine had just sent him video of—*whoa*. "You could say that."

"I should never have tried a brand-new spell in an emergency." Nadia leaned against the side of the building, her face still streaked from her earlier tears. They stood in the alleyway behind La Catrina, in the harsh circle of light from a nearby streetlamp; everything else around them was dark.

There were shapes and shadows around them only Mateo could see—like faces made of darkness, staring all the while—but he was learning to put those aside when he could. Right now Nadia needed him. "You were trying to help Mrs. Prasad. You did your best. You couldn't have known that was going to happen."

"I could've known if I had enough practice." She pushed her thick, black hair back from her face, like a little girl awakened from a nightmare. "Instead the exact same demon I was trying to expose? He had to fix everything."

"You said he just . . . gave you an extra minute. You're the one who saved the day."

"If Asa hadn't done it, Mrs. Prasad probably would have killed somebody, and it would have been my fault."

Mateo took her by the shoulders. "No. Nadia, come on. Snap out of this. You and I both know who's really responsible. Elizabeth is the one who killed Jeremy. She's the one who put a demon in his place. This is her fault. Only her fault. So stop beating yourself up about it, okay?"

Nadia shook her head. "It's not that simple."

"Yeah, it is." He folded her close against his shoulder. His fingers were woven through the thick silk of her hair, cradling the back of her head. He tried to imagine all the thoughts within her brain, the countless strands of hope and grief and love and fear interwoven there, so infinitely more complex than he could ever begin to understand. And yet there was nothing he wanted more than this—to know her. His lips against her temple, Mateo murmured, "You try to take care of everyone, all the time. Then you get mad at yourself when it's impossible."

"Someone has to stop Elizabeth, and there's no one else."

"Which is why you need to relax sometimes. Let us take care of you for a change." He kissed her forehead, then her cheek. "Tonight—okay, you made a mistake. Everybody makes mistakes. Yeah, there was a big scene, but it sounds like it's going to blow over."

Nadia's dark eyes gazed up into his, still so hesitant, so doubtful, that his heart ached to see it. Why did she keep taking the weight of the world onto herself, until she nearly broke under it?

"It's not just that," she whispered. "Every time I run into something else I don't know, it reminds me that I lost my teacher."

She said no more; she didn't have to. He knew her only teacher in witchcraft was her mother. When they'd first met, Mateo had thought Nadia was coping reasonably well with her mother's abandonment of the family. He'd slowly learned that wasn't true. In some ways she had only just begun dealing with it.

"I'm sorry," he said. "It sucks. I'd change it for you if I could."

"I know." She wound her arms more tightly around his waist, and then brought their mouths together in a kiss. Mateo opened his lips, kissed her deeper, breathed in the scent of her skin.

They'd had so little time. That first night, after the fire, they'd gone back to her house—

Her mouth under his, her body next to his. Their skin smelled like woodsmoke and blood. Mateo wrapped in her embrace, feeling her body shake with emotion and exhaustion. "I love you," said and heard, over and over until their voices mingled together. Curled together in her bed, still clothed and too tired for more, but somehow complete. Knowing they'd be together, completely, before long—

But that certainty had been an illusion.

Since then, they'd had to take care of Verlaine, deal with Elizabeth, confront the new demon in their midst . . . it felt like the whole world was trying to tear Nadia away from him almost as soon as he'd found her.

But there was no way he was going to let that happen.

Mateo slipped his hands beneath the hem of her sweater to grasp her right at the waist, his fingers against warm, bare skin. Nadia made this little gasp against his throat that did something to his pulse, made him go warm all over. He leaned into her more, the two of them fusing together in their embrace.

When they broke apart, Mateo was breathing hard, but he had to smile. "Feeling better?"

"Yeah." Nadia laughed, a little self-conscious—but he saw that flush in her cheeks. "You know how much I love you, right?"

"Maybe as much as I love you. But maybe not. Because I'm not sure that's even possible."

The back door opened; Mateo and Nadia broke apart, at least enough to be decent. It was Dad, who said nothing but gave them both a look. "I hate to be the bearer of bad tidings, but you just got an eight-top."

"Eight?" Large parties were the worst. Besides—"It's almost nine o'clock! We close in half an hour."

"They're here, and they're hungry, and unfortunately for young love, I let the other server leave early tonight." His dad pointed a finger at him. "Could've been you if you'd asked first."

"Okay, okay. I'll be right there." As the door swung shut, Mateo turned back to Nadia. "I'm sorry. This sucks."

"It's all right."

"You're sure you're okay?"

"Lots better," she promised, even though that wasn't exactly the same thing.

"What are you going to do now?"

"Find a spell I can use to take down Elizabeth," Nadia said. "And figure out how in the world I'm supposed to practice that before I use it against her."

It was as though Mateo's embrace had healed her. Restored her. Nadia returned home energized and ready to work. Even though she had to go through an entire paternal interrogation the moment she walked in the door (*"Are you kidding? An ax? What is it about this place?"*), Nadia's mind never stopped racing with possibilities. By the time she was back in her attic, she was already halfway into a plan.

Weirdly it was the whole fiasco tonight that had set her on this path. Nadia now knew she shouldn't try to find a new spell, however powerful, and use it against Elizabeth. It took time to get to know a spell, to learn how to work with it and discover all the possible repercussions. She'd forgotten that tonight—not much chance she'd ever forget it again.

What Nadia needed was a familiar spell, one that was totally known, totally reliable . . . but could be made stronger, and used for a sneak attack.

Such as a spell of forgetting.

Nadia had used these spells only sparingly; her mother had warned her that if she ever used them on her parents she'd be in Big Trouble, and since Mom had possessed the powers to double-check whether she'd been spelled, Nadia had never broken that rule. But she'd pulled it out to make people at school forget cruel nicknames they'd invented for her and her friends, to break up a near-fight one time on the "L," and even to get out of detention for talking in class, once back in Chicago . . . a successful spellcasting she'd never shared with Mom.

Last month, a witch in town had used this spell against Mateo with near-disastrous results. She hadn't known Mateo was a Steadfast, hadn't known he would make her spell far more powerful than it had ever been before. Instead of forgetting that he'd found another witch, Mateo had forgotten everything: his name, how to speak English, how to stand, nearly how to breathe.

Nadia doubted a spell of forgetting could wreck Elizabeth that badly. Surely she would have some defenses. But if Nadia intensified the spell, and had Mateo with her, they could probably take away some of Elizabeth's memory. A lot of it.

Including, no doubt, much of her magic . . . quite possibly whatever magic she was using now to hurt Mrs. Purdhy. Enough to undo whatever her real plan was.

It was worth a try.

"Watch your back, Elizabeth," Nadia muttered as she got to work.

As he rode his motorcycle home, Mateo did his best not to see the dark magic that still bound Captive's Sound.

He was Nadia's Steadfast. That meant he had a window to magic's true nature, one even a witch couldn't match. His first few days as a Steadfast, the signs and portents had terrified him, but by now they were all too familiar.

Every time he looked at the sky, he saw the strange, roiling film between the town and the stars—the thing that seemed to seal them off from the rest of the world. Every time he glanced at the town hall, there was a strange, glowing energy around the building, almost like fire. Lines blazed deep in the ground, the concentric rings that centered in on the site of the Halloween carnival—the leftover target from Elizabeth's attempt to kill them all.

By now, Mateo could gun his motorcycle motor and drive past things like that without a second thought.

However, it became harder when he went home and got ready for bed. Maybe Mateo was learning how to be a Steadfast, but there was no learning how to bear the Cabot curse.

His Steadfast abilities allowed him to actually see the curse now, every time he looked in a mirror; it writhed around his head like a dark halo, one made of snakes and thorns. When Mateo looked at it, he knew that Elizabeth's curse ticked within him like a time bomb. He knew that eventually, like his mother, grandfather, and great-grandmother before him, like all his ancestors going back to colonial times, he would go mad from the burdens of his visions—the ones that showed him slivers of the future.

Mateo could avoid seeing himself in the mirror as he washed his face and brushed his teeth. He could take a couple of Tylenol PMs in the hopes of sleeping more deeply.

But he couldn't keep himself from dreaming.

Verlaine lay crumpled on the ground, crying so hard that the sobs racked her body. "How could you?" she said, to someone or something he couldn't see in the blur. "You had to take this, too. You had to take the only thing I ever had."

He tried to push forward, to see who it was who'd done this to Verlaine, though he still didn't know what had been done, what she might have lost. Instead Verlaine seemed to disappear as he stumbled—not through the strange, misty blur that had surrounded them before, but through a forest. The dead of night. Twigs snapped under his feet, and thick oak trees and pines surrounded him on every side like the bars of an oversize cage.

In the distance he saw the arc of a flashlight sweep through the gloom, and he ducked down. It was very important not to be seen. Why? He didn't know, couldn't remember, but fear had seized his heart, made his pulse feel like the thumping of fear itself trying to escape from inside his chest.

But he wasn't afraid for himself.

Nadia stood nearby, hiding behind the trunk of one of the trees. When she peeked around the corner, a shape in the darkness moved, swinging at her viciously. The blow sounded solid, even wet—the

crunch of bone in blood. She fell so limply that he knew she was
dead.

"*Nadia! No! Nadia—*"

Mateo woke in his room, breathing hard. He'd dreamed about losing Nadia before.

This was the first time he'd ever dreamed that she was truly dead.

And he always saw the future.

Not that anybody on Earth or in hell would care, but Asa was having a terrible night.

First he'd had to go to the emergency room with his parents. (He'd decided to think of them that way for simplicity's sake; besides, the idea of having parents again was novel enough to be entertaining.) Apparently the doctors decided his mother must have had some completely new reaction to the blood-pressure medication she was taking, and wanted to keep her overnight for observation.

"You promise I didn't hurt anyone?" She'd been teary-eyed and shaky as they settled her in her hospital bed, fixing foam-and-Velcro cuffs around her wrists and ankles just in case she snapped again. "I don't know what came over me."

"You were just sick, Mom. People will understand." Asa smiled at her, trying to be reassuring. It didn't come naturally to him, but clearly that was what was needed.

How strange, to be able to do that and feel . . . *happy* that she was comforted. Maybe that was some echo of his feelings for the long-ago human mother he could no longer remember. Maybe it was human nature, soaking into him through this human shell.

Regardless, Asa thought he liked it.

Then he and his father had to leave her there and go home, which meant another couple of hours of running interference on the phone ("He can't talk right now. We're all very shaken up; I'm sure you understand. Can I take a message?") while his father Googled the blood-pressure drug to see if it had caused psychotic breaks in anyone else, then called his lawyer to talk about suing GlaxoSmithKline.

Once Asa finally had a minute, he went upstairs to take a shower. There was just *something* about misfired magic that felt sticky against your skin, like flop sweat or spilled syrup.

He stripped off Jeremy Prasad's designer clothes—the two-hundred-dollar jeans, the cashmere sweater, even the Calvin Klein underwear. How ridiculous, and yet . . . he had to admit, he looked good in those clothes.

As he stood in the bathroom, steam from his shower filling the air, he took a moment to admire his new possession. This body was exceedingly well made, wasn't it? Long and lean. Taller than either of his parents, thanks to a trick of genetics. Thick, black hair that curled slightly; tawny skin; angled brows that strongly framed large, dark eyes. Sculpted muscles that gave him strong arms and good abs—and the magic that ensnared him here kept this body from aging or degenerating, so he didn't even have to work out to keep this. Jeremy had done all the sit-ups for him.

Then he felt it—a sickening dip and sway as though he

were at sea in a storm. Asa tried to right himself, but the sensation wasn't coming from the room or the chair; it was coming from within.

It was as though something was turning him inside out, blinding him to his real surroundings, stretching him thin and forcing his attention on one point, one thing—

Elizabeth. She sat cross-legged on her floor, surrounded by glinting points of broken glass. It was as though he were with her, and yet he wasn't.

He realized she had conjured this, making at least a shadow of him appear before her. But why did it have to hurt so much?

"Would it kill you to get a cell phone like everyone else?" he snapped.

She ignored this. She ignored pretty much everything she couldn't use. Even the fact that he stood naked in front of her was meaningless to Elizabeth. "There was a disturbance tonight. Magic far too strong for its purpose. You were near it, weren't you?"

"But not responsible."

"Nadia?"

"Even though her Steadfast was nowhere near her. It turns out she's significantly out of her depth."

Asa told her the whole story, exaggerating Nadia's panic slightly; it made the telling better, and it seemed to amuse Elizabeth, insofar as anything that ancient and evil could be amused. When he got to the part where his mother had started swinging an ax around, she actually laughed out loud.

74

"Good," she said. "The sooner she recognizes her own limitations, the sooner she'll understand that she has to turn to me."

He didn't understand the urgency behind Elizabeth's desire to convert Nadia Caldani into her apprentice, but it wasn't his to question. "What next?"

Elizabeth smiled slowly. "She won't come to me for her own sake. Nadia will only turn to me to save another. The question is who."

7

ELIZABETH WALKED THROUGH THE STREETS OF CAPTIVE'S Sound—ignoring those who waved and smiled at her, knowing they would remember her smiling back anyway—until she reached the old blue Victorian house on Felicity Street. There she knocked and waited for an answer.

Nadia's father opened the door, and this time she really did smile.

He returned the smile, but vaguely. Her protective glamours would allow him only to think of her as one of his daughter's friends, a sweet girl with chestnut curls. "Elizabeth—that's the name, right? Nice to see you."

"Hi, Mr. Caldani. Can I come in?"

"Sure." For a moment, his expression clouded; probably he was wondering why she was here in the middle of a school day. But Elizabeth knew that confusion would resolve in an instant. Her glamours would make him sure that she'd never be anyplace she wasn't supposed to be. Mr. Caldani stepped back, allowing her to come inside. "You weren't mixed up in that carnival business, were you? Sounds scary."

"I saw the fire." It had surrounded her. Elizabeth had meant for it to kill her—had meant to die for the liberation of the One Beneath. Such glorious light. "Honestly, it was kind of exciting."

"It wouldn't have been as exciting if you were in it, trust me. Now, what can I do for you?"

"Nadia said I could borrow her copy of *Sense and Sensibility*. It's in her room, but she couldn't get away to come here with me. Can I get it?"

"Sure. No problem." He paused again. Was he wondering if Nadia even had a copy of that book? Elizabeth didn't know whether it existed, nor did she care. All that mattered was that Simon overcome his natural resistance to allowing a near-stranger into his daughter's room, even when that daughter wasn't home. He would, of course; he couldn't help himself. "Come on. I'll show you the way."

Together they went up the narrow, winding stairs, the ones illuminated by sunshine through an old stained-glass window. The house was a comfortable one, and—she could sense—it was beautiful in its ramshackle way. Elizabeth remembered when the only houses in towns had been the ones settlers built themselves, when she had lived behind paper windows, atop dirt floors. She had heard of a concept called *nostalgia*—a longing for how things used to be—and thought it was merely further proof that humans were fools.

No one with any sense would want to go backward. You could only look ahead.

"Here you go," Simon said as they went through a door at the top of the stairwell. "Nadia's bedroom."

Elizabeth smiled as she turned around. The walls were a soft, warm orange, the bedspread plain white and immaculate. Pressed flowers and leaves filled simple silver frames hung upon the walls. To anyone else, this would look like a simple, pleasant space; to her, it was a sign of an intelligent witch's work. Orange was a color neutral to spells in a way that blue, red, black, and white weren't; the neatness indicated a dedication to both Craft and secrecy. But the plants in the frames—that was a brilliant touch. Elizabeth lifted her delicate hand in front of the frames in turn. "Willow. White sage. Lavender. These plants are all for protection, you know."

"Protection from what?"

"Bad dreams, for one."

"Huh." Mr. Caldani looked nonplussed. "Nadia's really not the superstitious type. Let's see. Here's where the books live."

The shelves were overladen with books new and used, paperback and hardback. He began searching through them, which gave Elizabeth a chance to touch her quartz ring.

Mr. Caldani muttered, "*Sense and Sensibility*? I'm not see-ing it—but hang on. It could be anywhere in here."

She looked at him, concentrated, and cast a spell of desire.

Light flashed in the room, though Mr. Caldani wouldn't

be able to see it. All he would be able to see—all he saw now, as he slowly turned to see her—was how beautiful Elizabeth was.

How incredibly, irresistibly beautiful.

Now he would be blinded to the fact that this was his daughter's room, his daughter's friend; he would only see Elizabeth's willowy body, the perfect oval of her face, the brilliance of her eyes.

He is mine, Elizabeth thought. *Nadia, your father belongs to me.*

"There's no rush to find the book," she murmured as she stepped closer to him. "We can hang out in here for a while."

Mr. Caldani swallowed hard. He was struggling. Fighting it. Sometimes they fought.

"Is it on this shelf, maybe?" Elizabeth stepped next to him, so close that she nearly fit in the angle between his body and the bookshelf. Her shoulder brushed against his chest.

"I—hmm. Don't see it."

"I'll check down here." She sank to her knees by his side, but Mr. Caldani immediately backed away. Elizabeth frowned. "Are you okay?"

"Yes, of course. But I, ah, have a conference call for work that starts soon, and really—you know, just get Nadia to bring it to you tomorrow at school. How's that?"

Elizabeth hesitated, then rose. "All right." She strolled out without a backward glance, saying nothing besides a very ordinary farewell; she pretended not to hear the strain in

Mr. Caldani's voice as he wished her a good day.

The warden-crow circled overhead as Elizabeth walked back home. She hadn't completed her task today; the spell hadn't been strong enough to overcome his resistance. Few men would have resisted temptation so successfully.

But there were spells that could take away any man's will, if she needed them.

Nadia seemed to rely strongly upon her family. If she continued to complicate Elizabeth's plans—to defy the right and natural path in front of her—then the very things Nadia relied on were the ones that would have to be crushed into oblivion.

When Elizabeth walked out the door, Simon Caldani shut it, dead-bolted it, and sank to the floor.

What the hell is happening to you? That wasn't like him. Had never been like him. Simon had always thought guys who dated women much younger than themselves looked a little pathetic; he'd rolled his eyes when one of the other partners at his old firm brought a twenty-two-year-old date to the Christmas party. But at least twenty-two was legal, for God's sake.

She was his daughter's age! He'd never imagined he was even the kind of guy who *could* find that attractive, much less the kind who actually *would*. The more Simon thought about that moment upstairs, the weirder it seemed to him. Normally he'd never have let anyone in Nadia's room without her permission, even a friend. And when he'd found himself attracted to Elizabeth, it was almost as though some kind of . . . trance had come over him, as crazy as that sounded.

The fact is, it's been way too long since your wife left.

Simon thudded his head against the door, disgusted by himself, and sure of only one thing: He was never, ever going to be alone with that girl again.

"It's just an experiment," Nadia said as they waited their turn for "suicide" runs across the gym. PE was such a joy.

Verlaine didn't look convinced. "An experiment *on me.*"

"Well, yeah."

"Explain to me again why this is necessary?"

Nadia had known this would be a hard sell, but they had to do it. She needed the experimentee to be someone she knew, somebody who could be questioned thoroughly afterward without it raising too much suspicion. The only other possible candidate was Mateo, and his mind was under enough strain with the burden of the Cabot curse. So she had to get Verlaine on board.

Before she could say another word, though, the coach blew his whistle; their fifth turn was up. So she and Verlaine had to run to the first free throw line, back, half court, back, second free throw line, back—suicide runs *sucked.*

But as they went, Nadia managed to speak loudly enough for Verlaine to hear her over the thump and squeak of tennis shoes on the court. "I have to—try to make—Elizabeth forget stuff. Right?"

Verlaine nodded; her pale skin was already flushed red.

Panting, Nadia continued, "But I have to make sure—I can pinpoint—the spell. Make her forget first—what I want her—to forget most."

"And this means—I have to forget something?" Verlaine said between gasps.

"Got to be—one thing—you'd like to forget. Right?"

They were on the last leg, the full-court run, and neither of them spoke until they reached the finish. As they collided with the padded back wall, Nadia scooped her sweaty hair away from her face. Verlaine said, "Could you make me forget the time I messed up at my third-grade piano recital, and the whole room went quiet while I tried to think of what to play next, and in that total silence of that crowded church, I farted louder than anybody else you ever heard in your life?"

Nadia bit her lip so she wouldn't laugh. "I can try."

"Then okay. Because that memory is one I could live without."

They didn't get a chance to try it until after school. For safety's sake, Mateo didn't join them; Verlaine had sensibly drawn the line at maybe forgetting how to breathe. They walked toward Swindoll Park, which was more or less back to normal now that the charred remains of the haunted house had been demolished. Verlaine hugged her 1950s satin bomber jacket more tightly around her as she sat on the steps of the bandstand. Nadia stood about a dozen feet away.

"Come on," Verlaine called. "Let's get this show on the road. It's cold out here."

"I'm so taking you to Chicago some January so you can

see what real cold is," Nadia called back. In truth, she was hesitating—unsure at the last moment.

The key to focusing a spell is choosing the most specific ingredients, while devoting your mind to precisely what you want erased, Nadia reminded herself. So. Hand on garnet charm, ingredients summoned:

Evidence of absence.
Proof of love's existence.
Proof of love's death.

She had to go for simple, precise examples of each one. Brief moments that had pricked her like a knife's point—

Half of her parents' closet, empty now that her mother's stuff was gone.

The time she'd played hide-and-seek with three-year-old Cole and simply didn't bother seeking him, because she was so desperate for some time alone. And then feeling so bad she'd tricked him—only for him to hug her as tight as ever before they went to bed.

Reading that email from her mother's lawyer, the one where she'd learned Dad actually begged Mom to see their kids, and Mom ignored him—

The flash was subtle, the sort of thing that could seem like a trick of the autumn sunlight. After a moment, Verlaine blinked. "Did you do something?"

"I think so?" Nadia said. "Do you remember your third-grade piano recital?"

Verlaine frowned. ". . . I guess I must have had one."

"You don't remember?" When Verlaine shook her head no, Nadia clapped her hands together. "Yes. Yes! We did it! Oh, wait." She froze. "Do you remember how to play the piano at all?"

"Nope."

Oh, no. She'd gone too far, taken too much. Deflated, Nadia slumped against the nearest tree. "Verlaine—I'm sorry."

"What are you talking about? I only took piano for two years. I forgot years ago how to do anything besides find middle C. After third grade I never wanted to take lessons anymore." Verlaine shrugged. "I don't know why. Hey, were you going to make me forget something?"

"We're good," Nadia said with a grin.

In Verlaine's opinion, the Wikipedia entry on demons needed some serious editing.

It included every single mythology and folklore about demons, whether they were ancient Hebrew "hairy beings," Greek divine spirits, pre-Islamic lesser gods, or one of those creepy things that climbed inside little kids and made their parents call an exorcist. *See also: devil, fiend, ghoul.*

She sighed. It wasn't as though she expected a tab titled *Real Demons*, which she could click down to for the straight story, but still—there was so little information, and so much of it contradicted itself.

Of course she had checked sources beyond Wikipedia. However, it turned out that searching the internet for "real demons" was basically a shortcut to all the crazy of the world, right there on your computer screen. Verlaine now knew more than she'd ever wanted to know about various death-metal bands, wannabe Satanists, actual Satanists (who sounded much nicer than the wannabes), a fashion label, and several extremely delusional individuals. But she was no closer to knowing any more about the truth of what Asa was, or what he might be capable of.

The only authoritative sources Verlaine had on the supernatural were Nadia, whose word she trusted, and Elizabeth, whose word she didn't trust at all but whose actions spoke for themselves. Elizabeth had summoned a demon to help her do evil; Nadia said demons were the servants of the One Beneath.

But still, if they didn't ask to be His servants—if it was something they were created for, or got trapped into—

—if Asa was as much a victim of Elizabeth's black magic as Verlaine was herself—

She pushed her laptop away, disgruntling her cat, Smuckers, who had been napping on the bed beside her. "Sorry, buddy."

Why was it so hard to believe that somebody could be destined for evil? Jeremy Prasad had gotten most of the way there on his own, no possession required.

Yet it haunted her. Verlaine couldn't shake the idea of being *forced* to serve something so hideous, so hateful that it would burn and crush and kill. Maybe Asa didn't mind; maybe he enjoyed it. That might be how demons were, at least once they got . . . demonized.

As she sat cross-legged on her quilt, staring down at her

glowing laptop screen, Verlaine wondered why this got to her so badly. There was no question that Asa was working for Elizabeth, even that he seemed to enjoy taunting them about it. Why should she care? Her old crush on Jeremy Prasad wasn't that strong; she'd really only ever liked his body. Guiltily she realized she hadn't even mourned his death. Well, he wouldn't have mourned hers.

"Like the word *enslaved* on its own shouldn't be enough," she muttered. Slavery was evil, no matter who was in the shackles.

Then she heard a rustling in the hedge next to the house she shared with her dads. Though the sound made her ears prick up, Verlaine thought little of it; probably one of the neighborhood dogs got out again.

Then she heard it again—and louder. And that wasn't a dog. That sounded like footsteps.

"Uncle Gary?" she called. "Uncle Dave?" Verlaine hurried from her room—but Uncle Dave had his headphones on, because apparently his World of Warcraft guild had a major raid tonight, and Uncle Gary was on the phone with his sister in Nebraska. She considered making one of them hang up, or both, but that was stupid. She'd heard footsteps, no more than that. It was legal for people to walk around in their neighborhood. Even this late at night. This close to the house.

Verlaine snapped on the outside lights. Once again, some rustling—*all right, that's enough.*

She grabbed a flashlight from the hall cabinet—the big, heavy one that would hurt like hell if she swung into the side of someone's head. Then she fished around in her purse and found her rape-whistle key chain, the one Uncle Dave made her promise to carry at all times, and stuck the whistle between her lips. Verlaine hesitated for one moment with her free hand on the doorknob, wondering if this was a good idea or not. Very not. As in, actually intensely dumb.

Either it's nothing out there, and you need to see it's nothing before you can go to sleep, she rationalized, *or it's some dark-magic mojo that can get you even through your walls. So you might as well go outside.*

The outdoor lights shone in tight beams, which meant some places were extremely bright and others were still dark. Verlaine edged down the front walk, then toward the side of the house where she'd heard the rustling—right by her room. She swept her flashlight in front of her, but saw only the feeble brown grass. Her heart was pounding, even though it was nothing; it had to be nothing—

A hand closed over her shoulder and she gasped, the whistle falling from her lips, but then she sagged back. "Uncle Gary!"

"Honey, what are you doing? Did you hear something?"

"No. I mean, yes, but it's probably nothing."

"Well, let's see." He took the flashlight from her and stepped in front. Verlaine couldn't help feeling amused at the thought of Uncle Gary putting himself between her and the forces of evil—if he only knew!

Then she realized he'd do it even if he did know, and she hugged him from behind. He laughed. "Now, what was that for?"

"Just for being awesome."

When they got to the side hedge, Uncle Gary pushed some of the branches aside. "Look at that. Somebody vandalized Bradford's little garden. Who would do that to a gnome?"

The garden gnome that usually watched over their neighbor's vegetable patch had been torn up—no. Melted. It had melted right where it stood, like it had been exposed to some terrible heat.

She remembered Asa, and the unearthly, demonic heat that emanated from him every time he came near.

As Uncle Gary went next door to give them the bad news, Verlaine prodded the melted stuff with the toe of her shoe. Then she looked over at her house. This exact scorched spot was the very best place to see the light from her bedroom window.

Asa walked home through the dark, hands in the pockets of his black coat. He'd been playing spy for Elizabeth— tracking and observing Nadia and her closest friends, the better to learn their habits and vulnerabilities.

With Nadia and Mateo that was simple enough. But he found himself getting distracted when he watched Verlaine.

There was something about her that intrigued him.

He found himself walking home without seeing the houses around him, or the stars overhead. In his mind he saw only the silver fall of Verlaine's hair.

8

NADIA SAT BENEATH THE PROTECTIVE BLUE CEILING OF her attic, poring through the Book of Shadows that had belonged to Goodwife Hale centuries before. So much information was written down in here—spells Nadia had never heard of before, the history that had told her the truth about Elizabeth Pike—but there wasn't anything about whatever had happened to Mrs. Purdhy a couple of days ago.

She *had* been able to find specifics about demons, but almost wished she hadn't. They were only called upon for the darkest, most dangerous magic. And now he was following Verlaine.

Probably he's following all of us, Nadia thought. *Spying for Elizabeth.*

Well, let Elizabeth learn what she could. If Nadia perfected this spell of forgetting, Elizabeth would lose this information as well as all her magic.

Right now, though, she was distracted. She'd gotten an email from Faye Walsh today, asking Nadia to schedule a conference. There was no reason for them to have a conference. Not unless Ms. Walsh was about to start asking questions Nadia couldn't answer.

The way she'd stared at Nadia after the incident at town hall—had Ms. Walsh guessed the truth? Did she somehow know Nadia was a witch?

"Naaaaaaadiaaaaa!" Cole yelled from downstairs. "Dad says we all need to get out of the house for a while!"

Probably that really meant that he'd botched making dinner again. But eating out meant going to a restaurant, which meant Mateo. "Be right there!"

"See, buddy?" Nadia ruffled Cole's hair as the entire family got settled in their booth at La Catrina. "We made it just fine."

"Something always happens when we try to go here." Her little brother looked around at the skeletons on the walls; he didn't seem to care that they were all happily playing guitars or dancing. "Every time."

"Not this time. We finally get to try the best Mexican food in town for ourselves." Dad clapped his hands together. He seemed cheerful—way too cheerful, really, unless he'd had a serious jones for Mexican food the last couple of months and was now more excited about empanadas than any other man on Earth. Nadia felt like he'd been in a weird mood all day, or at least since she got home from school, but probably it was just work crap. Lawyers seemed to deal with that a lot.

Across the room, she finally caught sight of Mateo at the same moment he saw her. Even though he had platters of fajitas in his hands and balanced on his forearms, he grinned at her through the steam.

That was all it took. It was as though the world was in black and white until she saw Mateo, and then it was in color—all the vibrant gold, red, and turquoise of La Catrina coming alive around her, like Dorothy stepping into Oz. As though she'd only listened to the noise of knives on plates and dull conversations and now she could hear the music, Mateo showed her how vivid the world around her really was, how beautiful, if she'd only see.

When he came to their table, he was wearing a smile so broad it almost made her laugh—though probably she looked just as stupid. He only glanced away to slide some crayons and a kids' place mat to Cole. "Glad you guys stopped by."

"The hero himself," Dad said, and held out his hand to shake.

Mateo shrugged as if it had been no big deal, when in fact he'd helped her dad pull Cole out of their wrecked car, then rescued Nadia himself. That was the first time his visions had led him to her, the night they'd met. "Good to see you, Mr. Caldani. Now, do you guys want to hear tonight's special?"

Nadia ordered her usual without even thinking about it, the better to concentrate on how Mateo looked in his black T-shirt.

Her dad finished, ". . . and a margarita. Could definitely use a margarita. Nadia can drive home, can't you, honey?"

"Sure thing." That, too, was surprising. Dad rarely drank around her and Cole.

"Okay, coming right back with your drinks." Mateo finished writing on his notepad, ducked down to kiss Nadia on the cheek, then hurried to check on yet another new table nearby . . . Kendall Bender, in fact, though instead of her usual troop of loyal Plastics, she was with her family. There seemed to be about a dozen of them, from grandparents to an older sister in a college sweatshirt; they'd be keeping Mateo busy.

Dad raised his eyebrows. "Wait a second. I thought Mateo Perez had a girlfriend."

"Oh. Well—he didn't, actually. There was a girl he was hanging around with, but it wasn't, I mean—" Nadia didn't even know how to explain the whole Elizabeth situation in a way her father could understand. So she just shrugged and grinned. "Well, he has a girlfriend *now*."

"Uh-*huh*. This is major news. When were you going to tell me?"

Nadia laughed. "When I thought you wouldn't freak out about it the way you're doing right this second?"

"Aw, come on. This isn't freaking out. This is—normal dad curiosity. You know it's okay with me that you're dating, right?" Her dad leaned forward, suddenly way more intense than the situation called for. "Mateo's a great guy. You couldn't have done any better. And besides, a normal, healthy love life is . . . healthy. And normal."

She was beginning to think that her dad might be talking about more than her love life now, which wasn't something she wanted to add to her list of worries. "Yeah. Sure."

Cole looked up from his coloring. "When you kiss him, does he put his tongue inside your mouth?"

Dad pointed a finger. "You think you're pulling the innocent-little-kid routine, but we can see right through you. Right through to your bones, just like one of the skeletons on the wall! Want me to get a sombrero for you? Then we can put you on the wall, too." This made Cole start giggling, and saved Nadia from having to answer that question.

"Be right back," she said as she scooted out of the booth. Her dad, now coloring with Cole, just nodded.

In the bathroom, Nadia ran her fingers through her hair, checked her outfit, straightened up. It wasn't like Mateo cared—he'd seen her covered with soot, soaked with sea- water, you name it—but still. The more a guy thought you were beautiful no matter what, the more you wanted to be beautiful for him. *If you liked me all grimy with cobwebs, you won't even be able to handle me now.*

"Oh, hey," Kendall said, managing to reapply her lipstick and talk at the same time. "You sure do come here a lot. Like, all the time. I would've thought you guys would want Italian food sometimes."

Even by Kendall standards, this made no sense. Nadia frowned. "Why?"

"You're Italian, right? Caldani?"

"Actually, no." Dad usually said the name was Persian. That was an old habit, going back to when he was a little boy in the 1970s and his family had to deal with a lot of prejudice; the fact that his family had actually fled the Ayatollah Khomeini didn't stop people from blaming them for his rule. Nadia preferred the direct approach. "We're Iranian."

Mom's half was part Scottish, part Greek, but Nadia didn't bother mentioning that. It was too much fun watching Kendall's eyes get wider. "I thought you were American."

"We are American. You didn't think I was actually from Italy before, did you?" Nadia took another look at herself in the mirror. Gray T-shirt tucked into jeans, sari-print scarf knotted around her neck just so, earrings dangling instead of caught: Everything looked right.

"Well, no, *but*." Kendall said this like it somehow made sense. "Are you guys Muslim?"

"No. We're Chaldean Catholics. Well, at least in theory. Not many Chaldean Catholic churches around in the United States." There had been one in Chicago, but in Rhode Island, particularly Captive's Sound? Forget it. "What would it matter if we were Muslim anyway?"

But Kendall had already moved on to the subject that, clearly, had interested her all along. "So, looks like you and Mateo are a thing."

Nadia felt an irrational stab of annoyance. It wasn't like Mateo would ever in a thousand years go for Kendall—and to be fair, Kendall didn't seem to be into Mateo, either. But she was always sticking her nose in where it didn't belong.

Still—Nadia was proud of loving Mateo, being with him. Why not tell Kendall? "Yeah. We're together."

"Does Elizabeth Pike know?"

"Definitely."

"Bet she's not happy."

Halloween night, Kendall had seen Mateo under Elizabeth's spell. Nadia decided to bunt. "They decided they're better off as friends."

"Interesting" was the only reply, in a tone of voice that told Nadia the entire school would hear about this by tomorrow morning, if not within the hour. Kendall Bender was sort of a one-woman amplification system for gossip.

Good, she decided. *Let the whole world know.*

She said, "See you," and left the bathroom as quickly as she could, giving Kendall a smile so warm it would have to confuse her.

As she went back to her family's booth, Nadia glanced over her shoulder to see Mateo taking the check to yet another table. He had the most wonderful lopsided grin, and he seemed to be kind to everybody, even customers who were questioning the tab. This wasn't a guy whose love she had to fear.

There's no spell to break. Mateo wouldn't leave you. He's not going anywhere.

Kendall's voice rang out, sharp with fear, cutting through all the other chatter like a knife. "Riley?"

When Nadia looked over at the Bender family's table, she saw the older girl, the one in the Brown sweatshirt, putting her hands to her throat. That was the sign for choking, and Mateo ran toward the table—but he froze just as Nadia gasped in horror, just as Riley opened her mouth and black liquid began dribbling out.

Everything was a blur after that. Kendall screamed, and Mateo grabbed his phone to dial 9-1-1, and Cole began crying. Although Nadia swept him into her arms, she never took her eyes away from Riley Bender. The panic in her eyes, the gruesome smell of death, the burns that dark, tarry stuff left on the table: All of it was just like what had happened to Mrs. Purdhy, who was still in a coma at the hospital.

And if this was the same thing that had happened to Mrs. Purdhy, that meant . . .

Nadia turned to see Elizabeth standing in the doorway of La Catrina. Even as everyone else ran around in a panic, Elizabeth walked slowly through the crowd, weaving her way through the onlookers. Mateo didn't see her—he was on his knees trying to talk to Riley while her family held her head upright so she wouldn't choke. But it seemed to Nadia like he ought to feel Elizabeth approaching, like a chill in the air or a tremor of the earth. Cold snaked through the place behind her, around her.

"Hi, Nadia," Elizabeth said as though nothing were going on. "Hi there, Mr. Caldani." Her father's face went very red, for some reason.

"What are you doing?" Nadia whispered. "Why are you doing this?"

Of course Elizabeth didn't answer. She only stooped

beside the Benders' table, right by a smoldering puddle of the black liquid. Once again she dipped her fingers into it and painted it onto her upper arm, ignoring the searing of her own flesh. Nobody around her noticed that, or thought it was odd. As always, her magic protected her from unwelcome attention—while she was choking Riley Bender from the inside out.

Riley slumped over into the booth, unconscious. Her family's wailing was drowned out only by the sound of ambulance sirens approaching. Elizabeth rose to her feet, and there was nothing for Nadia to do but hold on to Cole and watch her go.

9

MATEO WANTED TO ASK NADIA WHAT HAD JUST HAP-
pened, but right now it was more important to keep between
his father and the outraged Bender family.

"What the hell are you serving in this place?" Mr. Bender
demanded. "My little girl's on the way to the hospital right
now because of you!"

"Stay calm, my friend. Stay calm." Dad was handling the
situation pretty well, in Mateo's opinion, but it didn't matter.
Mr. Bender had lost it.

"You put, what, chemicals in the food? What?"

"Daddy, please!" Tears were streaming down Kendall's
face. "Riley didn't eat anything. The same thing happened
to our teacher at school. It's some kind of disease." Nobody
else seemed to hear her.

"Somebody is responsible for this!" Mr. Bender yelled.
It was just possible to see the panic behind his anger, but it

wouldn't matter what he was feeling if he broke Dad's face.

"Tony, come on." Kendall's grandmother started pulling at Mr. Bender's arm. "We have to go to the hospital. The ambulance is going to leave any second." That finally seemed to get through to him, and he turned. Mateo sighed in relief; his father did the same.

Then Nadia put one hand on his shoulder. She must have just handed Cole off to her dad. "Mateo, did you see—"

The golden light behind her. The column behind her so like a tree. The fall of her hair, the expression on her face. He'd seen it before.

Mateo yanked Nadia down to the floor mere instants before Mr. Bender's fist slammed into the column—just behind where her face had been. The paint cracked, creating a spiderweb around the brand-new dent.

"Hey, hey!" Now Mr. Caldani was furious, too. "What are you doing? That's my daughter!"

"I—I thought—I was going for that other kid, the one who brought her the food—" Kendall's father pulled his hand back; he'd struck the column hard enough to cut open his knuckles. If Nadia had still been standing there, she'd have suffered a black eye and a broken nose at the least, maybe even a concussion. He remembered the wet crack of bone he'd heard in his dreams and shuddered. Mateo leaned his head against her shoulder for a moment, grateful to have kept her safe. At least the curse was worth something.

"Daddy, Riley never ate anything!" Kendall wailed. "Why won't you ever listen to me?"

Mr. Bender looked like he was in shock. Dad put one arm around Mr. Bender's shoulders. "Listen to me, my friend. You're not yourself. Your child's sick. Let's go look after her, okay? She needs you now."

It worked. Mr. Bender finally went to the door, surrounded by his family, though he still seemed to be in a daze.

"Whoa." Nadia slowly rose to her feet, and Mateo rose with her. "How did you know he was going to do that? Oh, wait. Was it one of your dreams?"

"Yeah. I didn't understand it until just now." He ran one hand through his hair. This was—not good. At all. "Did Elizabeth do this?"

"She was here. You didn't see her, but I did."

"Why? Why go after Kendall's sister?"

"I still don't know." Nadia looked so lost, so sad, that Mateo wanted to take her into his arms.

But then her father was there, still irate at the man who had nearly hurt her, and her baby brother was sobbing. Mateo's dad came up behind him. "We're going to have to comp drinks and appetizers for every table," he muttered, "just to make up for the disturbance, and if people start believing she actually ate something here that did this to her?"

"She didn't. People will know that. It's okay."

"Wish I could believe you. But come on, help me clean this up. What the hell is that gunk on the floor?"

Before his father could bend down to examine the smoldering black stuff, Mateo caught his arm. "Don't touch it, Dad. No matter what you do, don't touch it."

Nadia had meant to go home with Dad and Cole; by now Cole was sobbing. Ever since Mom left, he got scared so easily. Something like this meant nightmares for sure. If she sang him to sleep, or rubbed his back, maybe it would help.

Just as they got to the car, though, Nadia looked up and saw a figure sitting on a corner bench, pale in the nighttime gloom. As always, Elizabeth wore a white dress. She hadn't gone home; she just sat there with her hands folded, as though waiting for a bus.

"Go home without me," Nadia said quietly to her father. "I'll be there soon."

Dad was too distracted to argue. "Yeah, check on Mateo. Tell his dad to talk to me if that guy tries to sue. I can find a good torts lawyer for him."

"Sure."

Nadia crossed the street, walking toward Elizabeth. In a town as small as Captive's Sound, even this spot by one of the main intersections was quiet and almost deserted. Nadia didn't see anyone else any closer than the La Catrina parking lot; their only audience was a crow that had perched on a nearby lamppost and seemed to be watching them with odd, grayish eyes.

Elizabeth's pale face and curling hair made her look like a pre-Raphaelite painting, soft and dreamy, but there was no mistaking the menace just beneath the surface. Like that Ophelia picture, Nadia thought . . . if the girl climbed out of the river and decided to kill Hamlet instead.

As Nadia took the final steps and stood in front of Elizabeth, she was able to see the new burns on her shoulder—two lines that crossed the ones she'd made when Mrs. Purdhy collapsed, but at an odd angle. She willed herself to remember the pattern, to memorize it.

"You're killing people," Nadia said.

"They won't die." Elizabeth motioned toward the other side of the bench, inviting Nadia to sit by her; Nadia remained standing. If Elizabeth cared, she gave no sign. "At least, not yet."

"Then why are you hurting them?"

"If you knew more about witchcraft, you would understand. That's why you must become my student."

Nadia had to laugh. "Why would you ever, *ever* think that could happen?"

"Mateo isn't here now. There's no need to posture for his benefit. We can be entirely honest with each other." When Elizabeth leaned forward, her usual hazy inattention to the mundane world around her vanished; Nadia felt the full sharpness of her attention. "You've taken yourself almost as far in the Craft as you can go on your own. Already you're working at the very limits of your knowledge, and you've seen the dangers, haven't you? Face facts. You make mistakes. Some of them are merely amusing, but some of them go beyond that."

They'd taken Mrs. Prasad away in a van. Apparently she was still under twenty-four-hour psychiatric observation.

Her son had already been killed; would she wind up in an institution, too?

"I'm still learning," Nadia said, as evenly as she could manage. Anger bubbled beneath the surface, but she was trying to keep it under control. The less Elizabeth expected a fight, the more shocked she'd be when she got one. "Every witch learns throughout her lifetime."

"From her teacher."

"And from experience. And the spells of other witches."

"Which they learn in covens, not from some notes Prudence Hale wrote four hundred years ago." Elizabeth cocked her head, a movement uncannily like the crow perched nearby. "You must acknowledge that you will never fulfill your true potential as a witch without a teacher, and I'm your only chance."

"Okay, then, I'll never fulfill my potential," Nadia snapped. "Maybe I won't be as strong as I might have been, but—that doesn't mean I can't be good. And it definitely means I don't have to work for the One Beneath, or ever work with you."

Elizabeth's smile was easy, even contented. "You can say that so easily only because you haven't even begun to grasp what your true potential really is."

What did she mean by that? Deep within Nadia's revulsion and anger, another emotion flickered—curiosity.

But Elizabeth continued, "I am engaged in magnificent work, Nadia. Work that can reshape everything we have ever known about magic. You should help me. One way or another, you will help me. You can't imagine the glory waiting for you if you join me—though I can tell you what will happen first, if you continue to resist."

Nadia was very aware of the weight of her bracelet around her wrist. If Elizabeth cast a spell at this moment, could she counteract it? Did she intend to just strike her down, here and now?

Instead Elizabeth said, "First, I'll go back to your house, just like I did yesterday. Your father didn't mention it, did he? But not because he forgot. I promise you, he'll never forget yesterday afternoon."

"What did you do to him?"

"A spell of desire."

There was no such thing as a love spell; love sprang into being of its own accord, and that was all there was to it. But there were spells of desire—spells of lust, basically. Mom had always said it was wrong to use them outside of an existing relationship, "just to spice things up once in a while." They would be effective on anyone, though. A spell of desire put someone in your bed. Nadia remembered the way her father had wanted a drink, how flustered he'd been when Elizabeth walked in, and thought for a moment she might throw up.

Elizabeth shook her head. "Nothing happened this time. I didn't use much; I didn't think I'd have to. Upstanding men are so rare. Your father resisted very bravely. But it's in his head now—the idea of having me. Your mother left him months and months ago; he must be very lonely. If I go back to him, why, I might not even need the spell that time."

At first Nadia couldn't find her voice, but then she managed to say, "Leave my father out of this."

"It's too late for that. At this rate, I'm very close to going to Ms. Walsh for a counseling session, when I'd confess that I'd been pressured into an affair by one of my friends' fathers. I wonder what your life would be like if he went to prison for statutory rape? Would you be old enough to take custody of Cole full-time? Though of course you'd have to drop out of school and work to support you both. Even if you did find a job, you couldn't keep that lovely house, I'd imagine. There are some cheaper apartments further inland that might do. Then again, maybe you're not old enough after all. Would Cole go into foster care?" Elizabeth frowned, momentarily confused. "Or do they still have workhouses? I can't recall."

"You wouldn't dare!"

"What is it you think I wouldn't dare to do?" With a shrug, Elizabeth said, "You know, I could simply falsely accuse your father. Everyone would believe me."

They would. Part of Elizabeth's power was the deep enchantment she somehow held over most of the people in Captive's Sound. Nobody ever saw the horrible things she did, or questioned the fact that she'd been present for nearly four hundred years. Instead she was excused, accepted, and adored.

"But I wouldn't do that, Nadia. I would make sure he was really, truly guilty. Then the whole time he rotted away in prison, the knowledge of what he'd done would be there within your father. As I said, he's a good man. He'd never understand why he committed such a terrible sin. It would destroy him, slowly, from the inside. Even when he did get out of jail, he'd never be the same."

"Why are you doing this?" Nadia wished she could think of a spell horrible enough for Elizabeth, anything as gruesome as she deserved. "Why do you care if I work with you or not? The One Beneath has you already. Why would He need me?"

Elizabeth's eyes narrowed, the first sign of anger Nadia had glimpsed in her. "I'm only explaining what will happen if you don't join me. But you will. Then, instead of punishments, there will be rewards."

"There is nothing you have that I want. Listen to me. I'm going to figure out what you're up to, and I'm going to stop you. I don't care how hard it is or how long it takes. *I will stop you.* And if you don't leave my father alone, I swear to God, I'll find a way to make you sorry."

"We'll see, won't we?" With that, Elizabeth rose and walked away, never even glancing back. But Nadia felt as though she was still being watched, maybe because of that crow with the strange eyes, the one that never stopped staring at her.

Let her go. Don't argue any longer. Soon you're going to steal her memories. Steal her magic. And she won't be able to do anything to your father or to anyone else you love. To anyone, ever again. Let Elizabeth walk away tonight. Next time—the tables will be turned.

Nadia took one last look at the burns on Elizabeth's shoulder before she was swallowed up by the darkness. Imagined

106

the pattern burning itself into her retinas to leave a shadow, like staring at the sun too long.

Elizabeth came home to find Asa waiting for her, as her servant should; instead of kneeling and awaiting her bidding, however, he was reading a book by candlelight.

"You let yourself be diverted by human cares," she said, kicking shards of the broken glass in his direction.

He didn't flinch. "If you didn't want any distractions, maybe you shouldn't have sheathed me in someone who has homework."

"Don't let your human body deceive you into thinking that this world is anything more than a shell." Elizabeth went to one of the few pieces of furniture she still used, a chest of drawers so dilapidated that it leaned to one side and creaked as she pulled it open. "A shell we have already cracked."

"I can't help noticing that Nadia Caldani isn't with you." Asa smirked at her. Insolent beast.

"She will be." Elizabeth's fingers touched the thing she sought—a piece of human bone so old that it felt powdery in her hand. "Have you watched them as I bid you? Or are you too preoccupied?"

"I have watched. Their vulnerabilities are obvious, their schedules predictable. I know the vehicles they travel in, the comings and goings of their families, what they order at Burger King, so on, so forth. Which of them will you turn me toward first?"

"All three."

"Ambitious. You're not giving Nadia another chance?"

"I don't want you to destroy them. I want you to sow discontent." Elizabeth closed her fist tightly around the bone; motes of dust escaped between the cracks of her fingers. "She resists because she believes herself supported. Beloved. Take that away, and she'll be able to see reason."

"Tear her friends apart. Understood." Asa grinned. This was the kind of task demons were best at.

The quartz ring on her finger felt warmer against her skin as she called up ingredients for her spell:

Death in ice.
Hatred forever hidden.
A child never born.

Old memories sliced through her, so familiar that she could bear them without flinching.

"Please," the young man whispered. He was lost in the woods, a blizzard freezing the world around them, while Elizabeth stood and watched him from within a protective fire. "Please help me." He had no more strength to speak after that, could only lie there as his skin turned blue and the tears in his eyes froze.

"You will not raise your voice to me," her husband growled, lifting his arm in a way that meant only a threat, not a blow. Elizabeth wanted to use her spells to strike him down, but no man could ever see magic, could ever know that it existed, and so she meekly nodded and gave him a smile, that he might believe himself loved.

"Why won't it come?" The girl writhed in her childbed, trusting

Goodwife Pike to help her. There were tisanes of certain roots that might have brought the baby, certain spells that would have done more, but Elizabeth knew she would need this memory someday, and so she merely mopped the girl's brow and waited for the hours and pain to bear her down to death.

Elizabeth turned her hand upside down and opened her fingers. The bone dust remained suspended, a small, swirling cloud. She stepped back and let it rise until it steadied at eye level.

Asa looked bewildered, as well he might; this magic was obscure even for her. "What is that?"

"Something for Nadia Caldani," Elizabeth said.

"Another warning?"

"Indirectly. Call it a sign of things to come."

Mateo was dreaming.

He knew when he was in one of the visions by now. But that didn't make them any less immediate, less real—or less frightening.

The waves churned beneath the boat, twisting his gut with nausea. Overhead lightning split the sky. Mateo hung on to the sides of the boat and screamed, "Nadia!"

She didn't hear. He could see her in the distance, a dark, small shape almost lost in the whirling gray clouds and water. Her hair whipped and snapped in the wind, like a scarf of silk streaming behind her.

He had to get to her somehow. He had to get to her in time.

In time for what?

The boat suddenly rocked as though it had struck a shoal, but when Mateo turned he saw Gage sitting next to him. Gage's dreadlocks didn't blow in the breeze; his expression was stoic. It was as though nothing happening around them had the power to move him.

They were going too fast now. Their boat was slicing through the water at a speed so great it seemed to steal Mateo's breath away. Nadia was coming closer, closer—but soon he would race by her and she wouldn't even see him—

"Drop anchor!" Mateo shouted to Gage. "Drop anchor now!"

Gage lifted the heavy metal anchor, raised it high, then smashed it down toward Mateo's head—

Mateo woke with a start. In that first moment, he could only think, *Vision.*

But it still felt very real. Too real. Like, for instance, the flat, hard surface beneath his back—and, when he opened his eyes, the night sky above.

Cold wind made him hug himself tightly as he sat up and stared in disbelief. He was no longer in his bedroom. Instead Mateo lay in the rowboat tethered to the nearest dock. His hands were scraped and raw; even in his dreams, he'd tried to undo the ropes, to actually live out the vision playing within his head.

Was it a vision or was it real? Terror seized him at the thought of Nadia out there on the water alone—

No. It had to have been a vision. His boat had never left the dock, he was wearing a T-shirt and pajama pants that left him shivering in the cold, and Gage was nowhere to be seen.

But the vision had drawn him out of his house. Made him

do something dangerous. If someone had come upon him during the vision—someone Mateo might have thought was hurting Nadia—

I could have done anything. Anything. And I wouldn't have been able to stop myself.

Mateo shuddered as he realized: This was how people began to go mad.

10

AS PEOPLE PUSHED PAST THEM IN THE HALLWAY, HURRY-
ing to their morning classes, Nadia smoothed Mateo's hair
back with her hands. "Night terrors can happen to anybody," she said. "Lots of people try to act out parts of their
bad dreams. You don't know that it had anything to do with
your curse."

"It wasn't a regular nightmare," Mateo insisted. "It was
one of the visions, but this time it made me do something dangerous. Almost crazy." He still looked shaken,
and Nadia caught others staring and whispering. *The mad
Cabots, the ones who always went insane*—that was the reputa-
tion Mateo had had to live with his whole life. Now he'd
come to school with his clothes slightly askew, his entire
body tense, going on and on about his rude awakening that
morning. Nadia realized now that this was one of the ways
the curse worked against its victims: It scared them. Then

when others saw how unstable they looked, that began the cycle of alienation, whispers, rejection. Someone left so alone while scary things were happening to them—well, no wonder they freaked out.

But Nadia knew the truth. Mateo wouldn't have to bear this alone.

"Listen to me," she said, reaching up to take his face in her hands. "The curse dies with Elizabeth's power. Got it? When we take her down, you won't have to worry about the dreams getting stronger. You'll never have to worry about them again."

Verlaine hesitantly raised her hand. "So, do we have a firm date for this take-Elizabeth-down plan?"

"Tomorrow night?"

"Whoa." Verlaine's eyes widened. "I was being sarcastic. Are you kidding? Tomorrow night?"

"Yeah. I'm ready." Was she? Nadia had learned how to focus the spell of forgetfulness more sharply; at this point, further delay probably just gave Elizabeth more time to catch on. Now that Mateo's condition had worsened, her resolve hardened into certainty. "We need a location over water— it's not like I couldn't cast the spell without that, but over water would be ideal." And, in this case, nothing less than perfection would do. "We could take a boat out, but it's been so windy. The sound's too rough. Is there, like, a bridge we could go to? One nobody is likely to drive over while we're there? Someplace out of the way."

Mateo and Verlaine, the two locals, exchanged a look. It

was Mateo who said, "I guess there's Davis Bridge."

"Out to Raven Isle," Verlaine added. "But do we have to actually be on the bridge? Because it's pretty run-down. Nobody's used it to go to Raven Isle for years now, not even on a dare."

Nadia brushed this aside. "It doesn't have to stand for much longer. Tomorrow night, and that's all."

She felt suddenly free. Imagine—forty-eight hours from now, they might be free from Elizabeth forever. Mateo smiled tiredly, and she knew he was trying hard to believe it, too.

When Novels class was over, Verlaine was able to catch up to Asa on the way out. "You need to tell me what's going on with Mateo."

Yeah, okay, they were going after Elizabeth tomorrow night—but Asa didn't know that, and Verlaine figured the more information they had to work with, the better.

"Why would I ever do that?" Asa shrugged on his backpack as though the books weighed nothing; he turned and walked backward through the hallway, never running into anyone. The crowds just parted around him, perhaps sensing the strange heat from his skin. "You're desperate for someone to talk to, aren't you?"

That hit too close to the bone. Verlaine stopped walking. "At least I'm not Elizabeth's slave. And if I were, I'd try to *do* something about it. Not just sit and smirk and pretend I'm something besides her dog on a leash."

So *that* was what it looked like when you wiped the smile off that face. She'd never scored a point off Jeremy Prasad, but apparently she did better when it came to demons from the furnace of hell.

Asa had stopped walking, too, now. He leaned toward her, close enough for her to feel that searing heat, to see the blaze in his dark eyes. "You think it's so simple, throwing off the shackles of the One Beneath? You think you understand damnation? Slavery? Eternity? You understand *nothing*."

"I understand that you hate Elizabeth as much as we do," she shot back.

"Meaningless. Irrelevant. And foolish, too. You're still mostly arguing with the worthless boy who used to live in this body, instead of with me. I don't think you're ready to understand what I am, or what I can do. But you will." Asa's smile was feral now. Dangerous. Verlaine realized she was holding her books in front of her chest like a shield, but she managed to keep a straight face, even as he whispered, "You think you have nothing to lose. But you are so, so wrong."

Nothing to lose. Those words kept ringing inside her mind, taunting her, as Asa strolled away.

Verlaine tried to distract herself and take part in journalism class, but that went about as well as it usually did. "So, we should try to find out what Mrs. Purdhy and Riley have in common. Did Riley come to see her, maybe? You know, talk to an old teacher? This could be some disease she brought home from Brown. And we ought to see if there have been any reports of illnesses there that involve weird black . . . stuff."

It was like she was sitting in a bell jar, none of her words escaping. Desi Sheremata, who had inexplicably been named editor despite hardly caring about the *Lightning Rod* site, pulled up a sample home page that was all old photos of Riley Bender from previous years' annuals. The headline, centered over a picture of Riley in her homecoming crown, said *Our Prayers Are With Her.* "I was thinking we could have a text box where people write in their good wishes for Riley, you know?"

Everyone else nodded and smiled, like that was a really great plan instead of not journalism at all. Mr. Davis only said, "We'll want to moderate comments. Even with a tragedy, people will troll."

Especially with a tragedy. People seemed to get uglier in response to real emotions, at least in Verlaine's experience. Because nobody ever much noticed when she was hurting unless they wanted to make it worse for her.

Nothing to lose.

Verlaine raised her hand. "What about the investigative piece on the Halloween carnival? We're still running it, right?"

"Nobody actually got hurt," Desi huffed. "So it's kind of old news."

"It wasn't even two weeks ago!" Okay, nobody else here knew it had actually been the work of one of hell's minions, aka Elizabeth Pike, but still, a huge fire in the middle of town had to count as newsworthy if anything did.

Desi folded her arms. "I think you're more interested in a byline than in what happens to Riley Bender."

This was pretty massively unfair, given that Verlaine was one of the only people trying to deal with the person actually responsible for hurting Riley—but she couldn't say that. Even if she did, nobody would listen. Instead she scrunched down in her desk and folded her arms in front of her chest. A few people snickered, but then Mr. Davis got them all talking about which pictures of Riley would be best for the montage.

So much for asking whether they were even going to try to cover the not-quite-an-ax-massacre at town hall. Only in this room did attempted murder not count as news.

A byline? They thought she only cared about a byline? As if anybody would have paid attention to her regardless. Verlaine only wanted people to start thinking about how weird Captive's Sound actually was, to recognize that all these events were part of a larger, scarier pattern. But Elizabeth's magic wouldn't let them see that.

Just like Elizabeth's magic wouldn't let them see Verlaine for herself.

Nobody pays any attention to anything I do, no matter how hard I try, no matter how good it is. Even my best friends hardly notice me—and I know they don't mean it, but it doesn't matter, because the magic works on them, too. I might as well not even talk. Or show up.

Or exist.

That was usually the point where Verlaine reined herself in. Where she told herself that everything could change, that someday she'd go off to college and people would be nicer. Thinking about college and the better life she could create for herself there was the only way she made it through Rodman High.

But now she knew—it wasn't true.

Nothing was going to change in college. Nothing was going to change, ever. The magic Elizabeth had worked, the magic that prevented anyone from caring about Verlaine— that was permanent. It would last forever.

No one would ever, ever care about her any more than they did right now, today. She was going to spend the rest of her life on the outside looking in. This horrible, clawing loneliness inside her, the thing she battled every single day . . .

The loneliness was going to win.

Verlaine drew her knees up in her chair and huddled into a ball, right there at her desk, because otherwise she would break down and cry.

Nobody noticed. And she knew nobody would have noticed if she'd cried, either.

Nadia used one of Cole's purple markers to try to draw the shape again. Last night she'd made notes, but they weren't quite right. Were the lines on Elizabeth's shoulders a little more—curved, maybe?

"This tea tastes a little funny." Her dad squinted down at

118

the cup she'd made for him. "Are you sure this is the same stuff?"

"Absolutely," she said. *Just with a special ingredient added.*

She put down the marker and touched the pearl charm on her bracelet. Betrayer's Snare was another spell she'd never cast before; it could only be used in certain situations, and she wasn't sure whether the seduction Elizabeth was attempting was even one of them. Tonight was her first chance to cast it—you needed the moon at three-quarters to be sure the spell would take root.

Hopefully, as of tomorrow night, Elizabeth wouldn't be an issue any longer. But Betrayer's Snare couldn't hurt Dad, and Nadia didn't want to take any chances.

An unkindness returned.
An unwanted message received.
A danger unseen until too late.

Nadia kept her eyes on her father as she pulled up the memories:

Toddler Cole pulling her hair one time too often, shouting at him that he was a little brat, and watching his face crumple.

Mom saying "It's better this way" as she walked out the door for the last time.

Jerking back in horror as cobwebs closed over her face and body, entrapping her in Elizabeth's run-down old house, and Nadia realizing Elizabeth's Book of Shadows was an enemy in its own right—

Nothing happened. Dad still looked vaguely preoccupied. The only way to tell if Betrayer's Snare worked was if the person you were trying to protect stayed safe. Right now, Nadia thought, that didn't feel very comforting.

Cole came back into the room. When he saw that Nadia had stopped coloring, he started whining, "You didn't draw the zebra. You promised you would make a zebra!"

"I'm on it, buddy." Cole acted out when he was tired, and he was probably the most exhausted member of the family—which was saying something. He'd been torn apart last night, sobbing until after two a.m. Nadia and her father had taken turns sitting with him. It had been hard for her to focus on calming Cole down. She kept remembering Elizabeth's taunts, noticing how her dad's mind seemed to be . . . someplace else. She knew it wasn't anything Dad had control over. He was in the grips of a spell most people couldn't have fought off even this long. But still—*yuck*.

Was it only a few days ago that she'd been grossed out by imagining her dad dating again? If he took up with some normal forty-year-old woman now, Nadia thought she'd offer to babysit every night of the week. Anyone but Elizabeth. Anything but that.

"You're not drawing my zebra!" Pouting, Cole grabbed the red marker and deliberately made an ugly mark across her design.

That should have earned him a time-out. Instead Nadia gasped. "Cole, that's good. That's really good."

"It is?" He seemed too surprised to remember he was in a bad mood.

"It is!" Nadia grabbed the piece of paper and bolted for the stairs. "Dad, can you take Cole Patrol for a minute? I'll be right back down!"

She took the steps two at a time, yanked down the attic ladder, and climbed up as fast as she could, pulling the ladder up behind her. Goodwife Hale's Book of Shadows sat there next to her jar of Hershey's Miniatures, and Nadia helped herself to a Mr. Goodbar as she started flipping through.

Slowly, slowly—the pages are fragile—there. Nadia's eyes widened as she smoothed out the crumpled paper she and Cole had both drawn on. Although she couldn't yet be sure, it looked a lot like this symbol Goodwife Hale had sketched four hundred years ago. If this was what Elizabeth was trying to create—

Nadia quickly copied the symbol into her own Book of Shadows, making sure she matched every line, every angle. Beneath it she wrote the same words Goodwife Hale had written:

This sign shall mark His path.

The whole next day, Mateo could hardly pay attention in class. Part of that had to do with how people were still staring at him; more of it was the memory of waking up outside in the cold, alone, damaged from nightmares he knew would soon come back.

But as the hours wore on, as he slammed through homework right after school, his excitement grew. Nadia felt so sure about this spell of forgetting. Mateo knew firsthand just how powerful that spell could be. Yeah, it seemed almost too simple—but sometimes the most complicated problems had simple solutions. In fact, the simple ones were often the hardest to see.

If they could take Elizabeth out, lift this curse, protect everyone, make sure Nadia would be free from her corrosive influence forever—

And then what? Elizabeth would still be alive. She wouldn't have her powers anymore; she might not even remember being a witch. What if she just turned into an ordinary girl?

Could he stop hating her? Could he even . . . help her?

His entire mind recoiled from it. Elizabeth had murdered his mother. He could never forgive her, not for that.

They all met out by Davis Bridge just after dark. The wind was even sharper than usual, and Mateo shivered in his jacket.

"Guys—" Nadia stood there, gaping at the warped wood planks and battered metal frame that was, or had been, Davis Bridge. In several places, he could see through the wood to the churning water of the sound beneath. "You said this was a bridge. Not . . . an ex-bridge."

Verlaine shrugged, apparently comfortable in her leopard-print coat. "Over the water, you said. Over the water, we provided. Besides, yeah, it looks scary as all get-out, but it's stood for more than a century. What are the chances it's going to plunge into the ocean tonight?"

The wind blew harder, and the entire bridge shuddered in the gale. For a few long seconds all three of them stared at the bridge. Finally Mateo said, "Maybe we should get a boat after all?"

"No." Nadia squared her shoulders. For someone so little, she could look fierce when she made up her mind; Mateo *loved* that look. "We're here. This is the time. Let's try it."

Verlaine was the one who suggested they should spread out, so the bridge didn't have to support the weight of all three of them in any one spot. Although Mateo wondered for a moment whether Verlaine needed to be out there at all since she wasn't a Steadfast, that hardly even took shape as a conscious thought within his mind. Nadia was going to do something dangerous; they were going to be by her side. That was all there was to it.

He drew Nadia close and gave her a quick kiss. When she smiled up at him, he whispered, "For luck."

He went first, inching out along one of the steel beams that seemed less crooked than the others. The last light of day clung to the edges of the clouds on the western horizon; otherwise inky blue had claimed both sky and sea. Mateo glanced down to see the whitecapped waves beneath him, then decided not to look at them again. Nadia came next, walking more confidently on the battered old boards than Mateo thought was wise—but she didn't fall through, didn't even stumble. Verlaine took up the rear, barely edging out onto the bridge. But she was far enough for Nadia to reach in a few steps. If any one of them ran into trouble—or, God forbid, the bridge started to collapse—they could form a human chain to keep them all safe.

The wind snatched at Nadia's hair, sending her black locks swirling upward, away from her heart-shaped face, as she closed her eyes. Mateo found it fascinating to watch her cast a spell. No, she didn't utter spooky incantations in Latin or anything like that—but still, there was something about her expression at that moment. That ultimate concentration, the way she seemed to forget all the cares of this world and become part of the next: It captivated Mateo. Sometimes it frightened him a little. But it was always, always beautiful.

Then he saw magenta light spiraling out from her, like a flower unfolding amid the storm, and Mateo knew his Steadfast power had revealed her true power at work— battling Elizabeth at last.

Elizabeth was depositing the eyes of her latest crow in her jar when she heard a rustling from the back room.

Cocking her head, she walked through her house to find her Book of Shadows fluttering on the floor, like a dying bird. As she knelt by its side, however, it fell open to almost the first page, to one of the spells she'd learned as a child: a spell of forgetting.

Even as she looked down at it, she felt a strange fogginess descend upon her thoughts—as though she were sleepy, or dizzy, or—

Instantly she called upon a spell of repulsion. The fog dissipated in an instant, and Elizabeth gaped in shock at Nadia's audacity. That child had thought to undo her with one of the most basic spells . . . and had she not been warned, it could even have worked. The memories Nadia had selected must have been strong; no doubt she was on a bridge or in a boat, using the fluidity of the water to strengthen her magic further. It really could have worked, which enraged Elizabeth.

And yet she was reminded: Simplicity was sometimes the best weapon.

So Elizabeth cradled her Book of Shadows in her arms as she rose to her feet again and cast another very simple spell: a spell to move water.

"Did it work?" Verlaine cried.

"I'm not sure," Nadia said. The wind was so sharp she felt as though it were trying to carve her flesh from her bones. Yet still she didn't budge. It seemed to her as though she ought to feel some change in this town, some sign that Elizabeth had been affected.

Then she felt the bridge rock beneath her feet. She staggered to one side and heard Verlaine cry out.

"Nadia?" Mateo called. The bridge swayed again, as though it were a horse trying to buck them off. "The waves are higher—it's like the tide's trying to come in all at once!"

It didn't work, Nadia realized. *Elizabeth knows. She's doing this.*

And the bridge collapsed.

11

NADIA DIDN'T SO MUCH FALL OFF THE BRIDGE AS FALL through it. Wood splintered around her, metal scraped her skin, and then ice-cold water splashed over her, surrounded her, dragged her down.

Despite her terror, Nadia stayed focused; she'd been a lifeguard once, and she was a strong enough swimmer to propel herself even through this mess. When she broke the surface, though, jagged metal stuck up in all directions, and broken boards littered the water. "Mateo!" she screamed. "Verlaine!"

Then she saw a flash of silver white—Verlaine's wet hair, slicked down her head and back like a veil, as Verlaine pulled herself onto dry ground. The spell she'd cast had left a powerful magical resonance—that and whatever Elizabeth had cast—because for one moment, when Nadia looked at Verlaine, she saw her.

Really saw her. For one split second, Nadia looked at Verlaine without dark magic in the way and knew just how much she loved her friend, how good Verlaine had been to fight with her all this time.

"Verlaine—" she whispered, overcome by such overwhelming emotion that it outweighed everything else . . . until she heard Mateo splashing behind her.

Nadia turned back and saw him struggling in the water; it looked like his clothes were caught on something, keeping him from getting to safety. She swam to him, ignoring the boards that scraped her flesh, until they were side by side. Together they were able to tug him free and make it to shore.

All three of them ran, teeth chattering, back to Verlaine's car. She turned on the heater, which was some help, but for a few long seconds they just sat there trying to thaw out enough to speak.

"We—we should go—to my place," Mateo managed to say. "Dad's working. You guys can—change into some of my sweatpants. Something like that."

"Good thinking," Verlaine said as she hugged herself tightly. "Uncle Dave and Uncle Gary wouldn't know what to think if I came in like this. Nadia, I take it our plunge in the sound means the spell didn't work?"

"She stopped me," Nadia said, and it was so hard to admit it out loud, even when they all knew it already.

Mateo simply put his arm around her and said, "We knew it probably wouldn't be that easy."

Nadia just shrugged. She was still too upset to say anything else.

It wasn't that Elizabeth had beaten her. Although Nadia had hoped to win, she had known all along that defeat was a strong possibility. What hurt worst was that Elizabeth had shut her down in *seconds*. The best plan Nadia had been able to come up with—for Elizabeth, it had probably been no more than an annoyance.

Lifting her face to her friends, Nadia tried to brace herself for their disappointment. But Mateo smiled at her like he knew everything in her heart and wanted to make it better for her if he could. He couldn't, but Nadia loved that he wanted to try.

Meanwhile, Verlaine wrung water out of her long hair and sighed. "Well, this sucked."

During his brief time in Captive's Sound, Asa had sized up Kendall Bender as—insubstantial. Not terribly bright, not stupid, enamored of her own judgment: an entirely ordinary human being. But grief had awakened something else in her, something entirely individual.

The girl seemed to be in a daze as she wandered through the hallway, despite all the balloons and stuffed animals decorating her locker, despite all the questions about her sister. Her sandy hair wasn't even brushed. Probably she'd come to school straight from the hospital.

Asa stood very near the now-unused chemistry lab. (The school had closed it due to potential contamination, though nobody could say what the contamination might be. Instead the class sat in study hall and watched "science documentaries," which were mostly designed to amuse the brain-dead.) He was close enough to feel the enormous power lurking there—the wild, dark energy not far below the surface. It reminded Asa of pain. It reminded him of home.

Yet that darkness did not reach out to him, nor would it ever. The One Beneath did not speak to mere slaves.

A dog on a leash, Verlaine had said. Maddening girl.

Let her call him what she would. After last night's disastrous attempt on Elizabeth's life, no doubt Verlaine, Nadia, and Mateo were licking their wounds. They were doubting themselves now. That made them vulnerable.

He'd watched long enough. Waited long enough. The time had come for Asa to begin his work.

So here we go, Mateo thought. *Plan B.*

The butler opened the door, and his eyes widened in surprise. Mateo usually avoided Cabot House, showing up once a year for inspection/birthday wishes/weird, creepy, passive aggression from Grandma/a savings bond, before getting out again as quickly as possible. This was his third visit in three months.

Mateo tried to keep a straight face. "We meet again."

"Mrs. Cabot isn't expecting you," the butler said in his creaky voice. His weedy, white eyebrows seemed to be frozen in an expression halfway between surprise and disapproval.

"Just dropping by. Let her know I'm here, okay?"

He had to wait for her in a long room filled with ornate old furniture that hadn't been used in a while. A fine layer of dust grayed and softened every line, as though the room had been draped in a veil. Mateo felt more like an intruder in a museum than a visiting grandson. That was pretty much par for the course.

All along the brocade wallpaper hung Cabot family portraits from decades and even centuries gone by. A few of them showed signs of damage from the fire that had damaged the upper stories of the house back when his mother was young. This frame showed some blackening; this picture was stained with soot. But the one that interested Mateo showed not the damage, but the person who had caused it.

There, in a Colonial-era portrait, stood members of Mateo's family in knee breeches, full-length dresses, and powdered wigs—and next to them stood Elizabeth Pike.

Not Elizabeth as he knew her, of course. She'd spent most of the past four centuries aging backward from the old woman who'd made a deal with the One Beneath. Only now did she again look like a girl of seventeen. In this portrait Elizabeth still had gray hair, the more solid body of someone past middle age, but the painter must have been skilled, because the face remained unmistakably hers. Maybe it was the shape of her eyes; maybe it was the way she tilted her head just slightly.

No. What made Mateo so utterly sure this was Elizabeth was the expression the painter had captured in her eyes:

contempt. Elizabeth thought everyone else in the world was beneath her, only fit to do her bidding.

"Mateo." He turned to see Grandma standing in the door. She rarely stood any longer; it surprised him that she had the strength. Her ebony cane was clenched firmly in one frail hand. As always, she angled herself so that only one side of her face showed—the side without the horrible scars from the fire. "Your young lady appears to have heeded my warning."

"Nadia and I are still together. Thanks for asking." Mateo wasn't going to waste any time trying to make this woman like him. Instead he simply stepped close and held up his phone. "Listen, I need to know if you've ever seen this."

He brought up the picture Nadia had taken of a symbol drawn on yellowing old paper—a sort of wreathed circle made up of a few dozen curving lines that crisscrossed one another. At first Mateo had thought it looked vaguely Celtic, but that wasn't quite right. Really, it was more like a drawing by this guy they'd studied in art history, M.C. Escher. Lines you thought led somewhere didn't; angles that shouldn't have existed did.

"That?" Apparently startled out of her usual gloom, Grandma nodded. "I've seen that design before."

Usually Mateo hated that his grandmother lived in the past, that he was buried under so much horrible family history, it felt like it could crush him. But her obsession had finally paid off. "Where?"

"It's an old knife—part of the family silver, though it

resembles no serving piece I've ever seen. But I recall the symbol well. I thought it was some Cabot family crest, fallen out of use."

"Any chance I could have that knife?"

Immediately she turned to frost again. "If you're looking for items to hock, I'm sure there's something more valuable in the house."

"I'm not pawning anything, okay? You can have it back soon." In theory, anyway: Nadia might have to use it for some spell that would turn it to ash or God only knew what. He'd deal with that if and when it happened. "My friends and I want to look at it. That's all."

"I'm not sure you should be trusted with a knife."

"Come on. I work in a restaurant. Nothing but knives. So if I were looking for weapons, this is the last place I'd come. Right?" On second thought, Mateo wasn't sure that was the ideal argument for him to make—but Grandma seemed to be considering it.

She didn't know the whole truth about Captive's Sound. Mateo was pretty sure she had no clue that witchcraft even existed. Still, she believed in the family curse—which was enough for her to know that the supernatural was very, very real. Slowly she shook her head no, then called for the butler to find the knife.

He noticed that she was leaning more heavily on her cane; her fingers trembled on the handle. Tentatively Mateo took hold of her elbow. "Hey. Do you want to sit down?"

"Don't touch me," she snapped.

"Okay, then." He stuffed his hands back into the pockets of his letter jacket, took a couple of steps back.

When Grandma spoke again, however, her words were soft for once. "You meant to help. I realize that. But you're cursed, Mateo. I swore after what your grandfather did to me that I would never again be touched by that curse if I could possibly avoid it."

Which was why she'd frozen out his mother. Why she'd only begrudgingly acknowledged Mateo's existence once a year for his whole life.

But now that Mateo stood this close, he could see the other side of his grandmother's face despite her attempt to keep it turned toward the shadows. The welts had never healed, not after decades. It looked as though claws had raked across her skin, twisting cheek and eyebrow and jaw into mockeries of themselves.

Elizabeth had made her suffer, too.

Quietly he said, "None of us chose this, you know."

For one moment his grandmother looked at him—straight at him, not trying to hide her damage—and he saw just how lonely she was. They both suffered the same isolation because of the curse; they both mourned his mother, and hated being set apart from the world. Was that only pity in her eyes, or did she maybe, finally understand him a little?

But Grandma sniffed. "I chose this when I was fool enough to marry your grandfather and bear him a child. I won't choose it again."

When she pulled farther back, Mateo let her go.

The butler reappeared with something large and flat wrapped in a sueded cloth; the heft of it surprised Mateo as he took it. When he flipped back one corner of the fabric, he saw a long, silver knife—more like a dagger—almost black with tarnish. Although the pattern was almost hidden in the blackness, he could tell it was the same. "This is great. Thanks for loaning it to me."

"There is no need to return it in person," Grandma said. "If you must come here, try to send advance word."

She still feared him. Mateo shrugged it off as best he could, heading for the door. "Right. Got it. By the way, make that guy polish the silver sometime. What else does he do all day?"

Now that Cole had been pacified with what had to be his nine thousandth viewing of *Lilo & Stitch*, Nadia had a chance to unwind.

Well. If extreme moping could be considered unwinding.

Mateo and Verlaine had been so positive and encouraging, but Nadia's heart still stung from last night's failure. She still thought the idea had been a good one, in theory—but Elizabeth had charms and protections Nadia could only guess at.

What if she's just too strong? What if there's no way for me to take her on? Is it like—like when Cole tells Dad he wants to wrestle? Dad makes a good game of it and they roll around on the floor, but it's not like he can't pin Cole in an instant as soon as he's ready.

Maybe that's all Elizabeth is doing. Toying with me.

Then a rap on the window startled Nadia from her reverie.

She sat upright, brightening as she thought that Mateo must have come to see her. But why hadn't he come to the front door? Maybe he thought sneaking into her bedroom was romantic. If so, he was right.

Nadia rose and slid open her window—and realized it wasn't Mateo who'd come to visit.

"Mind if I come in?" Asa smiled. He perched easily on the tree branch; though the limb swayed in the strong wind, his balance remained perfect.

"Yes."

"Too bad."

With a leap, he landed on her roof, hands on the windowsill just between hers. There was no sound, as if he were light as a cat. Nadia jumped back, an automatic reflex, but one that allowed Asa to slip through the window and stand in front of her. He wore jeans and a dark gray sweater, the expensive kind with a soft sheen to it. In every way, Asa looked just like the spoiled rich kid Jeremy Prasad had been; only the uncanny grace of his movements and the knowing sharpness of his gaze betrayed his true nature.

"Willow," he said with a nod toward the pressed leaves and flowers on her walls. "Lavender. Minor protections, to be sure, but even little things add up after a while."

"What the hell are you doing here?" she said, keeping her voice as low as she could while still making it really clear Asa wasn't wanted. "Get out."

"First we should have a chat."

"Actually, no, we shouldn't. Get out *now.*"

"I'll leave in ten seconds." That sounded promising—until he lifted his hands and clapped. The sounds of Cole's movie from downstairs stopped in an instant; the music playing on her computer did, too. Nadia didn't even bother looking at her clock. She already knew time was standing still. Asa folded his arms across his chest and leaned against her wall. "And yet we still have plenty of time to talk."

"I don't know what it is you think you have to say to me. What, are you going to tell me how much fun it is to work for Elizabeth? We both know that's not true."

"Elizabeth is cold, cruel, and merciless," Asa said, startling her with his honesty. "Yes, she wants me to convince you to join her. To start learning from her. But Elizabeth has a weakness—arrogance. For instance, it never occurred to her that I might ask you to start studying with her for my own reasons, not hers."

Nadia sat back on the corner of her bed. This conversation was changing directions every second. "Why would I care about your reasons?"

"Because I think they're the same as yours." Asa stepped away from the wall, coming a little closer to Nadia, close enough for her to again feel that strange, unearthly heat. "Believe it or not, Nadia, we both want the same thing. We want to see Elizabeth crushed, defeated, destroyed *forever*. I can't do that. Maybe you can."

"But you both serve the One Beneath."

"Precisely. I serve Him, not her. And if you think the One Beneath doesn't accept deceit and backstabbing among His servants, then, I have to tell you, you haven't even started to understand Him." Asa's grin was fierce, almost frightening. "He loves her, you know. Insofar as the One Beneath can love anyone or anything, He loves Elizabeth. But He would glory in her devastation just as He would in anybody else's. We're all just kindling for His fires. There's no one He wouldn't burn."

Her heart was thumping wildly inside her chest, though her fear diminished by the moment. Asa was giving her the one thing she needed most, the one thing she couldn't get any other way: knowledge. "Okay. You want her defeated. So do I. Joining her doesn't do that. It only helps her win."

"Only if you play by her rules, Nadia. What if you played by mine?"

Asa leaned forward then, his hands on the bed, on either side of her. His face was very close to hers, the heat overwhelming. Nadia's eyes met his, and a shudder went through her, one so delicious that it took her a moment to remember she should be disgusted by him.

But she wasn't. Not even close.

Asa's smile broadened. He looked like a panther caught midpounce. "Don't feel guilty," he murmured. "You can't help yourself. Sin, temptation, craving, unmentionable desires: That's the stuff demons are made of. How else could we be so hard to resist?"

Flushed, Nadia pushed herself farther back on the bed to put at least a few more inches between her face and Asa's. She had to think clearly now. "Stop playing games and just tell me what you're suggesting."

"Join Elizabeth. Work with her. Learn from her. Learn all the magic she has to teach—and she has so much, Nadia, more than any other witch has ever possessed. Discover the countless spells a Sorceress has at her disposal. Tell her you must learn more before you swear yourself to the One Beneath; she'll accept that. It's how they all begin, really. You can start as only her student, no more. And you'll learn enough to destroy her long before the One Beneath ever has a claim on your soul."

Could that work? It sounded . . . plausible. Even coming from a demon.

Asa backed away, giving her a few moments to think. Nadia pushed her hair back from her face and stared down at her Book of Shadows. It so obviously belonged to a beginner: Crayola spells in the front, blank pages in the back. If she could learn more—become nearly as powerful as Elizabeth herself—

Demons tempted people. That was what they did. And they always tempted them down the path of evil, into the keeping of the One Beneath. So Nadia had every reason to doubt and distrust what he told her now.

Yet she also knew that the hatred in Asa's voice when he spoke of Elizabeth was absolutely true.

"If I become powerful," she said, "and I stop Elizabeth for good, that harms the One Beneath. You can't work against Him. It's impossible."

"True enough," Asa said. "I can't work against Him. But

I can assist in Elizabeth's destruction, which is what I'd very much like to do. After that—yes, He'll come after you, and I'll help Him. But that's going to happen no matter what, Nadia. At least my way you'd stand a chance, and we'd get to see Elizabeth go down in flames. Your way, you're just a stick of kindling for his next blaze. Think about it."

He clapped his hands again; sounds from the rest of the house rushed in, and Nadia let out a breath she hadn't known she was holding. When she looked up from her Book of Shadows, Asa was already gone. He must have slipped out the window again, without a sound.

Asa smiled as he walked away from the Caldani home. He'd made a good beginning of it, if he said so himself. Honesty always worked better than lies.

Of course, Nadia didn't know the other purpose behind the plan he'd suggested—pulling her away from her friends, from the people she loved. He was rather proud of having found a way to do Elizabeth's work and his own with a single stroke.

Well—not a single stroke. He had two more people to visit tonight.

Seduction was never accomplished in a single conversation, or on a single night. It had to begin slowly. You took people so far, then no further, and waited for them to travel the rest of the way to hell on their own. They always did, in the end.

12

MATEO SAT ALONE ON THE BEACH NEAR HIS HOUSE, BACK against a large piece of driftwood in the sand, earbuds in, music going. It was a cloudy night, one where he couldn't see the strange roiling stuff between Captive's Sound and the stars; the only evidence of magic visible at the moment was the strange glow surrounding the lighthouse. After the whole thing with Grandma, he needed space. Needed to feel like the world hadn't closed in around him. Right now he just needed to be alone.

But then he wasn't alone.

"Sorry, am I intruding?" Asa smiled as he leaned against the same bit of driftwood. "I suppose you can barely hear me over all the noise."

The music stopped. So did the waves, which remained midcurl, seafoam frozen in place like carved alabaster. Mateo yanked his earbuds out as he shifted away from the demon.

"What the hell are you doing here?"

"Just dropped by, figured we could bitch about Elizabeth, do each other's nails, make cookies—wait. No. That's girl bonding, isn't it? Sometimes I get it mixed up. No gender roles in hell, torment and anguish being more or less universal. So what do we do to be manly and brutish? Smash beer cans against our foreheads? Watch NASCAR? Crochet? What?"

Mateo decided to stay calm. The demon wasn't going to kill him, obviously. He would have done it long before tonight if that were his only goal. "What do you want?"

"It's more a question of what you want. You need answers, Mateo. I can give them to you."

"Like I'd trust anything you had to say."

"You should." Asa stretched his arms out across the driftwood, apparently enjoying himself. "You strike me as someone who's already seen the darker side of life. That is, you've seen the truth. I'm here to talk man-to-man. If I were you, I'd take advantage of the opportunity."

It couldn't be that simple, obviously. This all had to be some kind of a trick. But Mateo figured—okay, he wouldn't do anything Asa suggested he should do. He'd just listen to what the guy had to say. Then he could go over it all with Nadia later, and they'd figure out what Asa had been up to for real. They could turn Asa's words against him.

Keeping it casual, Mateo said, "There's one thing I've been wondering about."

"Ask away."

"Why can't I see that you're a demon? I'm a Steadfast. I see all kinds of magic, everywhere around town. Old spells. Sources of power. Elizabeth's true form—though she's changed since Halloween."

"Indeed she has. Elizabeth's not quite the woman she used to be," Asa said as he picked up Mateo's phone and started scrolling through the music library. "But, to answer your question, you can't see the truth about me in part because I can't see the truth about you. A Steadfast's identity is hidden from demons; even when I was in the demonic realm, and I knew Nadia had taken a Steadfast, I had no idea it was you. And no wonder, of course. A male Steadfast? Bizarre. Anyway, part of the magic that hides a Steadfast from demons also hides demons from a Steadfast. It puts a curtain between us. A veil. Blocks vision in both directions."

Was that true? It sounded like it could be. Maybe that was something there was no point in lying about. Asa might be a source of useful information—at least, once you weeded out the lies. Mateo tried again. "What do you mean, Elizabeth's not the woman she used to be?"

"Before Halloween, she was effectively immortal. Now she's not."

". . . She's not?" But Elizabeth had lived for centuries. Her power was almost limitless—wasn't it?

Maybe not. Maybe not.

Seemingly oblivious to Mateo's reaction, Asa continued, "Elizabeth Pike can die just like any other human being now. Which makes killing her a lot easier, by the way. Not easy, of course. She's still got four hundred years' worth of magic on her side. But easier! Now, let's see. What have you got on this music iPod . . . thing? I admit I'm out of touch after a few centuries in hell."

"Give me that." Mateo yanked back his phone; it was warm to the touch, like he'd left it in his dad's car on a blazing summer day. Asa shrugged.

Elizabeth could die. She could die just like any other person. Like Mom, and all the other people she'd made suffer.

Asa could have been lying, but Mateo didn't think so. He'd seen the change in Elizabeth for himself. The magic around her was no longer so dramatic, so blinding. She'd lost some kind of power, and if that was immortality—it made a whole lot of sense.

"I know that look." Asa smiled. "Someone's thinking about revenge."

"I never said—"

"Didn't have to. I'm a demon. I can smell vengeance. Literally, I mean. It's a little like blood. Metallic. Sharp on the tongue." Asa turned toward Mateo, all pretense of ease gone. The intensity of his gaze made it impossible to look away. "You want Elizabeth dead? So do I. My boss, also known as the One Beneath, will triumph with or without her. I'd prefer 'without her.' Want to hear more?"

"You're screwing with my head."

"Of course I am. I'm a demon. But that doesn't mean I'm not telling you the truth. Nothing screws people up worse than the truth."

It's probably all bullshit, Mateo thought. *But maybe it's not, and the part about Elizabeth being mortal again is definitely true.* "Yeah. I want to hear more."

Asa slid a little closer. The heat from him flickered across Mateo's skin, as though he were standing near a bonfire. "Obviously, Nadia wants to defeat Elizabeth through magic, to undo her spells or counteract them with spells of her own. She's a witch. Witches are trained to think that way. But Elizabeth's magic can't do her one damn bit of good if she's dead. If you want to stop her, I suggest a more direct approach. Stop worrying about whatever Elizabeth is or isn't trying to accomplish. Start thinking about how to take her *out.*"

Murder. Asa was talking about murder. Once, Mateo would have thought he wasn't capable of that, not unless somebody he loved was in danger, and it didn't seem like it would be easy even then.

Back then, he'd thought Elizabeth was one of the people he loved most.

I could, Mateo realized. *If it was Elizabeth—I could.*

He opened his mouth, closed it again. The words refused to come at first, but he got them out. "How do we get to her?"

Asa's grin broadened. "I like a man who isn't afraid to admit he wants revenge. I like it very much. You're wise to act now, before Elizabeth gets her claws into Nadia. Deeper into Nadia than they already are."

"What do you mean?"

"Oh, come on. She's been trying to recruit Nadia. You know this."

"Yeah, but Nadia would never go for that."

"She wouldn't? Are you positive?" Rising onto his knees, Asa made a great show of looking around the beach. The driftwood behind him had been scorched black. "I don't see her here with you now."

"We're all kind of freaked out after last night."

"If I were young and in love, I wouldn't let that stop me. Fate has given you absent mothers and highly distracted fathers. Why on earth aren't the two of you wrapped around each other in carnal delight—tonight, tomorrow night, pretty much any second you're not eating or sleeping? Or in study hall, once known as chemistry. Could you believe they made us watch *Code of the Ancient Maya*? How is that science?"

"Nadia and I don't need dating advice from Satan, okay?"

Obviously bored, Asa held up one hand and made the universal symbol for *blah blah blah*. "My point is that you've left yourself vulnerable. Left Nadia vulnerable. The only thing more compelling than love is power. Trust me: In hell you get plenty of lessons about that one. If magic is still the first thing in Nadia's life—not you—isn't it possible that she'll always choose magical power in the end? Even if that means giving you up?"

"This is the part where you start twisting my mind around," Mateo said. "I know what you're doing."

Asa just laughed. "Keep telling yourself that. The denial

can only go on for so long, but you might as well enjoy it while it lasts." He rose to his feet, brushing sand from his jeans. "I'll tell you another truth, Mateo. Another hard fact for you to ignore until it's too late. In every romance, one person loves the other more. Sometimes it's a lot; sometimes it's such a slight difference that nobody could ever tell—nobody, that is, except the one who's loved a little less. He's always aware of that patch of shadow where the sunlight doesn't fall. That fraction between how far he's reaching and how far away she is. The difference between loving and loving absolutely. Nobody else can even see it, but the one who does more than his share of the loving? Eventually he can't see anything else."

Mateo wanted to tell Asa he was wrong, but the words seemed to die in his throat. It couldn't be true . . . could it?

"Oh, look at the time." Asa made a great show of stretching and getting to his feet. "I should go. We're finishing Dickens tomorrow. It's a pleasure to have books again, you know. No libraries in hell."

As he heard the soft crunch of Asa's shoes against the sand, Mateo knew he should say something, anything, to let Asa know it wouldn't be that easy to tear him apart from Nadia. By the time he turned around, though, the demon had vanished as if he'd never been there at all.

Another exciting night here at the bustling media center of Captive's Sound, Verlaine thought.

She sat behind the desk at the town paper, the *Guardian,*

which came out only once a week and mostly just printed advertising circulars. Verlaine had an internship here, which meant less "covering news of importance to the town" and more "hanging around in case anybody drops off classified ads." They let her write stories, even ran them on the front page, but Verlaine had yet to see any evidence that either the editors or the citizenry appreciated her hard work.

They don't just ignore me. They ignore my writing. They ignore anything that comes anywhere near me. It's like there's this—chasm between me and everybody else in the world.

She took a deep breath, then another. Deliberately she wound her gray hair into a smooth bun at the back of her neck, which hopefully worked with the whole "sexy secretary" vibe she was going for with this 1960s rose-colored sheath dress. At least she was in control of her look.

But what did it matter how she looked, if nobody was ever going to look at her?

The bells on the door jingled, and she looked up—then scowled. "What are *you* doing here?"

"Would you believe a personal ad?" Asa said.

"No. Elizabeth pulled that trick last month. I wound up in the hospital for a few days as a result. Now I have a Taser and a much more selective policy about who gets to advertise in the paper." Verlaine did not have a Taser. In fact she'd gotten no further than thinking it might be a good idea to have one around. But Asa didn't know that.

He leaned against one of the counters and looked up at the endless musty volumes of back issues that lined the walls. "I wouldn't have thought this place could afford to be 'selective' about much."

Verlaine bit back her smile in time. "Yeah. Well. It's not CNN. But this is Captive's Sound."

"This used to be a much more interesting publication." Asa began strolling along the wall, trailing his long fingers over the ridges of the leather bindings. "Back in the day— even further back than these archives go, I'd imagine. When the printing press they worked on was one of the only ones in the New World, and more people knew the reason this paper was called the *Guardian*."

She frowned. That wasn't such an unusual name for a newspaper; usually it meant that the paper was a guardian of truth or liberty or something like that. What else could it mean?

And then she knew.

Slowly Verlaine said, "There's also a reason this town is called Captive's Sound, isn't there?"

Asa drummed his hands against the wall in obvious excitement. "You got there much quicker than I thought you would. Nicely done!"

Once upon a time, the people here knew they were guarding something. But what's captive in Captive's Sound?

"So many secrets," he said, strolling closer to her desk. His smile was brilliantly white against his tawny skin, and already she had begun to feel that strange heat. "So much waiting to be revealed. And I think you'd like to be the one who ripped the lid off."

"Yeah, right." Verlaine didn't like how close he was getting, so she rolled her desk chair farther back. "Like anybody would pay attention to anything I said. Elizabeth took that away from me. Or didn't you remember?"

It was hard to say exactly how Asa's expression changed. His smile didn't fade; his eyes never lost that black, mischievous fire. And yet she knew that he'd only halfway meant everything he'd said before—but what he said now was true. "I remember it well. I see it more plainly than anyone else does—even more than you, Verlaine."

She could have slapped him. "Oh, you can see my life better than I can? You think there's a better view than from the inside? Don't even pretend you know what this is like."

"Being forever alone? Forever unseen? I have no body of my own. No freedom. No chance my existence will ever change. I know what you endure far too well."

Of course. Asa was a slave. Maybe that didn't make him sympathetic, exactly—but it made him pitiable. Maybe he really did know what it felt like to be always on the outside looking in.

Asa's hands were spread across the counter, and he leaned over it, just far enough for her to again feel the warmth of him glowing against her cheeks. "You're so much stronger than anyone else knows. Nadia, Mateo—they try, don't they? But they never understand the courage it takes for you to support and love them when they can't love you as much in return. They never see how little the world cares for you, and how you dare to love the world back anyway. Nobody

149

reads what you write, and yet you write. Nobody looks at you, and yet you dress yourself like a goddess every single day. Nobody wants you, and yet you keep wanting. You stay hungry. You keep your heart open. You never give up."

She couldn't look at him any longer. Her throat hurt, and her breaths were coming too quickly, but she'd be damned if she'd let a demon make her cry.

"Verlaine." Asa's voice was soft, and he was closer to her now, leaning over far enough that they could have touched. Even kissed. What would it feel like, to be kissed by him? Would it burn her to cinders? "There are stories you could tell that would force people to listen. Let me share with you this town's real history. Let me tell you the truth about Elizabeth. Let the two of us try to find an answer together, without Nadia or Mateo or anyone else who can't see the truth for themselves. Believe in me. Trust me. *See me*, as I see you."

Slowly she put her hands on the folder in front of her, thick with old ad layouts and receipts. Her shaking fingers closed around the binding; it helped to have something to hang on to.

It helped even more to have something to swing.

Verlaine grabbed the folder and smashed it into Asa's face as hard as she could. He staggered backward, all the way into the nearest wall of back volumes.

"*Trust* you," she said as she came around the counter, still brandishing the folder in front of her like a weapon. "*Believe* in you. While you're trying to manipulate me in the most obvious way possible. Excuse me, but no."

"You should listen to what I've said." His grin remained in place as he rubbed the side of his jaw, but when she came closer to him, he began backing away.

"I heard you out. And I didn't hear anything worth my time."

"Don't tell me you weren't affected. That's a lie and we both know it. What you feel when you look at me—the way you parted your lips for a moment—"

"So what? You're hot. Big deal. It doesn't change the fact that you're a demon." Verlaine took another swing at him with the folder every few words, pushing him farther and farther toward the door. "A demon! And a liar, and Elizabeth's partner in crime, and a *total asshole*."

She shoved him out the door. The bells on the handle jingled again. And just like that, he seemed to have disappeared.

Inside she felt raw, torn apart. But Verlaine had become very good at putting her own pain aside. That was one of the few benefits of being on the outside looking in: You learned to take anything the world could throw at you.

"Well. Guess that showed him." She smoothed the front of her sheath dress and went back to her desk to finish her homework. "Bet he's not so smug anymore."

If she could have seen Asa at that moment, she would have seen him laughing out loud in sheer delight.

How brilliant she was. How fierce. Asa enjoyed fighting

151

with Verlaine more than he remembered enjoying time with anyone else.

He wanted to watch her from a distance, but he made himself pull back. If he paid any more attention to Verlaine Laughton, Asa thought he might actually become . . . fond of her. That would be disastrous. First of all, she was doomed. Bad long-term relationship prospects there.

Second, he couldn't save her from whatever danger would come. While there was a bit of wiggle room for him to betray Elizabeth, he could never betray the One Beneath. Rescuing Verlaine from mortal danger would be utterly forbidden. If he broke that rule, he would be forced to endure the worst torments of hell for what would feel like centuries. No girl could be worth that, not even one so daring and delightful as Verlaine.

Even one that made him feel as if he would find it painful when she died.

Yet Asa lingered awhile, watching her anyway.

He was still in a good mood the next morning as he walked through the halls of Rodman High; even the sight of Elizabeth falling into step beside him couldn't dim his smile. "Don't tell me," he said. "You just can't wait to watch a documentary on Albert Einstein."

"You know I have my reasons for coming here. How goes your task?"

"Let's see." Asa nodded toward the far end of the hall, where Nadia, Mateo, and Verlaine were all walking in.

They must have met up outside. Maybe they even came to school together. But even though the three of them walked side by side, even though they were smiling at one another, Asa could tell—there was a bit of a chill in the air that had nothing to do with autumn. Mateo didn't have his arm around Nadia. Nadia couldn't quite meet Verlaine's eyes. And Verlaine crossed her arms and scowled at both Asa and Elizabeth as the two groups passed.

"The suspicion is still subtle," Elizabeth said. "They doubt themselves more than one another. But I can see that the seeds have been planted. What next, beast?"

"Watch and wait." He imagined the elm trees that grew all over town, many of them so old they had pushed up the sidewalks in front of them and broken the paving stones into half a dozen planes and angles. The smallest seed could cause incredible damage, given time and the right conditions to grow.

She asked, "What did you tell them?"

"The most dangerous thing of all. The truth."

I laid out three possible ways to destroy you. Any one of them might work. All I have to do is hope at least one of them sees it. The faster they're driven apart, the faster they can stop focusing on one another and go after you. Your work and your undoing, and I managed it in just one night. You'll be sorry you called me beast *soon enough.*

Asa glanced over his shoulder at them once more. Really he should have been watching all three of them for signs of discord. Instead he only had eyes for the way Verlaine's long, silver hair flowed down her back.

Quietly he repeated, "Everything I said was true."

13

ON THE LIBRARY'S TV SCREEN, BLACK-AND-WHITE IMAGES of Albert Einstein flickered. The overhead lights were out. That meant Mateo's phone glowed too brightly—but since not even the substitute cared about what "chemistry class" was up to, that worked just fine.

"It's Latin," Nadia whispered as she squinted down at the picture on Mateo's phone. "At least, I think so. I've never studied it."

"Does Google Translate do Latin?" Mateo asked.

"I'll check and see." Nadia got to work on her own phone. "Even at full magnification, the words are kind of blurry. It would be better to see the real thing."

"Oh, yeah, I can see it now. 'Hi, I'm the unstable guy who brought a knife to school!' Let's not go there."

She put her hand on Mateo's arm; the pain behind that joke was all too clear. "Sorry. I wasn't thinking."

"It's okay. You should see it. Just—after school, you know?"

Still, he looked shaken and tired. Nadia rubbed his arm more gently, leaned close enough to whisper in his ear. "Was it rough? Dealing with your grandmother? I know how hard that is for you."

Mateo took a deep breath. "She wasn't as bad as usual," he said. "Which means she was awful. But maybe twenty percent less vindictive?"

"I say we call it a win."

He grinned, then pointed at her phone screen. "We have a translation. Okay, according to the internet, this Latin script means something like 'the road has three sections.'"

They met each other's eyes in mutual bafflement. Nadia said, "I was expecting something more ominous."

"It sounds more like directions from your GPS. 'In three hundred yards, turn left at the fortress of doom.'"

She only barely managed to hold back a laugh. "Maybe the internet translation is wrong?"

"Probably. Do we know anybody who speaks Latin? My priest, maybe—"

"Excuse me?" One of the hall monitors stood in the doorway and spoke to their substitute. "I'm supposed to bring Nadia Caldani to Ms. Walsh's office. I've got a note."

Nadia had been dodging Ms. Walsh and ignoring her emails ever since the incident at the town hall meeting. Of course, the emails had been just vague enough for her to feasibly not answer—*maybe we should talk*, etc. But apparently

Ms. Walsh could only be put off so long.

Mateo mouthed, *What's up?*

Ms. Walsh, she mouthed back. Even Mateo couldn't understand the fear every witch felt when there was a danger her secret had been inadvertently discovered.

She sighed and went with the hall monitor.

On the way, Nadia tried to remain calm. There was almost no chance that Ms. Walsh suspected her of witchcraft. After all, she could only know about witchcraft if she were a witch herself, and if she were, Nadia would have seen evidence of it by now. Wouldn't she? For a moment she doubted herself, but she knew the odds as well as anyone. There were very few witches in the world, and while there had been a coven in Captive's Sound, Elizabeth had apparently driven the coven deep underground.

Okay, this won't be about witchcraft, Nadia thought. *Then what?*

Probably it was about her mother leaving, or college applications, or something similarly depressing. It was all Nadia could do not to groan as she walked into the main office.

Ms. Walsh had the smaller office, nearest the door, but the principal and assistant principal both had their offices in this same area. Different sports and drama schedules were posted all around, and a few other people milled around the waiting area—including someone who wasn't a student.

"Well, look who's here." Verlaine's uncle Gary opened his arms for a hug, like they'd been friends forever; Nadia hugged him back. Even though they'd only met a handful

156

of times, one of those times had been when Verlaine was in the hospital and they were both scared to death; people got closer at moments like that. He had a broad smile outlined by a short, crisply trimmed beard; between that, his belly, and his usual good cheer, it was easy to imagine him playing Santa for little kids. "I know they can't have brought *you* in for detention. Never. Never ever ever."

Despite her tension, Nadia had to laugh. "Just meeting with the guidance counselor."

"It's that time of the year, isn't it? Verlaine keeps rewriting her Yale essay—four times so far, I swear. I thought it was perfect the first time. Didn't you?"

Nadia hadn't even realized Verlaine wanted to go to Yale, or that her test scores might make that a possibility. Verlaine had never even shown her the essay, because she didn't believe Nadia could care. "I'll ask her if I can look at it. Maybe she just needs a fresh pair of eyes. You know?"

"Some perspective. Yes. Exactly."

"I guess you probably need to talk to Ms. Walsh, too." Nadia's hopes rose. "It's fine with me if you go first."

"Oh, no. Just dropping this off." He held up a brown bag and a Hello Kitty thermos Nadia recognized. "Verlaine forgot her lunch, and I know she calls the cafeteria the Hall of Trans Fats."

"It's pretty disgusting," she agreed. *So much for getting out of this.*

Faye Walsh opened her office door, her smile betraying a little chagrin—Nadia had put off replying to the emails way too long. That alone had probably told her something was up. "Well, there you are," she said. "Come on in. Let's chat."

Nadia gave her a searching look. She'd always paid attention to how Ms. Walsh dressed simply because she was so stylish; today she wore a deep-orange pencil skirt and silky white blouse with a patterned scarf at the neck—basically outshining every other faculty member, and most students, by a mile. But today Nadia wanted to look for what Ms. Walsh *wasn't* wearing.

And it was exactly what Nadia expected: no rings, no bracelet, no charms strung on a chain around her neck. Every witch kept her raw materials close if she could, because that was the only way to ensure her ability to cast any spell at any moment. Back in ye olden times, that had sometimes meant carrying around a bag of stones and gems, but today it was easy to keep everything on hand as jewelry. If Ms. Walsh didn't do that, then Ms. Walsh wasn't a witch. She didn't know about the Craft. Whatever she'd seen at the town hall meeting, she hadn't glimpsed the truth.

Relieved, Nadia headed into the office to talk her way through whatever was coming—but then Ms. Walsh stepped past her, obviously dismayed. "Sir? Sir, are you all right?"

Uncle Gary stood at the counter, one hand to his throat in a gesture that had become all too familiar.

Ms. Walsh ran toward him, but not in time to keep him from falling onto the floor, sprawled out across the linoleum. "Call 9-1-1!" Nadia shouted. At least the paramedics could keep him alive.

He convulsed on the floor, gurgling and coughing, as streams of black liquid flowed from the corners of his gasping mouth. Nadia pulled off her cardigan and balled it under his head.

"Hang on," she whispered. "You'll be okay." It was a lie. To judge by the desperate panic in his eyes, Uncle Gary knew it.

The black stuff pooled beneath his head, burning streaks across his face and neck until it flowed and sizzled against the floor. Her cardigan began to smolder at the edges. Nadia tried to tune out the screaming of the secretary or Ms. Walsh shouting directions for the ambulance into the phone; the important thing right now was to focus on him, give him a little comfort if possible.

When the office door opened, Nadia looked up in hopes of seeing the paramedics—but instead Elizabeth stood there, unruffled as ever. Nobody else in the office even seemed to notice she'd walked in; her glamours protected her.

"What are you doing to him?" Nadia wanted to just get up and shake the truth out of Elizabeth, but Uncle Gary had clasped her hand, and she wouldn't leave him there. "Why?"

Elizabeth dropped to her knees just in front of Nadia, close enough that Nadia could see the soft dusting of freckles across her cheeks. The acrid smoke from the black stuff on the floor wreathed around her face. "You can have the truth. You know that. And you know the price."

Join Elizabeth. Work with her. Learn from her, Asa's voice whispered in her memory. *You'll learn enough to destroy her long before the One Beneath has a claim on your soul.*

As before, Elizabeth dipped two fingers into the gunk and lifted her hand to her bared shoulder. By now Nadia could see how the burned lines on her skin began to form the symbol she'd found in the Book of Shadows, the one that had some connection to Mateo's family. And those first lines—a regular burn would have begun to heal by now, but instead it seemed to have burned even farther into Elizabeth's flesh, which was so red and raw that Nadia winced to look at it.

This sign shall mark His path. The road has three sections. What was that supposed to mean? Was it a way of keeping Asa in the world?

There was nothing Nadia hated more than not knowing. Her ignorance was the reason Elizabeth could get away with this.

Nadia thought things couldn't possibly get worse until Verlaine ran in. Her expression as she looked down at Uncle Gary and realized what had happened—that was the worst.

Verlaine sat in a plastic chair in a pale, white hallway. In the distance she could hear the beeps and clicks of medical equipment, the hushed voices of doctors and nurses saying things she probably didn't want to hear. Around her, though, everything was silent.

She hadn't seen Mrs. Purdhy or Riley Bender collapse, but she'd listened to Nadia and Mateo's descriptions. Black tar that burned like acid. Smoke rising from the floor. The look of panic in their eyes—

"What's happening?"

Nadia's voice shook Verlaine back to something like normal. She turned her head to see Nadia and Mateo hurrying toward her. It was only just after school had let out; they must have rushed over on Mateo's motorcycle. Verlaine didn't move, just watched them.

They really wish they could care, she thought.

"Is Uncle Gary okay? What's happening?" Nadia repeated as they reached her. Maybe Verlaine looked even worse than she felt, because Mateo put a steadying hand on her shoulder as Nadia said, more gently, "Hey. Are you all right?"

"He's just like the others." Verlaine's voice was hoarse from the crying she'd done earlier; the words still seemed to stick in her throat. "He's in a coma. They can't wake him up. They don't know why."

Her friends sat down on either side of her. Mateo said, "Where's Uncle Dave?"

"Talking to the doctors." She coughed and wiped beneath her eyes, which were still damp from her tears. "When my parents died, Uncle Dave and Uncle Gary hadn't been dating that long. And back then, lots fewer gay people had kids, so they'd never talked about it, you know? They were hanging out. Going clubbing. They were only about five years older than we are now. So when Uncle Dave got custody of me, he thought—well, that's it. I've got a little girl now, and there's no way this guy's going to be up for that. But Uncle Gary stayed. He just kept showing up, and helping with everything, and changing diapers and taking me out in the stroller, like it was no big deal. Finally Uncle Dave broke down one day and was like, 'Aren't you going to leave me?' Uncle Gary said he wasn't ever leaving either of us. Not ever."

Mateo put his arm around Verlaine's shoulders, and Nadia took her hand. They were trying so hard. But they didn't get it. They *couldn't* get it.

They couldn't see what it meant to lead a life where only two people in the world could really see you, really love you—because they loved you before it all went wrong. Everybody else got to have friends, parents, brothers or sisters, boyfriends or girlfriends, this entire universe of people who could love them. Verlaine got exactly two—her dads— and now one of them had been taken away.

"This isn't the end." Nadia lifted her head, and she had that stubborn set to her chin that meant her mind was set on something. "I'm going to learn what's behind this magic, and I'm going to undo it." She paused before adding, "No matter what it takes."

"No matter what," Mateo repeated, but the way he said it—well, it reminded Verlaine of the days before she'd really known Mateo, when she'd thought he was dangerous and potentially insane. The days when he'd scared her a little . . .

A third voice said, "Verlaine?"

She looked up to see Asa standing in front of her; once again he'd approached without making a sound. He still wore his coat, as if he, too, had rushed to her side. Why did a demon who seared anything he touched need a coat?

"What are you doing here?" Mateo rose from his seat and

stepped between Asa and Verlaine, as if he could protect her. It was a nice thought.

"I didn't know it would be him," Asa said. "But I should have guessed. I didn't. I'm sorry. For what it's worth."

"It's not worth much." Verlaine leaned farther back in her chair. She felt tired, as though she'd been awake for days. Her temples throbbed from the crying she'd done, and all she wanted was to go into Uncle Gary's hospital room and curl up beside him on the bed. Maybe if she did, when she woke up this would only be a horrible dream.

Nadia got to her feet then to face Asa; apparently she was the only one here who had heard anything interesting. "What do you mean, you should have guessed?"

"If you expect me to explain Elizabeth's work, forget it. I've given you some very helpful suggestions—which you seem determined to ignore while she keeps going." Asa folded his arms. The black coat he wore was long and lean, zippered in a sideways slash across his chest, with a sharp collar that turned up in back. *He couldn't look more like a demon without putting red plastic horns on his head,* Verlaine thought.

Yet the look in his eyes as they met hers didn't seem demonic at all.

"Wait," Nadia said. She put up her hands as though she were holding something back, and her gaze turned distant. "Hang on. Elizabeth will keep going. She'll keep taking people out."

"Is that not obvious?" Asa frowned. "I'd have thought at

least that much would've sunk into your brains by now. I overestimated you."

Nadia didn't seem to pay any attention. "But the people she's chosen don't have anything to do with witchcraft. They aren't falling sick at one location or one time of day. So there's another purpose behind what she's done. It's like—it's like Elizabeth doesn't care who she hurts—but she has to hurt *someone*."

Asa's expression didn't change, but Verlaine could sense that Nadia was on to something. "Keep going," she whispered to Nadia.

"She's building on pain itself. There's only one thing you build on pain. Only one. That's not what she's doing. It *can't* be." Nadia's eyes were wide now, but not with exhilaration, even though she definitely, positively had to be on to something. Instead she looked afraid.

Very quietly Asa said, "I take back what I said about overestimating you." With one last glance at Verlaine, he stalked down the hallway; his shoes made no sound against the floor. Verlaine watched him go and thought the room was colder without him. There was no reason that should make her feel even more alone, and yet it did.

Verlaine said, "He's going because he can't help you work against Elizabeth."

"No, he can help us against Elizabeth," Mateo said, which surprised her. What did Mateo know about demons? "He just can't help us against—"

"—the One Beneath," Nadia finished for him. "Oh, my God. He's coming."

Verlaine shook her head. "The One Beneath can never, ever enter our world. You said so! Not without destroying every barrier between His realm and ours. Right? That has to be right."

"His realm is hell," Mateo said. "You mean, we're talking about hell on Earth?"

"Stupid!" Nadia's voice broke. "How was I so stupid? I should've seen it before. *The road has three sections*—but I never learned about it as a road. I learned about the three barriers between the One Beneath and our world. First He would have to break the boundaries of hell. Then He would have to create a bridge between His world and ours. Finally, He'd break through to our world and . . . end it."

Verlaine and Mateo exchanged glances. Even her misery about Uncle Gary was eclipsed by the dawning fear within them all.

Nadia was certain now. Everything about the way she stood, the determination on her face, even the way she now stepped in front of them both, made it clear that no doubt remained. "*That's* what Elizabeth did at the Halloween carnival. She broke the boundaries of hell. She completed step one. And now she's hurting all these people, keeping them in pain indefinitely, because she's using them for step two. She's using them to build the bridge for the One Beneath."

Verlaine shuddered as Mateo repeated, "Hell on Earth."

14

AFTER THEY LEFT VERLAINE AT THE HOSPITAL, MATEO had a crash course on the apocalypse.

He went home with Nadia, luckily arriving there while her father and brother were out, so they could skip the fake small talk and head straight to her attic. Nadia quickly found the symbol in Goodwife Hale's Book of Shadows and showed him the notes in her own that talked about the three barriers that stood between the world he knew and, as he put it, "total *Ghostbusters*-style, dogs-and-cats-living-together, mass-hysteria Armageddon."

"Pretty much." Nadia had yanked her hair back in a pony-tail, her eyes blazing with an energy that was part anger, part adrenaline. "It never occurred to me that Elizabeth would try this. I never thought it was something even a Sorcer-ess would want. They draw their power from the demonic realm. Destroying the barriers means even destroying herself. She's willing to die if it means she takes the whole world with her."

Mateo nodded. He knew now what he had to do, no matter how much it horrified him, no matter how hard it would be. "If she's willing to die, well, that makes it easier."

Nadia was fishing around in the jar of Hershey's Miniatures that sat in a row with her witchcraft supplies. "Makes what easier?"

"Going after her." Though he tried to say the words like it was a foregone conclusion, he knew he didn't quite manage it: "Killing her."

For a moment Nadia didn't answer him. She didn't even move, just sat there on her knees staring at his face like she'd never seen him before. Then she said, "Elizabeth might die as a result of her own magic, I guess. I'm not worrying about that."

"That's not what I mean." Mateo couldn't quite believe he was saying this, and yet he knew beyond any doubt this was the only way to win. "You want to stop her from working any dark magic, right? Well, there's one way to make sure she stops. And I think we ought to consider it."

"Listen—you're upset, you're freaked out for Verlaine, I get that—"

"I don't think you get it at all. Come on. You thought you killed her on Halloween! Why are you getting squeamish about it now?"

"I didn't *murder her* on Halloween," Nadia said. "She was the one who created the fire and stood in the middle of it. I just didn't risk my life to rescue her. Big difference."

Obviously Nadia wasn't thinking this through. "The point is, we're not exactly worried about keeping her alive. In fact, the longer Elizabeth lives, the more people she hurts, and the closer the One Beneath gets to eating our world alive. So why wouldn't we kill her?"

"What makes you think we *could*? Just her Book of Shadows nearly killed me when I went into her house to look for you. The protective spells she knows, the enchantments around every single place she travels—it's like she's at the center of a fortress, Mateo. We're not getting through that fortress without some high-level magic on our side."

"And that's exactly what she expects you to do! Outspell her, whatever you'd call it. She wouldn't expect us to just . . . take her out."

"You sound like you're talking about a video game," Nadia snapped. "Seriously, Mateo, what are you talking about? Stabbing her? Strangling her? Are you the kind of person who could do that to another human being?"

That caught him off guard. Once, in the final horrible hours before Halloween, the magical snares Elizabeth had used to bind Mateo to her had weakened. He'd rushed at her; he'd meant to strangle her. He'd tried to. And in the end he hadn't been able to follow through.

The result was that Elizabeth had opened this door for the One Beneath, and Nadia had very nearly been killed.

Instead of answering, Mateo said, "I've seen Elizabeth as she really is. You haven't. She's hardly even a human being any longer. I don't think she counts. So maybe—maybe it doesn't matter what we do to her."

Nadia shook her head and took Mateo's hands in hers. A lock of her shining, black hair fell across her cheek, only emphasizing the beauty of her heart-shaped face. His anger gentled as she said, "I'm not as worried about what it would do to her. I worry about what killing her would do to you."

How did she do that? Look into his eyes, say a few words, and somehow say the thing that stopped him cold, spoke to his soul? Mateo didn't know, but Nadia always seemed to find a way.

He squeezed her fingers more tightly, and when she smiled at him, unsure but hopeful, he decided they could try to think of something else. What that "something else" could possibly be, he didn't know, and he was pretty sure they'd have to come back to this conversation sooner rather than later. But maybe Nadia needed more time; maybe he did, too. For now, it was okay to just hear her out. "What other options are there?"

"Well. There's one possibility." She paused, as though she didn't want to say the rest. "I could tell Elizabeth I'm going to join her."

He jerked back. It was like she'd slapped him. "You didn't—you wouldn't, ever."

"Not for real. I mean, of course not. But if I just told her that I'd learn from her, work with her, I'd be able to find out what Elizabeth's really up to."

"We know that now. She's trying to bring the One

Beneath to our world, which is apparently a thousand different kinds of bad."

Mateo's voice had risen more than he meant it to, but before he could feel bad about it, Nadia started yelling, too. "I can't stop her from bringing the One Beneath here if I don't learn more about how she's doing this." She tossed her own Book of Shadows a couple of feet away, like it was useless instead of this priceless, secret thing. "Mom might have been a coldhearted bitch capable of leaving her whole family, but she wouldn't have done anything like this, ever. She wasn't able to teach me about magic this dark." Finally, almost as a whisper, Nadia said, "Mom wasn't this bad. No matter what, she wasn't this bad."

It wasn't as though Mateo couldn't hear how badly Nadia was hurting. Or that he thought she wasn't as scared as he was for Verlaine's dad. Instead it was like those words—*work with her*—were pounding a drumbeat that drowned out everything else.

Elizabeth had taken his mother. His grandfather. His chance at being accepted, ever, in this stupid, small town. She had blood on her hands and a demon on her side, and Nadia was willing to *work with her*?

Elizabeth was going to take Nadia, too.

"You say that now," Mateo said. "You think you can learn some high-level magic, make yourself stronger, and get out. But there's no way it's that easy, Nadia. You think Elizabeth started out this dark? I bet she didn't. I bet she believed it would just be a couple of spells, a little more knowledge, and then she'd be out. Next thing you know, she's not even human. And this time it's going to be you."

Nadia gaped at him. "You actually think I'd go dark? That I'd serve the One Beneath? How could you ever, ever say something like that?"

It had been meant as a warning, not an accusation, but at the moment, Mateo didn't care. His mind was filled with one horrible image: Nadia as the beastlike, inhuman thing he'd once seen as Elizabeth—golden, melting, ferocious, and brutal. If she changed, his Steadfast powers would force him to see exactly how quickly her humanity drained away. "I don't know. You want more power, don't you? You're always talking about it. How little you know, how much you wish your mom had taught you. You went diving in the sound to get this other spell book even though it nearly killed you." And then he said the thing he knew he shouldn't say but couldn't hold back. "You definitely want your magic more than you want me."

"What?" Her eyes went wide, like she had no idea what he was talking about. And she knew. She had to know. "Mateo, you're not making any sense."

"Yeah, I am. I love you more than you love me, and we both know it."

"Mateo, please." Nadia kept shaking her head no, which was meaningless, because everything he'd said was true. "Please, don't."

"I have to get out of here." He grabbed his backpack and headed for the door. Just as he pushed down the ladder, though, he hesitated. "I'll bring the knife by tomorrow. If you can use it to help Verlaine's dad, you should."

When Nadia nodded, he could see that he'd made her cry. Which made him feel like dirt—but he hadn't said anything that wasn't true. It didn't matter. He felt awful anyway.

Her voice shook as she said, "Did you just break up with me?"

Dammit, now his own throat was tight. "No. Because I love you and I can't help it. But I can't be here right now."

The attic door fell shut behind him, like he'd slammed it. He hadn't. Just sounded that way.

From the higher branches of the tree next to the Caldani home, two witnesses watched Mateo get onto his motor-cycle and roar away. One was the crow, which looked on with cobweb eyes, projecting every moment back to Elizabeth.

The other was Asa, who lounged along one long, crooked limb, the wood smoldering slightly beneath him.

"Damn, I'm good," he said to the crow.

The bird responded by flapping its broad wings and flying away. Asa sighed.

He couldn't see into the attic from this vantage point, and his myriad powers didn't involve X-ray vision. But Asa was close enough to hear Nadia's sobs. They told him all he needed to know.

They're further apart now. That makes each of them more likely to follow my suggestions. If even one of them succeeds, I rid myself of Elizabeth. And if they're parted, the One Beneath is more likely to win in the end. Instead of owing His triumph to Elizabeth, He'll owe it to me.

Maybe then I could be free.

He was lost in thought—rare for him, with his laser-like focus—but this dream was too precious to resist. If Asa were free, he wouldn't have to suffer in hell any longer. He wouldn't have to do the bidding of the One Beneath any longer . . .

. . . but he wouldn't be able to live in the human world, either. At least, not the human world as he now knew it. After the One Beneath's triumph, there would be little difference between this place and hell. Good-bye, internet; good-bye, blue skies; good-bye, Burger King chicken sandwiches; good-bye, loving parents; good-bye, Celtics games; good-bye, joy and laughter and Verlaine's smile—

The scent of woodsmoke around him grew stronger. Asa realized he'd lost his concentration enough to very nearly set the tree ablaze, and he wasn't here to start fires.

So he rolled off the limb, caught himself with one hand for a moment, then dropped silently to the ground, landing on his feet. The jolt would have broken bones in a human; for Asa, it registered as a thump, no more.

Night had begun to fall. In his black coat and dark jeans, he blended easily into the shadows, no magic required. He liked walking along the streets without being seen, without having to pretend to be Jeremy Prasad. Not that there weren't parts of that masquerade he relished—but sometimes he wanted the simple luxury of being himself, being able to enjoy this world for what it was.

Two weeks to Thanksgiving, a holiday Asa had never experienced. It seemed to involve eating, so he was game to give it a try. He ought to have the joys of this world while they were still here for the having. The more brilliant colors of the leaves had faded to brown, and already as many were on the ground as on the trees. Given the heat that radiated from him, he didn't need a coat; the one he wore was mostly for show, and also because he looked damn good in it. The mere humans around him were already beginning to don heavier coats, scarves, and those ridiculous knitted hats that made them look like garden gnomes.

Thinking of garden gnomes reminded him of the last time he'd become seriously distracted, enough to nearly start a fire—the night he'd watched Verlaine working on her computer. Her silver hair had fallen over her shoulders, and the light from her screen had illuminated the thin, fragile lines of her face. Her eyes had been wide, like she was drinking in every single thing she could learn, everything the world had to offer.

That memory was replaced by the one from this afternoon in the hospital, when she'd slumped in a plastic chair like a broken doll, all hope and joy gone.

Two people, he thought, anger rising inside him. *Only two humans in the world aren't ensnared by Elizabeth's spell. Only two of them can see Verlaine for what she really is: her fathers. She might have been allowed to keep them both. It was so little, and it was all she had.*

He thought of going back to her, but no. Verlaine would be with her remaining father now; they needed each other. There was little else for Asa to do but go home.

The mood was a little strained around the Prasad home at present. Mom had been allowed to come home two days earlier, having shown no further signs of dangerous behavior. (When not influenced by magic spells, Mrs. Prasad could come no closer to violence than cooking her superspicy curry.) Still, she remained shaken, and Dad kept agreeing to absolutely anything she said so as to avoid setting off another "incident." This of course irritated her more than any argument could, so both of them remained tense and cranky.

However, Asa did his best, telling funny stories about school that made them smile, and asking his mother what she wanted for her birthday next week. Her face lit up so brightly that he knew, beyond any doubt, that Jeremy Prasad had never remembered his mother's birthday in his life.

So. Errands for evil Sorceress: taken care of. Verlaine: in the best place she could be. Prasad parents: pacified.

And yet he still had to do forty-five minutes' worth of medieval history homework before bed.

I've known people from the fourteenth century, he mused as he started outlining his paper about the Hundred Years' War. *You'd think it would speed things up a little. But no. And I'm being forced to assist in an apocalypse I'd rather never see; could it at least happen before this paper is due? Of course not.*

Around nine p.m., his father appeared in the doorway of his room. "Hard at work, I see."

"History."

"Your mother seems well. Doesn't she?"

"Yeah." Then, thinking better of his casual reply, Asa tried to assume a more stricken expression, one that would make it clear he was anguished but finding the strength to carry on . . . something like that. Of course he knew his mother was fine, that she'd just run into an amateurishly executed couple of spells. But nobody else knew it yet, so a little more concern was called for.

"I just wanted to say, you've really come through these past couple of weeks. For your mother and for me." Mr. Prasad looked surprisingly moved. "You've made some changes recently. Keeping your room clean, not talking back, doing your homework. Don't think we haven't noticed. It meant a lot to your mom, you being there for her."

"We're family. That's what family does." At least, as far as Asa remembered.

Mr. Prasad smiled, slightly disbelieving. "You're finally starting to grow up, son." Then he shuffled off to bed.

Asa glanced at the screen saver on his computer, which was a collection of pictures Jeremy had taken over the past several months. Girls in bikinis either pretending they would flash him or actually doing it; him and his friends hanging on one another while drunk; one of a guy vomiting on the beach while Jeremy laughed: The sheer monotony of it was clear to Asa, even if it hadn't been to Jeremy. This was all just sensation—the most primitive kind—apparently selfish and certainly thoughtless.

Jeremy's face came up again, this time as he stood behind the wheel of a speedboat. He didn't seem to be watching where he was going—on the water at a speed that, to judge by the flumes of sea spray behind him, could be no less than sixty-five miles an hour. Really, it was a miracle Elizabeth had even gotten the chance to kill him; by rights, Jeremy ought to have died of pure idiocy long ago.

Asa murmured, "I'm a better you than you ever were."

15

"YOU SURE YOU'RE OKAY, SWEETHEART?"

Nadia did her best to smile at her dad. "Yeah. I'm fine." Then again—her eyes were probably red and puffy, and her throat was hoarse from all the crying she'd done. Coming up with an excuse would throw him off. "I guess I'm just upset about Verlaine's uncle Gary."

"He seemed like such a great guy. I kept meaning to ask them over for dinner some night, cook some burgers on the grill or something." Her father could only cook outside, over open fire; when he walked into a kitchen, it was a different story. That was why Nadia was the one putting a lasagna into the oven now. "The same weird thing that happened to that girl at"—he glanced over at Cole, who was in the living room watching *SpongeBob SquarePants* with rapt fascination—"at L-A-C-A-T-R-I-N-A?"

"Yeah."

"And the doctors still don't have a clue what that is? Doesn't look like any disease I've ever heard of. Something in the water, maybe? We have to get one of those filters." He sighed heavily and leaned against the kitchen counter. "I really should have gotten to know Gary better."

"He's not dead, Dad. He's just in a coma. So think positive and stop with the past tense, okay?"

"You're right. Sorry."

Dad wasn't looking so good himself lately. He hadn't been sleeping well, to judge by the late-night pacing in his room; his eyes were shadowed, and he'd lost some weight, despite Nadia's best efforts with waffles and pasta. The last time he'd looked like this much of a wreck had been in the first few weeks after Mom had left.

Nadia hated knowing why he wasn't sleeping. Every time her mind turned to the idea of what he was thinking about during those sleepless hours—who he was thinking about—her stomach twisted uncomfortably. Elizabeth's hold over him had closed around their home like a cold, thick fog no amount of sunshine could dispel. Betrayer's Snare might protect him if and when Elizabeth tried to strike at him again, but it could not undo the dark magic she'd used. That was beyond Nadia's power.

"I forgot something!" Cole yelled from the living room, without ever looking away from the TV screen.

She and Dad exchanged looks. Nadia said, "Oh, yeah? What?"

"I'm in the Thanksgiving play!"

"That's great!" she said, with as much enthusiasm as she could muster on a day as horrible as this.

Dad seemed to be trying just as hard. "So, are you a pilgrim or a Native American?"

"I'm mashed potatoes."

Had they heard that wrong? Nadia went into the living room. "What do you mean, mashed potatoes?"

"We're all different Thanksgiving food, and I'm mashed potatoes. Levi is the gravy, so we get to be onstage together. I need a costume."

"A costume?" Nadia turned to her father in disbelief. "How are we supposed to make a mashed-potato costume? What would that even look like?"

Dad actually grinned. "At least we don't have to make a gravy costume."

That made her laugh—too hard, like the joke was a lot funnier than it really was. But her feelings were all over the place, like her heart had been shattered and the fragments lay anywhere and everywhere.

Mateo was wrong about her not loving him. Her entire heart ached for him every second, like it couldn't beat without reminding her that he should be here with her, now and always. How could he think otherwise, even for a moment?

"Nadia?"

"Sorry, Dad. I guess I'm zoning out." She needed a minute. "Listen, I'm going to check on Verlaine. Dinner won't be ready for about another half hour."

He waved her off. "Do that. Give her my best. I'll just be

180

here trying to figure out why kids are dressing up as food."

Nadia retreated to her room. In a minute she'd text Verlaine. Right now she needed a moment to get herself together. She pulled her fluffy, white duvet over her, like it could shelter her from any of the crap that had happened today.

Instead she could pretend it was Halloween night.

That night, after the carnival and the fire and the terror of nearly losing each other, she and Mateo had come back here. Her dad and Cole had been in New York City, and he'd been able to call his own father and let him know he was okay, so there had been no one in the way, nobody to stop them from spending the night in each other's arms.

They hadn't made love. Mateo never had before, they didn't have any protection, and besides, they were both so exhausted they were shaking. Even after she showered, grime from the fire stained her skin; his cuts and bruises had needed even more bandaging than hers. So it wasn't exactly the ideal moment for wild, unrestrained passion. He'd stripped down to his underwear because he had nothing else, but she'd worn an oversize T-shirt that wasn't going to show up in a Victoria's Secret catalog anytime soon.

But they'd huddled together in this same bed, beneath this same blanket, and kissed each other until her lips were swollen, and raw from the little cuts of his teeth and hers. Their kisses tasted like smoke. She'd bent down over him, her hair falling around their faces like a curtain, and they'd smiled at each other as though they were keeping the most perfect secret in the world. His hands had woven through her hair, caressed every inch of her body, left her panting and yearning and yet completely, utterly content. When they fell asleep, arms and legs tangled and close enough to feel each other's breath against their skin, Nadia had reveled in the knowledge that this was only the beginning.

How could everything have changed so fast?

A terrifying figure rose from the ground—as though it were part of the ground come to life, some demon hatching from the earth itself. Mateo didn't run, didn't cower, but as he stood there, he felt only helplessness and fear.

Rain pounded down all around him; he and Nadia stood ankle-deep in mud. But they weren't in the forest or at the shore; instead they stood in the middle of the school complex, which was flooded inches deep. Water had plastered Nadia's hair to her forehead and cheeks, but he thought those were tears in her eyes. "Go," she begged. "Go now while you can."

"Not without you."

"I can't leave. He owns me. He owns me forever." Nadia pushed Mateo back. "Save yourself."

"Nadia—Nadia, no!"

Mateo awoke with a start. In the first instant he could only think of that horrible shape rising out of the mud, and the fact that Nadia couldn't get away—but then he thought, *Vision.*

Immediately after that he thought, *Where the hell am I?*

Cold bit into his skin as he drew up into a ball. Clad in

only boxers and a T-shirt, he seemed to be . . . at school. On one of the picnic tables outside. Great.

"Oh, man, check this out!" somebody called. Mateo turned his head to see a couple of jocks staring at him from the gymnasium entrance; apparently the basketball team had an early-morning practice. Double great. "This freak's half-naked at school!"

Derisive laughter stopped short as Mateo rose to his feet; the jocks got weird expressions on their faces as they ducked inside. Okay, being laughed at was a lot less horrible than being feared. Mateo winced—the courtyard was paved with gravel, which cut icily into his bare feet, and he didn't know how to even begin dealing with this. Call Dad? He hadn't grabbed his phone as he sleepwalked out the door. Walk home through town? The rumors would spread like wildfire—not like they wouldn't already, because the whole basketball team was probably texting up a storm—

"Mateo?" He turned again and saw a friendly face: Ms. Walsh, the guidance counselor. Nadia seemed worried about her, but right now she was smiling and taking off her own coat as she came toward him. "Are you okay?"

"I sleepwalk," he said. It was the truth, at least a sliver of it.

"Ugh. What a pain. I used to do that sometimes when I was younger—though it's been a while. One time I woke up in the shower of my college dorm." Ms. Walsh draped her blue coat over his shoulders like this situation was the most natural thing in the world. Mateo felt kind of stupid wearing a woman's coat, but way less stupid than he had parading around campus in his underwear. She patted his shoulder. "Good thing I came in early today. Come on. I'll drive you home."

"Thanks." Mateo hoped Dad would sleep a little later than usual this morning—maybe he wouldn't even have to know about this.

Ms. Walsh's Mini Cooper was ridiculously small, but Mateo was able to fit inside, even though it was a bit cramped. He was grateful for the lift, even more grateful that Ms. Walsh immediately put on the heater and didn't insist on awkward conversation. His mind wandered back to the horrible vision he'd had—a possible future, he knew. But as ever, he didn't know how much of the vision was literal truth and how much was symbolic. Once magic got involved, it was a lot harder to tell all that apart.

When they reached his house, Ms. Walsh said, "Forgive the question, but you're still seeing Nadia Caldani, right?"

"Yeah, of course." Echoes of yesterday's argument tugged at Mateo, but he knew his answer was true. Right now he was unsure how she felt about him—but he knew exactly how he felt about her.

"Let her know I'd like to see her, okay?"

That was a little odd, but right now, Mateo owed Ms. Walsh one, so he wasn't going to get into it. "Yeah. Okay. Thanks for the ride."

"No problem." She smiled like a woman with a secret. "We have to stick together, people like us."

❧

Elizabeth lay in the swath of fabric she used as a sort of bed. It hung in one corner, not unlike a hammock. The cloth was dusty and threadbare, and spiders had woven small webs around the spikes she'd hammered into the walls so long ago. All that mattered was that when she slept, she didn't have to touch the floor.

Floors were dangerous. The spells that could catch you from below—she didn't intend to fall prey to any of those.

The chill of autumn had begun to deepen. Frost lined the dawn-pink windowpanes. Snows came so much later now than they once had; Elizabeth could remember when it was not unusual to face the first winter storm in early October.

This room, though—this would be forever warm.

Elizabeth smiled at her metal stove, glowing with a fire that had nothing to do with combustion, brilliant in a way no darkness could ever dim. Its heat sank into her skin, working its magic, infusing her with everything she'd ever taken, everything she deserved.

The house began to creak and groan, as it sometimes did during a heavy storm—but the day promised to be bright. As Elizabeth lifted her head, the floor itself began to shake. The broken glass scattered about her floor began to skitter along the worn floorboards, and the glow from her stove brightened—brightened again—until it was nearly blinding.

Immediately Elizabeth dropped from her bed and went to her knees. Shards of broken glass pricked her flesh, drawing blood, but she paid the pain no mind. Instead she prostrated herself, accepting the blame.

"I will not disappoint you, my liege," she whispered. The light burned her eyes, even through her closed eyelids. "Nadia Caldani will come to me. I swear it."

The heat only intensified. His anger was growing; His impatience, too—this close to the end of His confinement, it was no wonder.

Nadia had something to give him that no one else did. Elizabeth understood. It wasn't that Nadia was more important, more beloved—only that she was a necessary step.

Purpose restored, Elizabeth lifted her head, allowing the light and heat to sear her. This small punishment was no more than she deserved.

"Not long now," she said. "I swear it."

The burning heat slowly dissipated. Elizabeth opened her eyes; everything had a sort of faded, red-gold look, as though she had stared into the sun for too long. She could see the trickles of blood around her cut knees.

As she rose to her feet, her resolve strengthened. It would have been simpler to do this more gradually—less complicated, less prey to difficulty—but the One Beneath had already waited too long to claim this world for His own. Elizabeth would not be the one to make Him wait even longer.

Then let it come all at once. Let it claim who it will. Let it begin.

16

NADIA HADN'T FELT THIS WEIRD ABOUT WALKING INTO Rodman High since her first day. Although people buzzed around her, talking and laughing, she could feel their glances glaring on her like a spotlight. Or maybe not a spotlight—one of those lamps from old movies, the ones the 1940s cops shone on suspects to make them talk.

And they made their whispers louder for her benefit. *Mateo Perez—that freak.*

He'd texted her that morning still completely beside himself because of what had happened. Nadia had played down the first sleepwalking incident, hoping against hope that it was an aberration, but apparently not. The sleepwalking was dangerous enough in its own right—*what if he'd wandered into traffic? If this happens in winter, he could freeze to death!*—but what worried Nadia most was that the entire town's paranoia about the cursed Cabot family had now focused on Mateo harder than ever. Mateo had enough burdens to bear; did he have to deal with this, too?

When she turned the corner toward her locker—and, not far away, Mateo's—Nadia immediately saw a familiar face, if not the one she'd been waiting for. "Verlaine! What are you doing here?"

Verlaine shrugged. "All I can do at the hospital is wait. All I can do at home is cry. So somehow Rodman is the least horrible place for me to be. That's new."

Nadia put her arms around Verlaine, reminding herself, *She needs this. She needs her friends. Be one.* As always, when she overcame whatever dark magic shadowed Verlaine, the impulse surprised her—and apparently Verlaine, too, because it took her a moment to hug back. But when she did, her grip was fierce.

"Nothing's changed?" Nadia asked.

"Nothing. Uncle Gary's still asleep. They put him in the same room as Mrs. Purdhy and Riley Bender; supposedly they're studying them all together. Really I think the doctors don't know what to do with any of them, and lining up the hospital beds makes them feel like they did something productive."

"It might be useful," Nadia said. "If you can get me in there, maybe I can try to figure out a little more about the magic at work."

"Oh, hey, yeah!" Verlaine actually smiled a little. "I didn't even think of that."

Maybe Nadia could help; maybe she couldn't. But she'd

managed to cheer Verlaine up, at least momentarily. Gently she teased, "I can tell you're worn out. You didn't even wear one of your vintage outfits today."

"Excuse me?" Verlaine gestured at the bedraggled stuff she wore. "Torn jeans? Flannel shirt? Nineties grunge all the way."

"I should've known it wouldn't be that easy to stop you." Nadia went ahead and stowed her stuff in her locker. As soon as she shut the door and turned her head, she saw Mateo.

She loved him so much that it was less like she saw him and more like he happened to her—every line of his face new, as if it were that first moment they'd met. Mateo's dark eyes met hers, and she opened her arms as she went to him.

They embraced fiercely, and he buried his face in the curve of her neck. Everyone in the hallway was staring at them, both at Mateo and the girl who wasn't afraid of him. Was Mateo the only one in the world who didn't know how much she loved him, that she would never give up on him no matter what?

But Mateo kissed her quickly then looked into her eyes, and she thought maybe he knew, too.

It was Verlaine he spoke to first, and Nadia couldn't blame him for pulling away and offering Verlaine a hug as well. "Hey, you're here. Are you all right?"

Verlaine hugged him back. "If by 'all right' you mean I can now go at least fifteen minutes without crying—maybe? We'll see. How are you? I heard you had another nocturnal adventure. Oh, wait. That kinda sounded dirty."

Mateo actually laughed. "Unfortunately, no. Unless you mean my feet. They were gross. I don't even want to know what I walked through."

He was joking about it. Nadia's heart swelled with pride at his courage, facing down both the curse and the sneers of those around them. She took his hand, and for a moment as he smiled at her, she thought everything was well between them again, the way it should always have been—but then Mateo's face fell.

She glanced over her shoulder and saw Elizabeth.

Her first thought was that Elizabeth looked terrible, which wasn't a thought she'd ever had about Elizabeth before. Evil as she was, a sort of warm glow seemed to follow her everywhere, enhancing a beauty that was all the more striking for being so low-key and natural. Even now she was beautiful.

But instead of the gossamer white she usually favored, Elizabeth wore a dress that—well, it had once been white, but now it was dingy, even stained. Her curls had lost some of their bounce. Band-Aids over her knees only slightly disguised a number of cuts. If it had been anyone else, Nadia would have asked whether she was okay.

It's like she's forgotten how to take care of a mortal body, Nadia thought. *She's tearing it up as she goes.*

Mateo suddenly straightened. His eyes took on the distant look that Nadia had learned to recognize as a sign that he was seeing something through his Steadfast powers—some working of magic that even a witch couldn't witness for herself. "Oh, my God," he said.

"What?" Nadia grabbed his arm then, not that he seemed to notice. "What is it?"

One guy in the hallway fell to the floor. Then a girl right next to them did the same. A teacher who came through the door slumped against one wall, coughed up the black slime, and slid down into unconsciousness.

People began screaming, freaking out, running in all directions. Gage immediately grabbed his phone to call 9-1-1; a few others stooped to check on those who had collapsed.

Elizabeth kept walking. As she went past one of the fallen, she would stoop just long enough to dip her fingers in the gunk; her skin smoking from the burn, she would then reach up to her shoulder. By now the scars on her flesh were ragged and horrible, but Nadia could recognize the symbol. It was complete; Elizabeth was just burning the marks deeper and deeper.

She didn't even pause as she walked past Nadia and Mateo.

And there was nothing—*nothing*—Nadia could do to stop her.

"What's going on?" Mateo said.

"Elizabeth's speeding up. Going faster. The bridge she's trying to build for the One Beneath—she wants it here sooner. Wants Him here sooner." That much was clear.

What wasn't yet clear was just how much faster Elizabeth had begun to work.

In front of La Catrina, Alejandro Perez took the clipboard from his supplier and started checking off the boxes. Then he frowned. "Hey, what's this? We asked for three cases of tequila, and you only sent us one?"

"We didn't get our own shipment in on time this week," said the driver, an amiable guy he knew only as T. J. "Gave you what we had, changed the bill, and we'll make it up the next time."

"So much for the two-for-one margarita special," Alejandro muttered. He'd been trying to think up various promotions to win diners back. Now that there was another victim of this mystery illness, someone who'd had the decency to collapse somewhere else, there was no more reason for people to assume the food at La Catrina could have anything to do with it. But all the same, it would take another few days for business to get back to normal. A margarita special might have made that two days instead of five. Even that much time made a difference to the bottom line.

Maybe a piña colada special? Not very Mexican—but in this town, authenticity didn't go nearly as far as a two-for-one deal.

He signed off on the modified shipment order, nodded good-bye to T. J., and started hauling in boxes. Too bad Mateo wasn't here, with his young knees and back; these boxes got heavier every year. But soon Mateo would go to college, get out of this stupid town, and be on his own. So Alejandro either had to get used to carrying boxes or start looking for someone else to hire.

That Gage Calloway is a good kid, he thought as T. J.'s huge eighteen-wheeler began lumbering onto the road. *Is he a senior, too, or would he be around next—*

The rest of the question died as he watched the eighteen-wheeler slowly begin to roll off the side of the road, brake lights never blinking once, until it plowed into the grocery-store parking lot. Metal screeched and glass broke as cars twisted, turned, and bent—finally slowing the truck to a stop.

Alejandro ran for the truck, a few other bystanders following close behind. His first thought was that T. J. must have had a heart attack. But when he reached the door and pulled it open, he realized the truth was far stranger than that. T. J. lay slumped over the steering wheel, feebly pawing at the dashboard while viscous black fluid flowed from his gaping mouth. His jeans had already burned away from the stuff, which was now eating into his skin. The smell made Alejandro want to gag.

"Everybody stay back!" he shouted. "Call an ambulance!" The various people now congregating around the truck mostly did as he said, though one girl insisted on coming close to help—that pretty girl Mateo used to be so close to, Elizabeth Pike. Of course she'd want to help—such a nice kid. But he couldn't think about her for very long, or about anything other than the blank staring horror on T. J.'s face.

Like the Bender girl, he thought. *It's happening again.*

Gage had gotten the hell out of school as quickly as he could; nobody was running around taking attendance while that was going down, and all the teachers insisted the students should clear out instead of trying to help. But as he walked across town, he felt more and more guilty for having ducked out.

What if you have Ebola? he asked himself. They'd shown a documentary about the Ebola virus in physics class (since Mrs. Purdhy wasn't around to teach it), about which he was still completely freaked out. *If you've been exposed to Ebola, then you're exposing everybody else to it, too! You'd be what they call a Patient Zero.*

Only then did it occur to him that if he could give other people Ebola, he would have to have it himself. That didn't help.

Okay. I'm going to assume I don't have Ebola yet. But it is past time to take some precautions.

He went to the drugstore downtown, where Mrs. Laimuns was Captive Sound's only pharmacist outside the hospital. She waved at him as he started searching the aisles. "Are you here to pick up your aunt Lorraine's blood-pressure medicine again?"

"Not this time, Mrs. Laimuns." Latex gloves—check. And hey, paper face masks, like people wore to the airport in Asia. He ought to grab some of those, too. As he filled his plastic basket, he reconsidered his answer to the pharmacist; going outside meant exposure to Ebola or whatever it was, so he should save his aunt Lorraine the trouble. "Hey, actually, I'll go ahead and pick up the—"

His voice trailed off as he realized Mrs. Laimuns was no longer standing behind the pharmacy counter. He couldn't see her at all.

Tinny Muzak played on the pharmacy sound system as Gage slowly walked toward the counter. "Mrs. Laimuns?" No reply.

He got to the drop-off window and leaned over to look inside. There, between rows and rows of medicine, Mrs. Laimuns lay unconscious on the floor, strange, black tar thick on her smock, sizzling against the tile.

In Kendall's opinion, it was like the doctors actually *wanted* this hospital room to be creepy. The overhead lights never seemed to be on, having three comatose people together made it feel less like a hospital room and more like a morgue, and the only proof she had that Riley still lived was the beeping of a half dozen machines.

Riley lay on the bed, motionless, with tubes taped into her nose and electrodes stuck to her forehead and chest. Nobody had washed her hair in days, and she didn't have on any makeup. When she woke up and found out that Kendall just let her lie there for days looking like this, Riley was going to be so pissed.

Well, that was the one thing Kendall could fix.

She glanced over her shoulder to see whether any of the nurses were coming; they'd just been here taking care of everybody's catheters—*so gross*—which meant nobody else should walk in for a few minutes. That was all Kendall needed. From her tote bag she pulled a packet of cleansing face wipes and her makeup bag.

"Here you go," she whispered as she carefully washed Riley's face, wiping around the tubes. "That's better, huh?"

Foundation and mascara would be overkill, definitely. But moisturizer had to be a good thing, healthy for the skin, and this one was tinted for just a touch of coverage. Kendall pursed her lips as she brushed the lightest bit of shadow onto Riley's eyelids, then a little blush onto her cheeks.

She finished by dabbing cherry lip balm on Riley's mouth. "There. You look so much better. You could go out like this, totally. Well, not your hair, which is, like, seriously unfortunate, but tomorrow I can at least bring in some dry shampoo."

Riley didn't look so scary any longer. She looked like herself—the girl who had ruled their high school while still being nice to everybody. Kendall wasn't as nice as Riley, and she knew it; someday, though, she hoped she might be.

For a moment she remembered sitting on the lid of the commode, opening her eyes wide as her big sister brushed mascara onto her lashes for the first time. But that just made her want to cry, and Kendall was sick of crying. Instead she patted Riley's hand and said, "I'll get some nail polish in here, too, because you're *way* overdue for a mani-pedi."

Kendall's head jerked upright as she heard voices in the corridor. Not normal nurse voices talking about ccs of fluid or whatever—people shouting. People who were afraid.

She went to the door of the hospital room to see half the staff hurrying down the hallway. Everyone was yelling stuff like *multiple incoming* and *everyone to the ER stat* and so obviously something very, very bad was going down. It was like a cliffhanger on *Grey's Anatomy*. Kendall wondered whether a plane had crashed outside of town or a gunman had shot up a store or something. That was the kind of thing it always was on *Grey's*.

Elizabeth Pike was hanging around, too, but that wasn't so weird. Kendall had seen her around before. Maybe she volunteered here or something.

Then as two nurses went past her, one of them stopped in her tracks. The other one looked back in confusion. "Diana? Diana, are you okay?"

The first nurse staggered against the wall, then slumped to the floor—and that black stuff was all over her, the same stuff that had choked Riley, the exact same thing happening again.

"Somebody help!" said the nurse now leaning over the fallen Diana. "We've got another one right here!"

Another one. She said another one. That meant the people coming into the ER—

Kendall looked back at the hospital room where her sister lay, between the other two patients, and realized they were only the first three. Only the beginning.

Faye Walsh was technically supposed to be in her office from eight thirty to three thirty every single day, but in reality, if she didn't have a student appointment, a fifteen-minute coffee run was okay with the principal, particularly if Faye brought a latte back for her.

The barista held up a cardboard cup and called, "I have a macchiato here for Larissa."

While the woman in front of her went to get her coffee, Faye pulled out her smartphone, just to double-check her schedule. If she could clear a half hour this afternoon, she'd try again to meet with Nadia Caldani. That conversation was overdue.

Someone near her gasped, and Faye glanced up to see the woman who'd just collected her coffee swooning to the ground, spilling coffee in every direction. But another puddle began to spread outward—the black, burning fluid she'd seen in her office a few days before.

The barista called 9-1-1; a few people bent down to try and help. Faye took a couple of steps backward and, unobtrusively as possible, used her phone to snap a picture.

It was important to document this, to get proof.

She had to be on the lookout for any evidence of witchcraft.

17

WHEN VERLAINE HAD LEFT THE HOSPITAL THE DAY before, it had been a place too quiet and mournful for her to bear.

Now it was bedlam.

At least a hundred people, maybe more, had crowded into the ER waiting room; everyone was demanding answers about their loved ones or this "mystery illness," and nobody had any answers to give.

Well, not any answers the crowd was going to get, anyway. The people who knew the truth could be counted on one hand, and included two witches and a demon. Verlaine figured that wasn't what anybody out there wanted to hear.

She and Nadia had managed to find a slightly less crowded corridor where they could at least hear each other talk. "Elizabeth can't have been everywhere in town at once," Verlaine said while they huddled near the vending machines. "Could she? Is there some kind of . . . time-turner spell?"

"Like I wouldn't be using that every single day if there were. And enough with the Harry Potter stuff, okay?" Nadia leaned against the wall, weary as though she were the one who hadn't slept. "I doubt Elizabeth made it to every single scene. But she would have made it to a lot of them."

"Has she completed that disgusting symbol thing she's burning into her flesh?" Verlaine supported tattoos, piercings, and other body modifications on general artistic principles, but actually using them to summon the forces of darkness was going too far.

"Yeah, but I don't think completing the symbol is a big deal. I think it's more about . . . strengthening the symbol. Calling on it. Reinforcing it. Every time Elizabeth burns it deeper into her shoulder, the symbol gets stronger. And so does her spell."

"Which means what? The One Beneath gets to enter our world?"

Nadia gave her a look like it was bad luck to even say that out loud. Maybe it was. Verlaine decided she'd be a little more careful with her words from now on, just in case. "No," Nadia explained. "This is just step two of her plan. What she's doing right now is building a bridge for Him. What she's building the bridge out of is pain itself."

"You mean all these people in this hospital—including Uncle Gary—they're suffering because Elizabeth can use that?" Verlaine hadn't known it was possible to feel so angry that her head ached and her hands clenched into fists so tight her fingers hurt. But if Elizabeth had been there at that moment, she swore she'd have been able to swing her fists right into Elizabeth's face, and no dark magic on Earth could have stopped her. "The pain these sick people feel is like . . . bricks, or stones. What she uses to create."

"Exactly. Her pain mirrors theirs. Makes it stronger."

"That's sick."

"That's dark magic." Nadia shoved the sleeves of her sweater farther up her arms, a restless, anxious move.

Verlaine realized there weren't going to be enough doctors and nurses to go around in this hospital. Who was going to take care of her dad? Fear cut into her deeper and deeper, a scratch turning into a cut turning into a wound.

Nadia lifted her head, and Verlaine turned to see Mateo coming toward them.

"Hey," he said, attaching himself to Nadia in his usual remoralike fashion. She cuddled into his embrace, and Verlaine wondered what it would be like to know you could be sheltered. Comforted. Cared about. "Okay, I tried asking around, but nobody would talk to me, so I just eavesdropped. Worked way better. They brought in almost forty new patients today. They're all in the same condition as Verlaine's dad—comatose, no explanation. The black junk burned their throats and did something to their lungs, but that's nothing people shouldn't be able to heal from. None of the doctors understand why the patients don't wake up again."

Nadia nodded. "Have they been able to analyze the black liquid?"

"They tried," Mateo said. "Apparently it destroyed the lab equipment. Somebody's calling the CDC."

"The what?" Nadia said.

Verlaine knew this; she'd watched *Contagion* on Netflix. "The Centers for Disease Control. They have hazmat suits and specialists and stuff, but still, they're not going to figure out what's really happening here."

"We know what's happening here," Mateo said. "And we know how to stop it."

At that moment, both he and Nadia got this weird look on their faces: stubborn and unsure, even though they never let go of each other. Apparently a plan was afoot, and once again, she'd been shut out of it. How incredibly not surprising.

At that point Mateo said he had to go back to La Catrina to help his dad, even though there was no way people in town would so much as leave their houses tonight for anyplace but the hospital. That meant it was up to Verlaine to give Nadia a ride home in the land yacht. Darkness had fallen, and though the lot was crowded with haphazardly parked cars, nobody else seemed to be around. Their footsteps sounded unnaturally loud, as did her car when she cranked it.

"Give it a second to warm up," Verlaine said, speaking of both her ancient car's motor and the still-cold air blowing through the vents even though she had the heater on. "Hey, is something going on with you and Mateo?"

Nadia huddled farther down in the seat, wrapping her down jacket around her until she seemed to be buried in it. "We don't agree on how to go after Elizabeth. And we had a fight, which I keep trying to tell myself isn't the end of the world. Couples fight, right? I guess after Mom and Dad—it's hard for me to realize that you can move on."

"You fought about Elizabeth?"

"That and other things." Nadia looked almost shame-faced, and Verlaine wondered what level of confession was on the way. But the conclusion was only, "Mateo thinks I don't love him as much as he loves me, and I can't figure out why he'd ever believe that."

Verlaine had to laugh. "Asa."

"Huh?"

"I would bet any amount of money that Asa screwed with his head. He's tried to screw with mine. Yours, too, I bet. Am I right?" Immediately Nadia looked abashed, and Verlaine shook her head. "Demons manipulate people. It's what they do. Asa says so himself. Sounds like he did a number on you two."

Was she really the only one of their group who under-stood him?

Nadia shook her head slowly. "Okay, that is—a pretty strong theory."

"So ask Mateo about what Asa's said lately. Bet that clears it up right away."

"I will. Thanks, Verlaine."

"Whatever." Verlaine scrunched down farther in her seat, ready to end the conversation but somehow not yet ready to drive.

"Are you mad at me?"

"No. Yeah. Kinda. Not mad at you, just—" Verlaine sighed. "It's hard being on the outside all the time."

"I know—it's got to be weird, but we try. I'm sorry we don't do better."

Verlaine was certain that Nadia was completely sincere, but at the moment she just didn't care. "Do you know what I'd give to have anybody feel about me the way Mateo feels about you? Anybody in the world?"

Nadia's face flushed. "Are you telling me you're in love with Mateo, too?"

"No! Of course not!" Sure, Mateo was handsome, but he didn't do it for her. Unfortunately her type seemed to be limited to either jerks in her class or demons from hell. Mateo was way too nice to qualify, not to mention undamned. "But if somebody ever loved me—if they even *could* love me—I don't even know what that would mean. I only know it would be the most amazing thing in the world."

Nobody spoke for a while. *Awkward,* Verlaine thought, and she wondered if she should put on the radio or something. Then, very quietly, Nadia said, "I see you sometimes. I mean, the real you."

"Huh?"

"When I cast a really powerful spell, or other high-level magic is happening around us." Her words came in a rush, but Nadia kept on, determined. "It's like—like just for a second, it blocks out whatever else is keeping us from seeing you for who you really are. The last time was when we were out at Davis Bridge, just after it collapsed. Obviously I couldn't say anything, because we were all swimming for our lives, and now it's hard for me to even remember straight. But I know it happened. For one second, I loved you so much—"

Hot tears blurred Verlaine's vision; her hands felt warm and weak on the steering wheel. "So it's true. What Asa said is true." *There really is something in me to love. It's in here. It always has been. Sometimes I didn't believe it but it's true, and it's been there all along.*

"What?"

"Nothing. Nothing." Verlaine shook her head as she wiped at her cheeks. "I'm okay."

Nadia wasn't deceived. "I made you cry," she said, beginning to tear up herself. "I shouldn't have said anything."

"No. I'm glad you did. I just—I can't right now, okay? I can't."

Instead of replying, Nadia just burst into tears.

For a few minutes they just sat there in the car and cried, no sound in the car except their sobs and the wheeze of half-warm air through the heater. Finally Verlaine punched at the glove compartment. Nadia jumped back, but Verlaine shook her head. "You have to hit it to make it open. Piece of junk."

She grabbed the packet of Kleenex from the glove compartment, handed a wad of them to Nadia, and started cleaning herself up. When Verlaine had pulled herself together enough to see, she realized that mascara had run all the way down Nadia's cheeks. "You look like crap, by the way."

"So do you."

Then they started laughing, which was probably a sign of hysteria, but whatever. It felt better than crying, even if it did make tears run down their cheeks again.

"Okay," Verlaine finally said, once they were back to themselves. "I need to get home to Uncle Dave, but I hereby decree that we need an emergency DQ run. There's no way I can deal with any of this without a Blizzard."

Nadia slumped back in her seat, obviously exhausted. "Please, yes."

They could fight the overwhelming evil tomorrow, Verlaine decided. It wasn't as though anything else could happen tonight to make the situation worse.

As Verlaine drove toward Dairy Queen, Nadia tried to sort through what to do next.

Talking about the collapse of Davis Bridge had reminded her of that crushing failure—but also of why it might have gone wrong. The more Nadia considered it, the more she became convinced that Elizabeth couldn't have simply sensed the spell on her own. By the time she recognized a spell of forgetting, it should have been too late for her to act to protect herself.

There were only two ways Elizabeth could have slithered out of that one. First, she had access to some form of protective spell that went beyond anything Nadia had come across. Second, she had been warned by someone else . . . or something else.

Demons could sense magic. Asa might have been able to

warn Elizabeth in time. But Asa wouldn't have bothered warning Elizabeth. He *hated* her—however manipulative Asa was, however many silky lies he'd whispered into Mateo's ear, Nadia felt sure Asa wasn't lying about his hatred for the Sorceress who took such glee in enslaving him.

The only other possible way Elizabeth could have been warned was by her Book of Shadows.

Spell books became sensitive to magic over time, even possessed magic of their own. After her spooky encounter with Elizabeth's Book of Shadows, Nadia felt certain that it had not only power, but a certain level of consciousness. It wasn't just the best weapon in Elizabeth's arsenal; it was her collaborator. Her ally.

In the past, both Mateo and Verlaine had suggested trying to steal it. Nadia had told them it was far too dangerous to consider, and she still believed that.

But what if she didn't try to steal it?

What if she tried to destroy it?

As Verlaine shouted their orders into the tinny drive-through speaker, Nadia sank deeper into thought, coming up with a plan.

"If you're taking too much of a loss on the margaritas, what's the point?" Mateo said. He was driving the truck, just in case his dad was able to talk the package-store owner into a free tequila tasting.

"The point is, we make it up by getting people back in the door. After all this craziness? Tonight, they're going to panic. Tomorrow, they're going to want to drink; trust me on that one. They come in for the two-for-one margaritas, but then they order dinner."

Mateo couldn't see it. Virtually everyone in Captive's Sound now had a friend or family member in the hospital. Nobody was going to go out for margaritas and nachos. Still, if Dad wanted to buy the retail-price cases of tequila at the place one county over, in the end, it was his call to make. "Sure, okay."

"Sure, nothing. You're itching to argue with me, but something's got you down." An approaching car's headlights briefly illuminated his father's face; he was studying Mateo intently, so much so that Mateo wished he could squirm out of the way. "You know I heard about the sleepwalking, right?"

He didn't want to talk this over with his dad. Not even a little bit. But he had to talk about it with someone, and there wasn't anybody else. "I was hoping it kinda got lost in the mass hysteria."

"Nothing gets past me. You hear that, Mateo? Nothing." This was almost laughable, considering that Mateo was now Steadfast to a witch, and one of his "oldest friends" had been outed as a Sorceress, and Dad had missed all of it. But Dad's voice was gentle as he continued, "Anybody can sleepwalk. Lots of folks do it. Doesn't mean anything, except I'm going to put on another set of locks, because I don't want you tripping on the steps. Are people giving you a hard time?"

"Only slightly harder than usual."

"Listen to me. It's all crap. Everything they say about that curse. Pure. Crap. I watched your mother go through this. All those years she had to take it alone—alone except for your grandmother, which if you ask me, was worse—but you don't have that problem, okay? You've got me. You've always got me."

Mateo knew a lot of guys didn't get along with their parents; sometimes he was extremely grateful to be the exception to the rule. "Okay. Good to know."

"And not just me! You've got your friends: Gage and that girl, the one with the weird hair—"

"Verlaine."

"Something like that. Plus you've got your girl, huh?"

Mateo remembered how Nadia's dark hair felt in his hands, the way she smiled at him, how she'd fought through the cold waves to save him from drowning—the memories shone inside Mateo like a shaft of light. "Yeah. I've got Nadia."

"Then hang in there."

Just when Mateo thought he might be able to stand telling his father a little more, he saw headlights approaching on the road—on both sides of the road. "Hey. That guy, is he passing or what?"

"Watch it. You get crazy people on the highway these days."

Ahead of them, blue and red lights began to flash. The police? They weren't speeding, so why would anybody try to stop them?

Mateo realized then that the cops weren't pulling over the

truck. They were blocking off the road completely.

As they reached the blockade, he also saw that these weren't just police cars. Behind them was a line of vans and trucks. Mateo pulled over to the side, and Dad rolled down his window. "Officer? What's going on?"

"Return to your vehicle," said a stiff voice through a megaphone. "This county is under quarantine, under orders of the Centers for Disease Control."

Quarantine.

The government thought Elizabeth's dark magic was a plague or pandemic. They were going to rope off Captive's Sound from the rest of the world to protect people from a disease that didn't exist.

But that meant every single person in town was now trapped there, within Elizabeth's reach, unable to escape.

18

VERLAINE HAD THE STORY UP ON THE *LIGHTNING ROD* home page by eight a.m.

Town Under Quarantine said the headline in the largest type that would fit on a standard page view. People could click through to see the photos she'd taken last night; since she couldn't sleep anyway, she'd driven along every road that led out of town as far as she could, until she reached the vans and barricades. The sight of government people in white coats conjured up a few conspiracy theories, but while they were fairly rude about making her go back, they didn't stop her from taking pictures. So apparently no top secret, illuminati-type stuff was going down.

Verlaine hadn't been able to nail down an interview yet, but she'd been able to find other records of CDC quarantines and how they worked. That gave her material for an info box about how nobody was allowed to leave town, but how these things normally only lasted a few days—until the scientists figured out just what kind of disease they were dealing with.

In this case, the disease was magic. The CDC was good at lots of things, but detecting magic wasn't one of them. That meant the quarantine might be going on a while.

She'd sent tons of material to the *Guardian* editors, too, assuming Mrs. Chew would ever go ahead and post it. In the meantime, though, anybody eager to learn more about what was happening in their hometown should be led to the *Lightning Rod* through a simple Google search. Mr. Davis couldn't tell Verlaine she'd overstepped this time. Even Desi Sheremata would have to notice the good work she'd done. The basic updates had gone up an hour ago, in which time the site had received . . .

. . . nine hits. And one comment awaited moderation.

Nine. A total of only *nine hits*. People in town had to be panicking. Medical vans were parked all over the place, everyone had a relative in the hospital, and nobody much could know what was going on. Didn't they have to be online, looking for information? Didn't they care what was happening to this town?

She tried to think of something constructive to do. The only thing that came to mind was the one comment she had to moderate, so she opened it up. It read:

Awful, how only the most beloved members of the community have been struck down. Mavis Purdhy with her twins

at home who need her—Riley Bender, the homecoming
queen—Gary Turner, a caring father—and now so many
more, but all of them so dearly missed. It's as if someone
wanted to cause as much pain as humanly possible.
Then again, this amount of pain isn't entirely human,
is it?—Asa

Great. Her only page views were coming from demons who wanted to taunt her.

Verlaine hit *Discard as Spam*, then flopped down on her bed, pulled a pillow over her face, and wished the entire world would just go away.

The last time Nadia had staked out Elizabeth's house, Verlaine had suggested that she was maybe pushing things too far.

So this time, Nadia hadn't told Verlaine about it.

She had ducked behind a neighbor's hedge, partly shrouded by a spell of shadow; this wouldn't make her totally invisible, but it would make people less likely to turn her way. Nadia wasn't sure how long she'd have to wait. She was pretty sure Elizabeth didn't get out much. Not likely to run to Costco, or join a book club. Still, obviously Elizabeth left her house sometimes, and the next time she did, Nadia intended to seize the chance.

Nadia had brought her phone and earbuds, a thick coat, and even a folding seat her dad used when he went camping; she was prepared for the long haul.

Which was why it surprised her so much when, not ten minutes later, Elizabeth's door opened.

Elizabeth had forgotten what it was like to feel weak.

The muscles in her body obeyed her only sluggishly; her skin burned with what she dimly remembered as fever. She wanted water to drink, so much that at first she thought her old thirst had returned—but it was just this sickness having its way with her.

"We call it infection," said the demon as he led her along the street. "Are you conversant enough with the twenty-first century to understand infection?"

It was what modern people believed in, instead of evil spirits. Fools. "I want it done with."

"Then come with me," he said. He spoke slowly now, as though to a child; Elizabeth wished to scold him for it, but in truth the fever made it harder for her to understand. "The only drugstore in town has been sold out of every useful item since yesterday. But my parents have supplies at my house."

"They are not your parents. It is not your house."

Asa's expression darkened, but he only said, "You'd better hope it's my Neosporin, hadn't you?"

They went to the Prasad home, where his parents greeted her with the same glazed delight all humans gave to Elizabeth. For some reason Asa didn't seem to like watching her charm them into adoring her. Was his humanity getting the better of him already? Had he learned to like these hapless people who were sheltering a demon's soul in their dead son's flesh?

When the human world fell, and Elizabeth stood beside the throne of the One Beneath, she would slaughter them before Asa's eyes. It would be a test for him, a test of his worthiness, a test he would certainly fail.

In the family bathroom, Elizabeth stared dully at a dish filled with shell-shaped soaps—what an odd thing to possess—while Asa worked on her burns. He muttered, "If you're going to burn gashes in your flesh that will never heal, you might consider keeping your own medical supplies at hand."

Elizabeth hadn't entered an apothecary's shop in nearly one hundred and fifty years, so she didn't recognize any of the items he'd taken from the medicine chest. No matter. He would fix this, and she could go on.

It was true that the seal had seared her arm terribly. His pathway had been burned into this world; all that remained was for the bridge to be built.

That bridge was weaving itself longer, stronger, and broader every single moment—

She first felt the warning—a shiver in the air that made her hair stand on end. Was it her Book of Shadows? Her sense of magic? As Elizabeth jerked to her feet, Asa sensed it, too. He began backing away as she said, "Stop time."

He hesitated. The insolent beast *hesitated*. His hatred of her was as obvious as his pride, and he would pay for both.

Elizabeth shouted, "Do it!"

215

Asa brought his hands together again. For a moment they glared at each other, before she turned and stalked out of the bathroom. His nursing appeared to be at an end, and she intended to deal with this latest interruption immediately.

They went past the Prasads, who were frozen in place in front of their television set. Wordlessly they walked side by side down the few blocks that led to her house . . .

. . . which was on fire. ·

The fire was frozen, of course. Each orange flame glowed still and slow, like electric lights rather than any natural burning. To judge from the fact that her house still stood and looked relatively undamaged, the fire could only have just started. And yet it had already spread throughout her house. Only magical flame did this.

"Where is she?" Elizabeth had to look over the area two or three times before she saw Nadia Caldani standing there. That spell of shadow had been well cast; even knowing of her presence, it was hard for Elizabeth to focus on her. But perhaps that was only the "infection" of which Asa spoke, muddying her mind.

Elizabeth walked into her house, easily stepping around the tongues of still fire. Every flame was frozen in place, each flicker like a sculpture of glowing gold. The heat remained, but Elizabeth could endure that. For one moment she simply stared at the brilliant light around her attempting to consume her home and spell book.

Asa paid the heat no mind, of course; he was used to hell. He didn't even take off his coat. "A spell of conflagration.

Nicely done. She could have gotten your Book of Shadows if we'd been only a few seconds later."

Conflagration was indeed a sudden and devastating spell. It worked faster than virtually any defense. With a demon on her side, though, Elizabeth had all the time she needed for a spell of negation.

A wish unspoken.
A promise broken.
The work of a lifetime destroyed.

She held out her hands, allowing her fingers to rest in the heat of the still flames themselves, as she brought the ingredients together. The light was so brilliant she could see through her own skin and muscle, revealing the dark outline of bone.

Lauren Cabot, determined never to marry, defying Elizabeth's wishes and insisting she had to go through life alone—never able to carry the curse herself lest she self-destruct before bearing the children Elizabeth needed to endure the curse next—and then one day turning her head to look at the handsome newcomer in town, Alejandro Perez—not daring to speak of her longing, but it was there, and in that moment Elizabeth knew the line would continue.

"You don't interfere with us," the witch said, "and we don't interfere with you." As if her weak, pitiful little coven could interfere with Elizabeth's great work. But she nodded and even smiled, only waiting for the moment to destroy them all.

Standing in the wreckage of the Halloween carnival, feeling the jagged tears in the world where the One Beneath's cell had been, thinking of every witch who had given her life's work, or even her life, to trap Him—but now at last His cell had been broken open and He might now walk free—

Instantly the fire went completely out. Her house wasn't even damaged; the only evidence of the spell of conflagration was a thin layer of ash lying over every surface. Asa brushed off his black coat with distaste. "What a mess."

But when he held up his hands to let time resume, Elizabeth shook her head. "Not yet."

Elizabeth walked outside directly to where Nadia stood on the sidewalk nearby, her bracelet of witching charms still clutched in one hand. The wind had caught her ponytail, and time had stopped at a moment where the intent on her face was very clear, very real.

"She's strong, this one," Asa said. "She'll do whatever it takes to save the soul of the boy she loves."

Elizabeth could not imagine a greater waste of time than saving someone's soul. "Begin again."

Asa clapped his hands, and time returned. Nadia startled; she had been staring at a house on fire, only to have it instantly go out—and see Elizabeth apparently materialize in front of her. When she glanced at Asa, though, she obviously realized what had happened. Her face flushed with anger. "If Asa hadn't been with you—"

There were other ways in which she might have saved her home and spell book, but no point in letting Nadia learn too much about her power until they were on the same side. "Asa is here," Elizabeth said evenly. "And so you failed again."

Nadia sagged against the nearest tree in disappointment— and Elizabeth smiled.

"Doesn't this make it even more clear that your skills are lacking?" She tried to say this pleasantly, to show none of her impatience. "That you have so much more to learn?"

"Not from you," Nadia said. "Never from you."

Asa chimed in. "I don't know where else you expect to learn anything. Certainly not at Rodman. After two weeks, I have no trouble pronouncing high school a total loss. Nothing they teach will ever be relevant to your existence ever again. Except calculus. They have calculus in hell."

Elizabeth ignored this irrelevancy. Her eyes never left Nadia's face. Though to any outside observer they looked the same age, she could feel all the centuries that lay between her life and Nadia's. What had it been like to be so young, to still have hope that the world could be made new and sweet, that it might comply with your will? She couldn't remember. Perhaps she had never been quite as young as that, even as a girl.

If she couldn't speak to Nadia as a young woman, then perhaps it was time to age her spirit. To show her what the world really was.

"So what are you going to do?" Nadia hadn't backed up even a single step; that took some courage. "Do whatever you want to me, but I swear to God, if you go after my father again—"

"If I go after him again, he'll enjoy it. At least for a little

219

while. But your father isn't the one you should be thinking about. If I were you, I'd realize it was well overdue to start thinking about your mother."

Nadia actually laughed. "My mother has nothing to do with this. She's not even here."

"Did you think that was coincidence?"

It was always so delicious, that moment of realization: the moment when people realized the trouble they were in was infinitely deeper than they'd ever dreamed—the moment when uncertainty or tension turned into real fear. Real fear was sweeter to Elizabeth than wine.

"You didn't do anything to her," Nadia said, trying to sound more certain than she truly was. "She left us. Just— left. Moved out. Got a divorce. Same old story. You didn't have anything to do with it."

"No, I didn't. And yet I know the truth about what happened—a truth you haven't even begun to guess."

Even more beautiful was the first real temptation. Nadia could have turned her back on all the wisdom and witchcraft Elizabeth had gathered during the past four centuries, but knowledge about her mother? That was the perfect bait for the hook. Nadia actually took a step forward then. Good. The best witches were always more strongly motivated by curiosity rather than fear. "Did you make her leave us?"

Elizabeth laughed. My God, the girl really was still a child. "No. Why would I? I didn't even know you then. But surely it struck you as strange. Even if your mother had come to despise your father—even if she couldn't stand the endless annoying burdens of motherhood one day longer—she remained a witch. Your teacher. Responsible for your training. Even if she had abandoned you as a parent, she wouldn't have abandoned you as a witch. At the very least, she would have found a coven to bring you along. But she didn't, did she?"

"I don't understand." Nadia looked halfway wild now. "You know she didn't—she just—what are you saying? Tell me. Just tell me!"

She slipped it in as swiftly and smoothly as she would have a dagger into the ribs. "Your mother didn't abandon you, Nadia. She *traded* you."

Nadia jerked back, stiff as though she were in physical pain. For whatever reason, she looked toward Asa, who shrugged. "It's news to me."

Pressing her advantage, Elizabeth added, "Your mother traded you for something she wanted more. More than you, your father, and your brother put together. She made a deal. It's as simple as that."

"What?" Nadia's voice shook. "What could she have wanted that much?"

"I didn't make the trade," Elizabeth said. It was close enough to an answer. "But can you imagine what kind of power might have been on the table? What knowledge, what gifts your mother might have received in return? I'm not asking for anything so dear—though maybe your mother didn't consider her family too dear, not if she made the trade so readily. No, you don't have to abandon anyone. All you have to do is see reason. Come and work with me. Learn from me. Together I think there's nothing we couldn't do."

Nadia turned to Asa. "Is she lying about my mom?"

"No," the demon said. "I can tell that much. Elizabeth has told you the truth."

For another moment Nadia hesitated, and then she turned from Elizabeth and began walking away. Not running, not fleeing the scene . . . just walking.

"She's in shock," Asa murmured.

"It will wear off. And then perhaps she will see sense." Elizabeth realized she was weaving slightly on her feet—the infection Asa spoke of, the one burning its way into her arm. The fever affected her still. "Help me inside."

He took her arm, his unearthly warmth almost comforting to her. November was indeed turning cold; she must see about that coat. As he walked her back into the house, Asa said, "You realize Nadia won't take your word for it. She'll investigate."

"Her mother doesn't speak to her. She can't leave town. There's only so much investigation Nadia can do." Elizabeth smiled. The One Beneath would be proud of her, glad His work was being carried out. "In the end, if she wants answers, there's only one person for her to turn to. Me."

Nadia felt as though she couldn't see, couldn't even breathe. And yet she made it back home and through the front door again.

At least there was no one she had to put on a smile for;

not even for Cole's sake could she have done that now. But Cole was asleep in her father's lap. Dad must have nodded off while letting his little boy watch cartoons after a long, sleepless night. For a moment, Nadia stood there looking at them—Cole in his Batman pajamas, his cheeks still round with baby fat, and her father with stubble on his cheeks and weary circles under his eyes even in sleep.

She traded them. Mom traded them away like they were nothing. Like we were nothing.

Nadia wasn't going to be treated like nothing any longer.

19

DESPITE HER MISERY, DESPITE THE NEARBY CDC WORKERS taking blood samples as she, Mateo, and Verlaine waited their turn, Nadia almost had to smile as she saw Verlaine gaping in shock. "Whoa. Whoa. *Whoa.* Wait the what the how the?"

Nadia repeated, "Elizabeth told me that my mother didn't just leave. Apparently she traded our family away for some kind of magical power; I don't know what. But I have to find out."

"*Traded* you?" Mateo held up his hands like he was trying to stop that information in its tracks; Nadia knew how that felt. "You mean she gave you away to get power of her own?"

Nadia nodded. "Gave up her kids, gave up her husband. All this time I thought Elizabeth was the only dark witch I ever knew, but now I'm wondering. Because who does that?

What kind of person does that?"

Her voice broke, and Mateo took her hand in his. That simple touch did her in. Tears sprang to her eyes, and it took her a moment to get her composure.

"You okay?" Mateo said.

"No." Nadia tried to laugh, but it came out strange.

Verlaine finally found her voice. "I don't get it. You said she traded you guys."

"Right. I don't know what for."

"Yeah, I understand that but, Nadia—who did your mother trade you *to*?" Verlaine glanced around the crowded gymnasium, making absolutely sure nobody was paying any attention; they weren't. Everyone was too tired and freaked out to notice what was happening right in front of their noses. Verlaine continued, "That's what a trade is, isn't it? An exchange. If she gave you guys up for something else, did she maybe swear you over to someone else?"

"That couldn't be true." The response was automatic, and as soon as it was out of Nadia's mouth, she began to doubt it. Was this situation somehow even worse than she'd thought?

Counting off on her fingers, Verlaine said, "You meant to stop Elizabeth on Halloween. Not only did you not stop her, you inadvertently wound up helping her. You've tried to kill her twice now. Most people wouldn't look at their attempted murderer and say, 'Hey, that's exactly who I want on my team.' Elizabeth's still trying to recruit you. She knows something you don't. Do you think—maybe—your mom traded you to, well . . ."

Verlaine pointed down at the floor. Nadia and Mateo both stared.

"By that I mean hell," Verlaine said. "In case it wasn't obvious."

"It was." Nadia's head had begun to spin. Maybe that was sleepless nights and stress messing with her, but she didn't think so. "I didn't even think that was possible."

"We don't know that it is." Mateo shot Verlaine a dirty look; she responded by shrugging, like, *Just saying*. "Listen. Your mother can't have traded you to the One Beneath. If she had, He'd already have you. Instead Elizabeth keeps trying to get you to join her. So you can't belong to Him."

She clutched at that fragile hope. "You really think so?"

"Yeah. I do." Mateo's hand tightened around hers, and Nadia managed a smile for him.

Verlaine just said, "Wait. How are you going to confront your mother? She's nowhere near here."

"I'm going to have to get out of town."

Mateo gave her a look. "You noticed the quarantine around the town, right?"

"Okay, yeah, that makes it harder, but still—I have to do it," Nadia insisted.

"I thought you didn't even know where she was," Verlaine said.

"I didn't. But after Elizabeth said that—I kinda went through my dad's stuff. Got an address. She's still in Chicago, actually. Twenty minutes from where we used to live."

"Which brings us back to where you're trying to get out of a town under quarantine." Mateo's eyes shifted sideways, toward the nearest set of medics from the CDC; they'd worked their way to a table not far off.

"I'm a witch. I have ways around barricades."

"Yeah, but after the barricades, you have to travel all the way to Providence, get on a plane, get a hotel room in Chicago, all of that. You're going to need cash. Do you have a credit card?"

"Oh. Right." Magic couldn't solve every problem. "No credit cards—Dad won't let me get one until college. I have a few hundred bucks in my checking account."

"Won't be enough," Verlaine said. "I can swing you some, though, no worries."

"Me too. Dad pays me the same as any other server." Mateo took a deep breath, as though preparing himself for a needle stick or something else that would hurt. "Don't worry. We can do it."

It was too much. Nadia hadn't realized how fragile her hold on her emotions was until that moment, when her throat choked up and her hands started to shake.

Verlaine leaned closer to her. "Hey. Are you okay?"

"I don't deserve you guys."

Mateo's fingers closed around hers. His touch anchored her again, as though she could once more feel the ground beneath her.

Verlaine said, "Well, no kidding. We *are* pretty awesome."

At least she could still laugh.

I shall never understand the madness of this world, Asa thought.

Captive's Sound had been turned upside down by these

strange people who wielded needles and microscopes, who would try to find a cure for Elizabeth's dark magic. They would try and fail, and yet he admired the effort. In his day—distant though that was, and fragile as the memories had become over centuries of disuse—humanity was helpless before plagues and pandemics. Sickness swept across the land unchecked, mowing down lives the way a scythe mowed wheat. Now humanity had found the tools to fight back against disease and death.

Not that you could ever defeat fate. Death waited; that would never change. But Asa liked that humanity fought anyway. Elizabeth would have called it misguided; he thought of it as valiant.

What bewildered him were the reactions of the towns-people. Fear should have galvanized them, stirred them to protect themselves. He would have thought at least a few would recognize the marks of witchcraft and begin to suspect others in their midst.

They would never suspect Elizabeth—her glamours had seen to that. But he'd expected to see at least a *little* random harassment of the innocent-yet-marginalized. Torches. Pitchforks. The classics.

Instead the people of Captive's Sound had been stunned into passivity. They'd turned as stupefied as rabbits caught in a hunter's snare. All around him, they shuffled along the sidewalks, staring at nothing. What little fire remained in them only sparked when they had to line up for supplies, food, and the like. Now that stores and restaurants couldn't receive new shipments, these people whose tags and vans read CDC were the only ones who could provide the basics of life. They couldn't imagine how much worse it would get.

They were about to learn, courtesy of Elizabeth.

He ought to have delighted in that, reveled in the explosion of fear and fury that was to come. Instead he could only think of Verlaine trapped in the midst of it. . . .

No. No more. Elizabeth could not glimpse this in him—this unbidden, overwhelming feeling that smoldered within at the very thought of Verlaine. That would be an excuse for further tortures, and this time, Verlaine might be made to suffer with him.

Besides, he'd just seen Mateo walking along the other side of the street, which meant he had work to do.

Asa strode across the street, ignoring traffic; horns honked, but naturally everyone braked to make way. At the sound of the horns, Mateo glanced over, then looked wary. He was learning.

"You seem to be in a good mood for a man under siege," Asa said as he fell into step beside Mateo. "I would imagine you've got a bit of time off. Maybe that's why you're so cheery."

"Time off?" Mateo stopped walking when they reached the ATM at the corner. He took out his wallet, then gave Asa a look.

"What, you're afraid I'll look at your PIN?"

"Like you wouldn't."

"It's three-four-nine-eight," Asa said, casually readjusting his scarf.

". . . How did you know that?"

"Demon. And yes, I figure you've got some time off, as La Catrina can't possibly stay in business like this."

"We've got another couple of days." Mateo at least had enough sense to go on with his withdrawal, punching the keys almost without looking. "Though tonight we're only going to be able to serve *tamales de pollo*, and tomorrow—maybe just piña coladas; I don't know."

"I should imagine people feel like getting drunk," Asa said amiably. "And my, what a lot of cash you're taking out. Curious thing to do, at a time and place when you can purchase virtually nothing."

Mateo stepped closer, and though he was a few inches shorter than Asa, and only a human, he managed to be threatening anyway. "Stay out of this."

"Someone's leaving town." Asa leaned in even nearer, until he could whisper and still be heard. "Someone's running far, far away, and I don't think it's you."

"If you tell Elizabeth one word about this—"

"You'll be as powerless as you are right now." Asa leaned against the edge of the cash machine. "Besides, when will you understand? I hate Elizabeth even more than you do. If Nadia's little excursion works against Elizabeth's will—well, I'd offer to drive if I didn't have hell's legions to serve, not to mention that medieval history test next week. Study buddies, you and me? Up for a late-night cram session?"

For a moment, Mateo looked so angry that Asa wondered if he'd be struck. "You leave Nadia alone," he said. "I swear to God, if you get in her way, I'll find a way to hurt you.

And don't tell me there's not a way. If there weren't, Elizabeth wouldn't have you doing her bidding, would she?"

With difficulty, Asa kept his smile on his face, but he could tell by the satisfaction in Mateo's gaze that he'd glimpsed Asa's anger, and his helplessness.

One of the ironies of being a demon was that you were infected with all the pride of hell just as you were humbled for eternity. That didn't mean Asa couldn't teach Mateo a lesson.

"Nadia's leaving town," Asa said. "Obviously she thinks she can learn something damaging about Elizabeth that way."

Mateo didn't speak. He wanted to contradict Asa, though; that much was clear in his poorly disguised smile. So Nadia was going after the mother, then . . . and they hadn't yet guessed what ammunition that could give them against Elizabeth. No need to enlighten them, either. Asa had something better in mind.

So he continued, "So, Nadia's going to talk to her mother. The mother known for deals with darkness."

That broke through the silence. "What do you know about it?"

Asa held up his hands in the time-out symbol. "Very little, and there's even less I could do about it. But remember what I told you about Nadia wanting power. Right now she wants it for all the right reasons, but how long will that be true?"

Mateo shook his head. "You don't know her."

"I know humanity. Better than knowing individuals any

day. Saves time, at any rate." He continued, "Ask yourself this, Mateo—if Nadia does what it takes to defeat Elizabeth, if she becomes what she'd have to be to bring a Sorceress down, then will she still be the girl you fell in love with? She might come back to you, but will she come back as someone you'd still love, or someone you'd fear?"

With that, Asa turned to go. For a moment he thought Mateo might follow him, but he didn't. The damage was done.

Mateo drove Nadia out on the back road himself, just after midnight. The barricades were up there, too, but without any streetlights or businesses around, they at least had darkness on their side. Once they went as far as Mateo thought safe, they shut off the motorcycle and walked it off the road, into the woods.

Nadia's backpack was slung over her shoulders, the straps pressing deep into the down jacket she wore. Her thick, black hair was in a loose knot at the nape of her neck, and her cheeks were so reddened by the chill that he could see the flush clearly despite the scanty moonlight. She looked not at him, but at the far-off checkpoint blocking the road. At this distance the barricades and vehicles were just dark shadows, nothing more.

"What did you tell your dad?" he asked.

"That I was going to stay with Verlaine for a couple of days to help out while Uncle Gary's in the hospital. Right now he can't get to his job anyway, so he can be around for

Cole. Verlaine's going to cover for me if he drops by there."

"Got everything?"

She nodded, and at last she turned back to him. "Thanks to you."

Mateo patted the handlebars. "You walk it at least half a mile past the checkpoint, out in the field. Then get it back on the road and go. You know the way to Providence?"

"Yeah. I go to the airport, put your motorcycle in long-term parking, and then I can pick up my ticket."

"And you remember everything I taught you about the bike. Really, riding it is easier than it looks."

"Right." But Nadia didn't look too sure. It hardly mattered; this was their only shot.

Only then did Mateo realize he was still thinking of this as their chance, their risk, not hers alone.

"Mateo—thank you."

He shook his head. "You'd do the same for me."

"Not just for the bike, or the loan, or the ride. For believing in me, despite everything."

The thing was, Mateo had his doubts. He didn't know what temptations Nadia was about to face, or whether she could resist them. Whether any of this would be enough to conquer Elizabeth or the One Beneath.

But he'd made a decision. Mateo knew he couldn't test Nadia; he could only test himself, and his love for her.

So he had to trust her enough to let her go.

"You can do it," he said.

Only now did he recognize the forest where they stood.

He'd seen it in his dreams. In that vision Nadia had said she might never return—but had that been a metaphor, a sign that she would not return as the girl he knew and loved, but as someone else entirely?

Nadia clutched at his jacket, pulled him close, and kissed him so hungrily, so hard, that he knew she felt the same desperation he did. For a moment he could only think of the first time their lips had met—when she'd been trapped underwater, and he'd had to breathe for her. It was like that now, as though they were keeping each other alive.

The wind picked up around them again, so hard it nearly knocked him over. They broke the kiss, clinging to each other in the gale. And yet there was something about this—a shimmer in the wind that meant it wasn't only natural. His Steadfast abilities told him another force had caused that . . .

. . . but in this Sorceress-haunted town, when wasn't magic at work?

He met Nadia's eyes again, willing himself to be strong for her. When he repeated the words, his voice was near breaking: "You can do it."

"If I can, it's because of you," Nadia said, and she turned away.

Then he watched her walking the cycle out off the paved road, into the dust and brambles all alone, until her shadow was just one more sliver of the night.

20

ELIZABETH STOOD AT THE SEASHORE, LOOKING OUT AT the old lighthouse tower. The gray clouds in the sky hung low, threatening either snow or rain. By now she owned a warm coat, a loose gray cape that reminded her of the cloaks she'd worn long ago; wearing it was her acknowledgment that she had to walk in this world for as long as it endured.

Not much longer now.

She could feel the bridge growing stronger beneath her. Already so much was being pushed up from the muck. The earth beneath her feet was only a shell now, and in time the shell could be broken—but first, first, the bridge had to be completed.

Every stone in the bridge was made of suffering, of sorrow. Her work had created so much pain, and yet still the path was not clear.

Faster, she thought. *I must work faster. Or else the One Beneath will begin to doubt me.*

This was hard, given what Elizabeth had done for His sake. But that was what it meant to be the servant of the One Beneath. His rules were as harsh as His instruments. His followers were born and shaped by blood.

"Faster," she whispered, holding her hand up to the sky. A flick of her fingers was enough to summon her crow. It alit upon her wrist, cobweb eyes unblinking.

Elizabeth curled her hand around it. She felt the brief flutter of its wings against her palm, and tried to remember what it had been like to feel afraid. The heart beat faster; that much she could recall. Even now the bird's tiny heartbeat pattered against her fingertips.

Then she sliced in deep with her thumbnail, swiftly enough that she was able to touch the heart before it stopped beating.

Verlaine was in the hospital when it happened.

As much as she wanted to be there for Uncle Gary, she had come to hate the hospital the past few days. The smell of stale air and disinfectant seemed to have burned its way into her nose, and the fluorescent lights made everyone look as sick as the three people connected to life support in this room. She'd been trying to get comfortable in a plastic chair for hours, to no avail.

And yet she would live like this forever if it meant they hadn't yet lost Uncle Gary.

She tucked her feet under her in the chair and adjusted herself yet again. Now she was angled to look out the window.

The view wasn't much—a bleak, gray sky over the parking lot—but at least it made a change.

Then the clouds . . . twisted.

The movement wasn't gentle, like clouds stirred by the wind. Instead their shapes shrank and clenched as though they were being wrung out by unseen hands. From every tree and wire, countless black birds swirled up at once, darkening the sky so that the weak sunlight dimmed almost to dusk. Verlaine shuddered, knowing this was Elizabeth's work.

But the horror only hit her when she heard Uncle Gary cry out.

It was a shout of pure mindless pain, and as she sprang from the chair to go to him, she saw his body begin to thrash. "A seizure!" she shouted. "Help, someone, he's having a seizure!"

Then the other two patients in the room began seizing as well—and alarms sounded from up and down the hall. Verlaine realized every single person struck down by the dark magic was in agony, all of them at once.

She's killing them, every one of them, right now, oh, God, I need Nadia and she's gone, there's nothing we can do—

"Somebody, *help!*" This time her voice was a scream.

The next hour was a blur of nurses running and CDC guys hovering and Uncle Dave dragging her out of the hospital room. She wanted to collapse in his arms, but he was crying so hard that she felt she had to hold him up. No time for her to fall. Verlaine had to be strong.

By the time a doctor came out to talk to the throngs in the waiting room, people were miserable and angry and wretched. Despite Verlaine's worst fears, nobody had died; they'd all stabilized back to the same coma state as before. Whatever pain Elizabeth had inflicted on them hadn't been fatal.

She's keeping them, Verlaine realized. *Like fireflies trapped in a jar. She's keeping all those people so she can torture them again and again, to build her bridge for the One Beneath.*

The only end to Uncle Gary's pain would come when Elizabeth had made him hurt so much he couldn't take any more, or when she'd brought about the end of the world.

Uncle Dave was staying behind, so she left. Numbly Verlaine walked out into the cold, not even bothering to fasten her coat. Misery knotted her up from the inside, so much that it felt odd to even stand up straight.

Still, she had to do something useful. Something helpful. Right now she couldn't battle the One Beneath or Elizabeth, or even help Nadia, so that left getting something for her and Uncle Dave to eat. So Verlaine lined up at one of the CDC supply trucks to get their house's rations. It wasn't that long a line—most people had a few days' worth of groceries to fall back on—but she and Uncle Dave hadn't been shopping since Uncle Gary's collapse. The only one in their house with food remaining was Smuckers, and even now Verlaine wasn't miserable enough to start eating Meow Mix.

After she took the sack of food, she began trudging back

238

home. Gas rationing had begun, which meant she couldn't fill the land yacht up until tomorrow; she had to hoof it today.

Verlaine didn't mind that—she felt as though she were beyond caring about anything—until a couple of guys fell into step behind her.

"Hey," one of them said. "Hey."

She tried to ignore this. In a town as small as Captive's Sound, nobody was a total stranger, but these guys were unfamiliar. They worked down at the dock, she thought.

"Hey, gray-haired girl. Hey, come on, talk to us."

"I'm busy," Verlaine said without turning around.

"Those rations you got there? Government chow? It sucks, huh?"

It did suck. The food the CDC handed out was like the stuff she'd sometimes put aside for a church food drive, then take back because it seemed cruel to foist it off on poor people: brick cheese, rice, beans, pasta, and lots of canned food, usually food you didn't even want when fresh, like beets. Verlaine figured it was better than nothing, but that was all it was better than.

"Hey, come on. You don't want to talk with us?"

"By now I'd think that would be obvious," she snapped.

Both of them just laughed, and the one who had been quiet up until now said, "You're not gonna share? You're not the only hungry person in the world, you know."

What a relief to know they only wanted the food. If it came down to it, she could drop the sack and run as fast as her legs would carry her. These two wouldn't come after her, because they'd be too busy scooping up this crappy canned food.

But then she and Uncle Dave wouldn't have much to eat. She'd have to try to tough it out.

"Why are you being so stuck up?" the first guy said. "We're trying to be friendly. You're too good to talk to us, share what you've got to eat?"

Walk faster, she thought, but she couldn't. Her body had burned through all its adrenaline at the hospital, and she had none left to match her fear. Exhaustion dragged at her, and she wondered whether she could run even if she had to.

The second guy, still quieter, said, "Why are you being such a bitch?"

Verlaine turned. "Why are you being such idiots? Listen. This is my food. Mine and my family's. You want yours? *Get in line* like everyone else!" She dropped one of the bags at her feet, reached into her purse, and pulled out the pepper spray. "Things are screwed up in this town right now. But that doesn't mean you can get away with anything you want. Now get the hell away from me before I burn your eyes out with this stuff, and don't think I won't."

That wiped the smiles off their faces. As they slunk away, Verlaine let out a sigh. She doubted they'd follow her—they looked pretty shamefaced—but still, she thought she'd watch them go for a while before she turned her back.

Then she heard a soft laugh. "You're more ferocious than I realized. I like that in a woman."

"Asa." Verlaine turned her head to see him standing off to the side, leaning against a parked car, utterly casual. "Wow, thanks for jumping in and saving me."

"Demons aren't big on saving people, as you might have guessed. Besides, you hardly seem to need rescuing."

She'd had more than enough attitude for one day. "I'm going home," Verlaine said. But even as she turned, she hesitated. She couldn't shake the fear that the dock guys might yet decide to come after her and her stuff.

"You know, I was just thinking of taking a stroll," Asa said, walking to her side. "I'd offer to carry your bags, but I'm afraid I'd burn through them."

Being walked to her house was as much of a favor as she was ever likely to get from him. Verlaine decided to take it.

They went together side by side, through a town so still and shadowed that it might as well have been the middle of the night, though really it was only just after noon. Asa matched the speed of his steps to hers, and they were close enough that the unnatural heat of his skin warmed her slightly against the cold.

Verlaine knew she should thank him. Yet he remained a demon, and Elizabeth's servant. She would thank no one working for the Sorceress who was even now torturing one of the people she loved most in the world.

When they reached the front step, Asa stood by her as she unlocked the door. It swung open, bathing them both in soft light; Uncle Dave must have left a lamp on. Verlaine was grateful for the illumination on this dark, weird day—until she saw Asa's face looking down at her expectantly, and wished she hadn't.

Because there was something about seeing him so . . . wistful, so eager, that turned her inside out.

"Help me put this stuff up," she said. Was it rude, to just order him around? He didn't seem to think so. Instead he just came inside and made himself busy beside her in the kitchen.

Wait. Should I not have done that? Is there something about not inviting demons inside your house? Or is that just vampires? Oh, crap, I hope there aren't vampires. I have to ask Nadia about that. Also about asking in demons, but I've already done it, so— okay.

Smuckers came and twined himself around Asa's legs, tail curling along his ankles and knees. Asa glanced over and saw Verlaine watching them. "Cats love demons," he said.

"Why is that not even remotely surprising?"

He laughed. He had a beautiful laugh—nothing like Jeremy Prasad's. Sometimes it was hard for Verlaine to remember that this was still Jeremy's body; everything about Asa's speech and laughter and movement was so different that he seemed to have transformed.

Asa wasn't all bad. He couldn't be. He deserved a chance. But could he be given one?

"Is there—" Her voice was hardly more than a whisper. "Asa, is there any way to free you?"

His hand froze, still holding a bag of rice, halfway to the shelf. ". . . Free me?"

"From Elizabeth."

"Only the One Beneath could do that. I serve at His pleasure."

"Then, from the One Beneath."

Asa turned to her then, his gaze impossibly sad. "Nothing any mortal could ever do."

"It's not fair, that you got—stolen into this. Kidnapped. Shanghaied."

"*Shanghaied.* An old word. I like that." Asa shook his head. "No. It's not fair. But it's the only existence I'll ever have. I've accepted it."

"Does that mean accepting everything that's going to happen here? Everything that's happening to my dad?"

"Don't you know I'd change that if I could? Most of this world—this stupid, corrupt world—who gives a damn what becomes of it? But I'd save the lot if I could, just because you live here."

It was too much. Verlaine stepped back from him. "You're toying with me. Again."

"I'm not. I wish you could believe that. Not that it makes any difference, I suppose. But we can't help wishing, can we?"

Their eyes met, and once again Verlaine felt it—that unmistakable surety that she'd finally been *seen*, that one person in the world could really, truly look at her and see the truth. That had to be some kind of demonic magic, like the burning of his skin or the voodoo he'd worked on her besotted cat. And yet she couldn't not revel in that unfamiliar feeling.

"Give me one thing," she said. "One truth, and I'll believe you."

Asa blinked. "What?"

"Tell me one thing that will help us against Elizabeth. Anything real. Give me that."

He stepped closer to her, until they were very nearly face-to-face. "All right," he said. "One truth."

"Say it," she whispered.

"You know that Elizabeth's responsible for the deaths of your parents," he said. "For the fact that no one else can see you. But do you know why?"

She hadn't expected his truth to be about her. Verlaine blinked, suddenly unsure. "No. I don't know. I've never known."

"Everyone in town loves Elizabeth, don't they? They adore her. She's only a dim shadow in their memories, a vague impression of the perfect girl."

"Well, yeah. That's her magic at work."

"But what part of her magic?" Asa reached up and brushed a lock of Verlaine's silvery hair from her cheek. "Elizabeth's not that lovable on her own. So she steals the very ability to be loved. She steals it whenever she feels she needs more, and who do you think she steals it from? The very people who have the most. The ones whose hearts would be pure, whose joy in living could be unbounded, the ones who nearly every single person would find themselves drawn to as if by the gravitational pull of the stars. In other words, she stole it from you."

Verlaine shook her head. "That's not me."

"It *is* you. Or, I should say, it ought to be. Who can feel joy when everyone else overlooks them? Whose heart can stay pure when they're tormented by loneliness, and by jealousy for the simplest human connection? No one. Though you've come closer than anyone else I've ever heard of. There's so much good in you, Verlaine—so much light, not even Elizabeth could take it all."

"Stop," she said, stepping back from him. "Please stop."

"The theft is an illusion, really." Asa's voice was desperate now. "You still possess it, this ability to be loved, but the light shines on her instead. Like a candle that's only visible in a mirror, do you understand?"

Verlaine shook her head. She was dangerously close to tears. "I don't understand any of it. You have to stop."

But Asa kept going. "The illusion doesn't work on demons. I know you, Verlaine. No one else in the world does, but I do."

"You could be making all of this up."

"You know better."

She did. But Verlaine had learned to deal with a hard world. She had learned to hold on to what she knew was true even when faced with hatred or indifference. She could hold on to it now, too.

"You're a demon," she said. "You're helping the person who's ruining my life. Whatever you feel doesn't matter. Whatever I feel doesn't matter. You're here on this earth to do evil, and I'm here on this earth to stop you. So—that's that."

Asa straightened. He looked even sadder than she felt, and Verlaine had the absurd urge to comfort him.

Or maybe that was only the urge to put her arms around him.

"That's that," Asa said, and he turned and walked out into the cold. The door shut behind him, untouched.

21

NADIA SAT ON THE 22 BUS, HEADING NORTH ALONG Clark Street, cell phone clutched in her hand. Texts from Verlaine kept scrolling along the screen, one after the other, each of them explaining what Elizabeth had stolen from her, and why. Although Verlaine's misery was clear even through textspeak, Nadia couldn't bring herself to feel anything— and for once, she didn't think dark magic had anything to do with it.

She was only ten blocks from her mother's new home. Nine blocks. Eight. A powerful numbness had settled over her, which Nadia knew was an attempt at self-preservation.

Only a few minutes remained before she faced the person who had hurt her more than any other. She couldn't afford to have feelings right now.

When she alighted at her stop, her boots sank down into days-old snow, already gray and crusty. Nadia had missed so many things about Chicago—Ann Sather, the "L," real pizza. But she'd forgotten about some of the sucky parts, like snow that never melted and only became grimier. Or cold that bit through your coat and your flesh to make your bones quiver. Days like today: Nadia had managed to blot those out.

It was amazing, the things you could make yourself forget.

She double-checked the address as she walked along the street. *Stupid,* she told herself. It wasn't like she hadn't memorized this from the moment she'd first seen it. But her hands had started trembling, and despite the cold, sweat made her skin sticky beneath her thick coat and socks.

What else can Mom do to you? Nadia told herself savagely. *How could this get any worse than it already is?*

The apartment building was a nice one, but there was no doorman, and Nadia was able to slip in as someone else was walking out. As the aged elevator shuddered its way upstairs, Nadia clenched her fists, spread her fingers, clenched them again. She was ready for this. She had to be.

Finally she stood at her mother's door. Only then did it occur to Nadia that Mom might not even be home; despite the ample settlement Dad had paid out in the divorce, she might have taken a job. Or just gone out, to shop or visit the Art Institute, something like that. Her mother had a life now, a life that didn't include her at all. Nadia hadn't thought of it because she couldn't imagine it. Their lives still had that jagged hole torn in the center, the place where she had been. Maybe Mom had moved on.

But she still knocked on the door.

Mom answered it.

They stood staring at each other for a long moment. Nadia didn't feel as though she could speak. All she could think was that Mom looked awful—even haggard. Her soft brown hair, which she used to always wear braided back in complicated, impractical, romantic styles, now hung lank around her face. She'd lost weight, though she'd been thin to start with. Instead of one of her rich cowl-neck sweaters in plum or rust or gold, she wore a plain T-shirt that didn't look very clean. Even though this was the first time she'd seen her daughter in more than half a year, her mother's face showed no reaction save a great tiredness.

Finally Mom said, "You shouldn't have this address."

"Don't blame Dad. I snooped through his things."

That should have earned her a scolding at minimum, but Mom merely shrugged. "I suppose it was inevitable. What do you want?"

What do I want? What do I want? *For you to explain yourself, you worthless, miserable, hateful—*

Somehow Nadia held back the angry words. "I want to know why a Sorceress says you traded me away."

"Dammit." Mom ran one hand through her hair. "A Sorceress?"

"Her name's Elizabeth Pike. She happens to be in the same town we moved to—in Rhode Island—" Did Mom even know that much, or care?

"Happens to be? There's no 'happens to be' about it." Her

mother sighed and stepped into her apartment. "You might as well come in. I'm only going to explain this once, and it's going to take awhile."

The apartment was nothing like Nadia would have expected. Mom loved color and texture, making things beautiful; she always spent enough on decorating and redecorating their condo that Dad sometimes got annoyed. But this space was bare and joyless. The furniture seemed to have been purchased from secondhand shops almost at random, because nothing matched, and while everything was in good condition, none of it seemed pretty or even cozy. Her walls were bare, the floor uncarpeted. Her witchcraft materials lay out in the open; apparently her mom didn't expect anyone to come in, ever.

It was strange not even to feel comfortable taking a seat. Nadia had been more at ease in a doctor's office.

For her part, Mom didn't seem to care whether Nadia sat or stood. She made herself comfortable on the sofa, hardly even glancing at her daughter. "It's no coincidence that you've been confronted with a Sorceress. The One Beneath has more influence in the mortal world than we'd like to think. Probably He . . . aligned the forces. Smoothed the way. Made it more likely your father would wind up there, dragging you along."

"I was *brought* to Captive's Sound? On purpose?"

"You've been put in the way of temptation. I expect they're tempting you now; that's the only thing that would bring you here."

"I'm not *tempted*," Nadia insisted.

"They've offered you power, though, haven't they?"

Nadia's temper snapped. "They offered to teach me. I don't have anyone else, not now that you abandoned our whole family. You know that. I won't ever turn to Elizabeth—*never*. But it would be nice if I could actually learn everything I need to know about witchcraft. You walked off without thinking about that, didn't you? Left me half-trained, forever. Do you have any idea how much that sucks? No, you don't. Mom, do you even know that Cole has nightmares, all the time, and Dad—he doesn't—"

"Stop this," Mom said. "No, Nadia, I didn't know any of that. And I don't care."

It felt like rage could actually make her head explode. "You *don't care*?"

Mom held up one hand. "You can scream at me pointlessly. Or you can get the answers you came for. Which do you want?"

Nadia took a deep breath, then another, then another. "Answers."

"I broke one of the First Laws."

So, she could still be shocked. She'd never thought her mother would do something like that—even after leaving her family. Yes, Nadia had broken one of the First Laws herself when she told Mateo about witchcraft, but that was different; she'd *had* to tell him when he became her Steadfast. "What—why did you—"

"I didn't know I was breaking it, you see. But it turns out

there are good reasons for the law that tells us we must never bear a child to the son of another witch."

"Wait. You mean *Dad*?"

"Normally witches know enough of each other to warn people away from relationships they shouldn't be in. Witches learn to recognize one another; you must have picked up on that by now." Mom sighed. "There are female relatives and coven members around to provide warnings if a mother has died, usually. But if that mother emigrated far from her native country, if she passed away long before she could find a new circle of witches, and she had only male relatives to survive her, men who could never have been told anything about the existence of witchcraft . . ."

Her father had told them the story. His mother had never really recovered after being uprooted from her native Iran. The political situation made it impossible for her to go back and visit, and both Nadia's *pedarjoon* and Dad believed her grandmother's sadness had robbed her of the fighting spirit she would have needed to recover from the sudden infection that had killed her.

Covens were secretive. Several existed in a major city like Chicago, but even those were wary of one another and unsure whether more lurked in the shadows. The likelihood that any American witch would have strong ties to a coven from Tehran in the 1970s—it was beyond remote. It was impossible.

"It's so stupid," Nadia said. She still stood in the center of her mother's living room, like the unwelcome guest she was.

"The secrecy about witchcraft. It cuts us off from knowing even the most basic things we should know about each other."

"That secrecy has kept us alive," Mom replied.

Nadia would have liked to argue that; at this point, secrecy was creating more problems than it solved. But she had to get her answers first. The rest could come later. "Okay, so, you broke one of the First Laws. It's not like there are Witch Police who come and shut you down." She paused. "Are there?"

"No. But these things carry their own penalties. Have you never asked why that would be one of the First Laws, Nadia? Why it's forbidden for witching bloodlines to intermarry?"

"I always figured it was so we wouldn't die out. So there would be more witches instead of fewer, like there would be if we intermarried all the time."

"A good guess, but it comes from a modern understanding of genetics. The First Laws are far older than that."

Something in Mom's voice was familiar now in a way it hadn't been before. She was in Teacher Mode, which Nadia had sometimes found frustrating, but now it encouraged her. Maybe, instead of the vacant-eyed shell who had greeted Nadia at the door, her mother would start acting like herself again. "Well, then, what?"

"A child born with the blood of two witches is—special."

"You mean, I'm more powerful?"

Nadia's fragile hopes faded with the shake of her mother's

head. "No. You're immensely powerful, Nadia. You have so much potential—but my mistake makes you better suited for a specific kind of magic."

"What is that?"

"Dark magic." Horribly Mom smiled, as if she could say that and only think of it as a bad joke. "Witches like you are the perfect servants of the One Beneath. His evil fits into your witchcraft like—like a key in a lock. No wonder He's using this Sorceress to tempt you, Nadia. Almost no children are born of two witching bloodlines, and they haven't been for centuries. He's been waiting for a servant like you for a very long time."

She wanted to tell her mother she was wrong, and yet Nadia knew instinctively, bone-deep, that this was the truth.

Quickly she turned from her mother and walked to the lone window in this long, thin, cramped room. She blinked against the thin, watery sunshine, stifling her tears. Elizabeth's desperate efforts to persuade her—the way Nadia's power had developed when she moved to Captive's Sound, where the One Beneath was at His strongest—even Asa's smug evasions of her questions, the ones that would have led her to understand this: All of it added up.

Nadia had been made to do evil. To be evil.

Did that mean she was doomed to follow in Elizabeth's footsteps, no matter what? No. Nadia refused to believe that her fate was already determined, out of her hands.

"Were you ever going to tell me about this?" She kept her

voice from shaking somehow. "Or is that one more thing you decided I didn't need to know?"

"I did what I had to do."

Nadia turned to glance at her mother over her shoulder. "You had to abandon us? You had to leave Dad, never even see me and Cole again?"

"I had to keep you safe." Mom's expression had become— lost, somehow. Her eyes stared past Nadia, through her, trying to see something that wasn't there any longer. "That was the most important thing to me then. I know that much."

". . . What do you mean?"

"The One Beneath doesn't always give His servants a choice."

A chill swept over Nadia as she remembered Asa. Once upon a time, he'd been human, like her; he'd been turned into a demon against his will, so that he might be the One Beneath's slave. She'd despised him for that, knowing that little good remained in demons after their transforma- tion . . . but that had been before she'd realized the exact same thing could happen to her.

Mom kept talking. "I knew He'd find a way to tempt you one day. But I could keep Him from controlling you. From forcing you to serve Him."

"Mom? What did you do?"

"I cast the only spell that could protect you. A spell of sacrifice."

Her mother had tried to protect her? The same one who had left without a backward glance? Nadia didn't want to believe it. Believing that could even be possible—it would rip off the bandages on her wounds, leave her bleeding and in agony about Mom's abandonment all over again. She whispered, "I don't know that spell."

"It's very advanced magic. Rare. The sort of thing a witch hopes never to cast once in her lifetime. Sacrifices have their own power, and only become stronger when mixed with magic. A spell of sacrifice will protect someone from being enslaved by the One Beneath, always and forever. But in order to cast it, a witch must give up the most important thing in her life."

Nadia whispered, "You mean . . . us?"

"I mean my love for you, for all of you. My very ability to love. That was the only sacrifice powerful enough to keep you safe. All the love I'd ever felt or could ever feel—I tore it out of my heart and laid it down."

Memories of those last few weeks they'd lived together as a family came flooding back. Mom had stopped smiling. Stopped laughing. She'd forgotten to sing bedtime songs to Cole, to come shopping with Nadia for a prom dress, even to kiss Dad hello when he came in through the door. Nadia had always known that was the beginning of the end—the moment when Mom's love ran out. She had never imagined that Mom had actually given that love away.

For her.

"I thought—afterward—I'd be able to go on like I had before," Mom said, forehead furrowed in concentration. "I'd just do everything I used to do, and none of you would ever have to know that my heart wasn't in it any longer. But you did know, all of you. You knew it right away."

"Not *this*—"

"No, not about the spell, but you knew I didn't love you. The way you all looked at me with those wounded eyes—I couldn't stand it. And you have no idea how irritating it is to live with people you don't love in the slightest. Like a college roommate, but worse." Mom laughed at her little joke; Nadia didn't.

Mom didn't even seem to realize that would hurt.

"That's why you left?" Nadia managed to say.

"More or less. I'd been emptied out. I was of no more use to you, and I thought it would at least be easier to live somewhere else." Her mother shrugged, like it was no big deal. "I didn't realize all the repercussions then."

"You mean, how it would affect Cole." Her little brother was the easiest one to talk about, the one most obviously betrayed.

Mom gave her a look, like she didn't know what Nadia was talking about. "How it would affect me," she said. "I don't love anymore. Not anybody, not anything. Once, I know, I used to take pleasure in my appearance, in my home. Now I don't even know what that would mean. And I used to have favorite foods, too. These days I only remember to eat when I get extremely hungry, and even then—what's the point?" Mom shook her head. "Sometimes I try to recall what it was like to feel love. To have that kind of joy in other people, in food or friends, or even in just existing. But I can't

257

even remember it clearly. All I know is that it was the only thing that made life worth living."

Their eyes met. Nadia knew she must look stricken; Mom only looked annoyed. She couldn't even understand what this moment meant to her daughter. Not even that was left.

Finally her mother said, "I gave all that up forever to keep you safe, and make sure your choices were your own. So I suppose I must have loved you very much."

Nadia nodded. By now her vision wavered with unshed tears, and Mom was just a blur, nothing more.

"I can't help you with your Sorceress." Mom rose from the couch, and Nadia realized that she was about to be asked to leave. "And I've done as much as I can do to shield you from the One Beneath. He could still trick or coerce you into serving Him; all I've done is keep Him from enslaving you. Now that He sees what you are, He won't stop until you're His."

"There has to be something I can do," Nadia insisted.

"If you want my advice? Don't go back."

"What? You mean, run away? Just leave my family?" How could she ever think Nadia would do that? Then again— Mom had left them, and she no longer even possessed the part of her soul that would have told her why that mattered.

"They'll manage. I have to say, your father's stronger than I thought." Mom stepped closer, and for the first time all afternoon, Nadia felt some flicker of intensity from her. If she couldn't feel love, she could still feel fear. "Nothing else will save you. If you return, the One Beneath will claim you. No matter how hard you fight, no matter what magic you try to perform."

Nadia swallowed hard. "You can't know that."

"Believe me or don't," her mother said, opening the door so Nadia could leave for good. "But mark my words. It can't end any other way."

22

"HOLD OUT YOUR ARM," ELIZABETH SAID.

Asa did it without hesitation. Though she could see in his eyes the foreknowledge of pain, he still obeyed instantly. That was what it meant to be the slave of the One Beneath.

The demon needed reminding of that. Besides, the next step required blood.

They stood together on the small scrap of island that surrounded the old lighthouse. Sun shone down brightly, making the day feel more like early autumn rather than November's end. Elizabeth pushed up the sleeve of Asa's black coat, exposing his tawny skin.

In most ways, her body had once again become like that of any other human being, but a few aspects of her ancient, once-immortal power remained. For instance, her fingernails remained far harder than they should have been, less like any aspect of the flesh and more like steel.

So Elizabeth was able to use her thumbnail to slice into Asa's flesh.

He sucked in a sharp breath through his teeth as she drew her nail up the length of his inner arm, splitting his skin along the middle, just above the veins. Blood welled from the wound, dripping down either side of his arm to fall on the shell-strewn ground beneath their feet. Asa pressed his lips together and adjusted his stance; Elizabeth knew he was bracing himself for what was to come.

She dragged her nail back along the cut to deepen it, then took both hands and pulled the flesh apart. Despite the heavier bleeding, she could now make out the very structure of the arm: muscle, nerves, veins, and arteries quivering. No need to delve all the way to bone.

Only a small cry escaped Asa, and that he stifled as best he could. Elizabeth wondered whether she should punish him for it regardless.

The spell was punishment enough, she decided. Quickly she brought to mind the ingredients for the summoning:

A call to war.
A fire at night.
A cry of purest pain.

"Hold," she murmured. Asa had begun to waver on his feet.

"Quickly," he said, voice shaking. "I might black out."

A rider on a horse, shouting about Fort Sumter, and stupid, ignorant boys dashing out of their houses to fight in a war that would shred their arms and legs and souls, take their lives before they really knew what living was.

The church blaze she'd created to consume that upstart coven, flames licking at the steeple, the screams of women whose attempt to defy her had been their final mistake.

Lauren Cabot, trembling at the shore before setting out to die, thinking of the little boy she left behind and unable to keep herself from screaming in misery.

Power lanced through Elizabeth, a shock as great as being struck by lightning. She felt the crackle of it all throughout her body and deep into the earth, high into the sky. There was no illumination, no outward sign of its strength, but she knew it was enough.

She had laid the foundation. Now the bridge was coming into being. Soon the One Beneath would travel to the very brink of the mortal world.

Asa stumbled to one side. "We have to stop."

"Beg."

"Please," he whispered. With his wound held open, blood pulsing from him with every heartbeat, his demonic pride could hold no sway. "Please stop. My mistress, I only wish to obey. Let it end."

"For now."

Elizabeth released his arm. Asa fell to his knees, clutching at the wound. She thought idly of infection, of the possibility of losing him to illness, but mortal concerns were distant to her, especially now that the end was so very near.

Mateo felt the change even before he saw it. The sensation was like static electricity crackling along his skin, but only on one side of his body. He turned into it and felt it grow stronger.

"Looks like our last night for a while," his father was saying as he surveyed the nearly empty freezer. "Not that anybody's coming in these days."

La Catrina had turned as ghostly as the rest of Captive's Sound. Fearing infection by the mysterious "disease" that had struck down so many, most people stayed home as often as they could. Rumor had it school would be canceled after Thanksgiving.

Right now, though, Mateo's main concern was that strange, flickering energy he felt—the one he knew wouldn't be evident to anyone who wasn't a Steadfast. The magical forces at work had shifted yet again.

If only he could ask Nadia . . . but he couldn't, and he had to begin to rely on his own new powers instead of always leaning on hers. Mateo squared his shoulders, ready to take control. "Dad, I need to head out for a little while. Is that okay? If anyone comes in, Melanie can cover."

"Big if," his father said, never looking away from the empty stores. "Go ahead. Take the whole night off. No point in both of us wasting the evening."

Mateo nodded and hurried out of the kitchen, taking off his black apron as he went. Just as he went out the front door, he nearly ran into someone coming in—Verlaine.

"Hey." She managed a smile for him, but it was clearly a struggle for her. "Listen, I'm kind of driving myself crazy at the house, and right now I don't think I can deal with the hospital, so I was wondering if I could just hang—"

"Drive me to the ocean."

Verlaine blinked. "Huh?"

He grabbed her hand and pulled her out with him. "Something's going on. I don't know what, but—it's by the beach. That direction. I can tell. When we get closer, I can see it."

"Oh, yeah, Nadia has your motorcycle." Verlaine's steps quickened to match his. "I was able to gas up the car today. So let's go."

For the first part of the drive, Mateo wasn't able to see anything out of the ordinary—at least, for a Steadfast. The same strange magical flickerings that marked the town were still there, though it seemed to him they burned more feverishly than before.

Really, if anything was unusual, it was Verlaine herself. She was back in vintage mode with her leopard-print coat and a white silk scarf tied around her hair, but the attempt at glam didn't disguise how exhausted she looked. Yet something had energized her, too. It reminded him of the way he felt when he was cramming for exams and drank coffee all night long. "You okay?" he said.

"I'm questioning the nature of love. I don't know whether I'm strong enough to do all the things I have to do. Also I'm wondering whether it's worth breaking into one of the houses on the Hill to get something to eat that's not canned beets. How are *you*?"

Mateo thought about that for a moment. "Uh, the same, actually."

They rounded a hill that brought them within sight of the sea, and then he couldn't think about anything else any longer, because something was taking shape beneath the water. Something vast, immeasurable, and awful.

"Can you see that?" he said, pointing at the darkness beneath the waves. It looked so substantial that he wondered whether it could be made only of magic.

"The lighthouse? The water? What?"

"Never mind. It's something only a Steadfast can see: this weird, huge shape under the water," Mateo said. "But trust me. It's not good."

"Crap crap crap crap," Verlaine muttered, flooring it.

They pulled up alongside the beach, not that far from Mateo's house. Together they dashed onto the sand, as if getting any closer would help Mateo understand what was going on. It was low tide, and they were well out into flat, drying sand before he stopped running.

Verlaine came to a stop beside him. "Tell me what you see," she said. "Describe it."

"It's like—like video you see on TV of whales. You know, this huge, huge shadow in all the blue. But this isn't alive. It's solid; I'm sure of that. But it's also like a hole. A hole so deep there's no bottom."

"We'll just pretend that made sense," Verlaine said. The

wind whipped the edges of her white scarf, which was brilliant in the deepening night. "Magic. It's weird. Okay. Where is this thing?"

"Underneath the sound. Almost the entire sound." The strange glimmering of energy he could see under the surface illuminated the outline of this shape. It came very close to shore, and went very far out to sea.

"I'm going to go out on a limb here," Verlaine said. "Are we talking about the bridge the One Beneath crosses to get into our world?"

"No idea. But yeah, that would be my first guess." *Nadia, I need you.* When didn't he need her? Right now, though, Mateo felt it so sharply it was an almost physical pain.

Then a woman's voice came from farther down the shore: "Steadfast."

He turned to see Elizabeth striding toward him. She looked even more ragged than before; it was as though she didn't remember how to brush her hair, or maybe even bathe. Her gray cloak whipped in the cold wind. Behind her was Asa, who followed haltingly, as if it was difficult for him to walk. His arm was wrapped in something, and clutched to his chest.

"Are you here to witness my handiwork?" Elizabeth said. Her lovely face betrayed no hint of the evil that lurked within. Her eyes sparkled with the deepest happiness.

"Go away." Mateo didn't feel like he had anything else to say to Elizabeth, now or ever.

Elizabeth went on as though he hadn't spoken. "I should

have known you were near. Your strength makes me more powerful."

He hated this—the fact that being a Steadfast meant he gave more power to any witch he came near. Though he was Nadia's Steadfast, bound to her and able to give her more energy than he would anyone else, Mateo couldn't prevent Elizabeth from feeding off it, too, like a leech. "I'd stop it if I could."

"There is one way," she said. "You could die."

Ignore her, he told himself, and he might have been able to, except that Verlaine stepped past him, heading toward Asa. "Are you okay?" she said, then turned to Elizabeth. "What did you do to him?"

Asa shook his head, and he smiled, though it was only a shadow of his normal smirk. "Verlaine, don't."

Verlaine didn't listen. She shouted at Elizabeth as though she was outraged. "What did you do?"

"Nothing that is not my right," Elizabeth replied. The lilt in her voice made him wonder if she was trying not to laugh.

She'd tortured Asa. Mateo understood that now. As little as he liked the demon, he hated the idea of torturing anyone or anything. "Every time I think I've learned just how disgusting you really are, I realize I haven't even seen the half of it."

Elizabeth didn't reply. For a few moments she gazed at Verlaine, who stood there with her fists clenched at her sides in impotent fury. "You're irrelevant. You—" She turned to Mateo, expression hardening. "It's been useful having a Steadfast around. But as you're sworn to Nadia, and she refuses to swear herself to me, you're simply a tool she can use to oppose my plans. And I think she's had use of you nearly long enough."

Mateo froze as he realized that, for Elizabeth, killing him would be no more than swatting an irritating fly. He had no magic to use against her, nothing, and in that split second he decided just to rush her—at least hurt her before she took him out.

And the night sky lit up all around them.

Verlaine screamed, and Mateo jumped, but instantly he realized Asa was as startled as they were, and even Elizabeth looked surprised. The brilliance coalesced into a sphere that surrounded him and Verlaine both. He'd seen this before, but where?

This was what he'd seen Halloween night, in the fire that had nearly killed him. This sphere—this protective spell that shielded them completely—that was how he'd been rescued by Nadia.

He turned, knowing where he would see her even before he heard her voice.

Nadia walked closer to them, her features becoming clearer as she stepped closer to the light. Her dark eyes focused intently on Elizabeth. "Mateo's mine," she said. "Don't ever forget it."

"You're back." Mateo couldn't stop grinning. "You're back and—you're *you*."

Nadia probably thought he was talking nonsense. But he

knew that whatever dark magic Nadia had learned about on her trip hadn't changed her; if anything, it had only made her stronger.

"We should talk, you and I." Elizabeth's voice sounded strange. If she weren't so damn powerful, if she hadn't been holding every one of the cards, Mateo would have sworn she sounded . . . desperate.

"There's nothing to say." With that, Nadia stepped through the protective sphere. Its shimmering surface sparkled around her as she broke through, then reformed behind her. When her arms went around him, Mateo embraced her tightly. He buried his face in the curve of her neck and the curtain of her black hair, just to breathe in her scent.

How could he ever have doubted her?

Verlaine called out, "Asa?"

"Never mind me, Verlaine," Asa said. His voice sounded more distant. Mateo didn't even bother looking up. "I'm not worth it."

"They're going." Verlaine's voice was quieter now, more intense; obviously she was speaking to Nadia. "Elizabeth's getting away."

"Let her go," Nadia whispered against Mateo's cheek.

After a few more moments, the sphere vanished, dimming until it was a faint glow, and then nothingness. Elizabeth was done. The danger was gone. It didn't even matter. Now Mateo just stood on the beach holding the girl he loved.

"Okay. Well." Verlaine sounded very distant. "Obviously I could set myself on fire right now and nobody would notice.

Right? Right. Catch you later." Her footsteps crunched through the sand as she walked away.

They wound up at his house, where he held Nadia while she sobbed out the truth about her mother. Mateo had spent much of the past month loathing the former Mrs. Caldani on Nadia's behalf. But she wasn't at all the cold, heartless woman he'd believed her to be—

—well, she hadn't been. Cold and heartless was exactly what she had become, but she had done it to save her daughter from damnation. No matter what, Mateo thought, her sacrifice deserved respect.

"I can never tell Dad," Nadia whispered. They lay in front of the fireplace, tangled up in each other. "So he'll never know the truth. Neither will Cole. I just wish they could know how much we were loved."

"At least you know. Right now, I get that it hurts like hell—but at least you got your answers."

Nadia propped herself on one elbow. The firelight behind her painted her black hair nearly auburn. Her wind-chapped cheeks were pink, her eyes swollen from crying, and yet to him she had never been more beautiful. "You thought I loved you less."

Mateo shook his head. "I listened to Asa, and I shouldn't have."

"Demons mess with humans' heads. It's what they do. But it's not the lies others say to us that destroy us. It's the lies we tell ourselves." Nadia's hand brushed along his cheek, trembling and tentative. "Never believe that I don't love you completely. I love you more than any power. Any secret. Anything else in the world I could ever hope to gain. I'd give it all up for you if I had to, to keep you safe—"

"You don't have to give up anything for me." He folded her close against his chest, willing her to hear his heartbeat and know it only belonged to her. "And I'll never doubt you again."

They began to kiss, first tenderly, then more passionately. Mateo closed his eyes, felt the softness of her in his arms, and the warmth of the fire.

His hands found the cradle of her waist and hips; his lips brushed against the line of her collarbone. Nadia's fingers slipped beneath his sweater, tracing the lines of every muscle. He felt as though she were learning him by heart.

"Do you have to be anywhere?" she whispered against his cheek. Her words were hardly any louder than her trembling breath.

"No." Mateo pressed his lips to the soft triangle of skin exposed by the deep *V* of her sweater. "Nowhere but here. Nowhere but with you."

For now, the evil they faced, the entire rest of the screwed-up world, seemed very far away.

Outside the Perez home, an unearthly wind whipped through the trees, shearing away the final leaves of autumn. Some people swore they saw heat lightning crackle through the clouds—even though the night was so cold that frost masked the windows and covered the ground. Sinkholes still unfilled after the strange events of autumn crumbled and quaked, filling in with new, soft earth, as though attempting to erase the town's scars. And the crows swirled up into the air, dark, shining wings glittering in the moonlight, disturbed by a force they could not recognize.

There were other rules about witches and Steadfasts, rules Nadia herself did not know. Rules her mother had never thought to teach her.

They would reveal themselves in time.

23

IT FELT LIKE A MILLION YEARS SINCE NADIA HAD BEEN home, not just two days. The windows glowed with light and warmth, welcoming her back.

As she came in, her dad called from the living room, "Nadia?"

"Yeah." He didn't sound surprised—then again, so far as he knew, she'd just been across town at Verlaine's. She smoothed down her hair, hoping he wouldn't notice that her lips were swollen and flushed; her entire body still hummed with excitement from Mateo's touch. Straighten the sweater, double-check the belt: okay. "I'm back."

"Is everything good with the Laughtons?" Dad appeared, a tape measure around his neck. "You know, we could have Verjane here for a couple days. Might give Dave a break."

Her mother's voice echoed in her memory: *Your father's stronger than I thought.* Nadia struggled to act natural. "I think she wants to stick close to home."

Her father nodded, like, *That makes sense.* From the living room, Cole called, "Nadia, you have to see me! Come see me!"

She stashed her backpack and went into the living room, where Cole stood with his arms outstretched, beaming proudly. He was wearing—what was it? Some kind of white sack, padded lumpily from the inside, and a white fluffy hat—

Mashed potatoes.

"We get to have the Thanksgiving pageant, and then there's no more school until the doctors leave!" Cole was beside himself with excitement. "That might not be until after *Christmas*! I look awesome."

Dad crossed his arms as he surveyed his handiwork. "Not too shabby, if I do say so myself."

"It's great," Nadia said. She thought about how her mom had always been the one who put together their Halloween costumes, or helped them with school projects. She'd meant to make this costume herself, but Dad had managed on his own. He'd come through. Cole was coming through. Both of them were getting over the worst abandonment of their lives, even though they could never know the real reason it had happened.

Cole frowned. "Are you crying?"

"No," Nadia said as she wiped at her cheeks. "But it's beautiful, you know? It's the most amazing costume I've ever seen."

"It's not *that* good." Dad chuckled as he pulled her into his embrace. More softly he said, "You've had a rough couple of days, huh, kid?"

Normally Nadia hated being called *kid*, but she'd let it go this time. "Yeah."

He ruffled her hair. "I think we all have. Did you eat?"

Mateo had given her the last food he had at the house. She nodded. "Did you guys?"

"Yeah. But we've still got flour and sugar and a little butter. Who thinks we need to make some cookies?"

Cole began dancing in celebration, which looked so goofy in the mashed-potato costume that Nadia had to laugh.

Just being with her family and loving them, weird as they were—she took it for granted sometimes. Or she had, before seeing what had become of Mom after all the love had been torn from her heart. *Never again,* Nadia swore. She'd never forget again. From now on, she could love her dad, and her brother, and Mateo the way they deserved to be loved. Black magic or no, she'd remember to love Verlaine, too.

The darkness had taken as much from her family as it was ever going to. Never again.

Today would be the final unraveling.

Elizabeth walked along the street, bundled in her gray cape like any other teenaged girl. People waved to her cheerily, each of them no doubt thinking how dear she was, how much they admired her. She didn't bother waving back; they'd remember her doing that anyway. They'd remember a smile.

Her new crow looped through the morning sky overhead.

The flight pattern wouldn't look unusual to any casual observer. Only someone watching carefully would realize the crow was flying in precise, geometric circles with Elizabeth at the center.

Mateo Perez, she thought.

Midway through the arc, the bird shuddered in the sky, its wings flailing for only a moment before it regained steadiness. Elizabeth lifted one hand as if to point at the exact place the crow had faltered.

In her palm was clutched a crumbling bone, one from the first Cabot she had ever cursed. It would help her reach the last.

CLOSED UNTIL FURTHER NOTICE

THANKS FOR YOUR LOYALTY

LA CATRINA WILL RETURN!

The exclamation point felt like they were trying too hard. Still, his dad had hand-made the sign, and Mateo didn't feel like making another one, so, okay.

He'd signed out of his first-period study hall, the better to finish closing the restaurant. The few useless scraps of peppers and guacamole had to be cleaned out of the fridge before they went bad; they had to take another tally behind the bar—stuff like that. Dad had worked late last night, leaving the finishing touches for Mateo. Hanging the sign on the door was the final step.

Mateo had never resented working at his father's restaurant.

Yeah, it ate up a lot of his spare time—and now that Nadia was in his life, he'd rather have spent that time with her—but still, Dad had always made it clear that the restaurant was what kept a roof over their heads. Grandma had disowned Mom when she got pregnant with him. They had to make a living. He had been expected to chip in as much as he could, as soon as he could, and that was just how things were. Really, it was better, being in touch with reality. Sometimes when Mateo heard his classmates bitching about not getting the newest phone or whatever, he wondered if they had any idea where money came from.

As he locked the door, though, he realized that he'd miss his shifts at La Catrina. Was it possible he actually liked it?

You're just turning into mush today, Mateo told himself. He remembered last night, holding Nadia in front of the fire. Just the memory of the way she'd felt against him made his gut tighten, his heart turn over—

The light blazed around him, through him, making him stagger backward against his bike. All around Mateo, the world seemed to bend and break.

What the hell? He fumbled for his phone, thinking he had to call Nadia and tell her something serious had gone wrong. But then images took shape in the light, images that moved and spoke, and he realized that they weren't the work of his Steadfast power. They were dreams.

His curse had broken free from sleep, and had sent the visions to torment him even now.

Nadia by the waves, wind whipping at her hair, screaming, "You don't own me! You'll never own me!"

Verlaine surrounded by the fires of hell itself.

Elizabeth with her arms outstretched, a smile on her face, triumphant.

Mateo tried to tell himself that none of it was real. He understood that the visions were only images of what could be—and yet he couldn't make out the shapes of the buildings and cars around him, couldn't even be sure that was really the ground beneath his feet. He slumped down until he fell, or seemed to fall; he couldn't be sure.

The crow continued circling. Elizabeth held up her hand, sending her power into it, and thought, *The little children.*

Once again, it fluttered in the sky, uncertain. It was like shooting a bow and arrow, Elizabeth thought, and the crow was the bowstring being plucked. Its feeble life directed her weapon and gave it speed as it flew toward its target.

But she didn't need the bird to lead her to the place she'd strike next. She was already there.

Elizabeth stood in front of Nadia Caldani's house and smiled.

"Okay, where's our pecan pie?" The substitute teacher, who was really nice but really old, kept looking through all the kids. Who was pecan pie again? Cole couldn't remember. All he knew was that his costume was the very best one.

"Mine's stupid," Levi said. His mom had just put him in a brown sweater and pants and hung a sign around his neck that said GRAVY.

It was definitely stupid, but Cole knew better than to say so. He tried to sound cheerful as he said, "It's okay." Also, he couldn't help thinking that at least Levi could go to the bathroom without having to ask someone to help him get out of his costume. Cole was starting to think he'd have to ask really soon, but he was embarrassed, and the teacher seemed like she was too busy.

Well, Dad would get here in a few minutes. All the parents would come to the pageant, and he could just go to the bathroom then, when Dad would take him.

He shifted from leg to leg and hoped Dad would get there before the pageant started.

The girl at the window—Abigail, in her cranberry-sauce outfit—started shrieking. Cole turned and saw all the birds. There were hundreds of them, hundreds and thousands, and at the sound of Abigail's screams they began hurling themselves against the window.

Cole screamed, too. So did most of the kids. But he could still hear beaks and feet scrabbling against the glass, see their wings beating so hard, like they could save themselves. It was like they were flying into the window, but Cole somehow knew they were being thrown. That they were in pain, dying, afraid, but they couldn't stop.

They couldn't stop until they got through.

One pane of glass cracked, and it sounded like lightning.

Elizabeth raised her hand to knock, but she didn't even get the chance. Mr. Caldani opened the door. He was nicely dressed, and in his hand he held one of those "cameras" people now had, which captured the illusion of an event for viewing later. Perhaps he was going to see his small son.

Or he'd been planning to anyway. His afternoon was going to go quite differently. This afternoon would make him her possession, and give Elizabeth her best, sharpest weapon against Nadia's heart.

She managed not to laugh.

"Hi," she murmured. "Did I catch you at a bad time?"

"Oh. I—no. Of course not. No."

"Can I come in?" Elizabeth stepped over the threshold without waiting for an answer. Mr. Caldani looked as if he wanted to object, but her enchantments kept him silent and struggling.

She was close enough now for him to smell her skin. Elizabeth willed him to feel the warmth of her—to believe she was the only warmth in this entire cold, useless world—to think he'd been alone forever and that he couldn't bear it one moment more.

Elizabeth smiled up at him, almost conspiratorial. "Shouldn't you shut the door?"

He had to know that was an invitation. He had to know precisely what she was inviting him to do.

Still Mr. Caldani backed away. Still he fought to hold on to his decency—it was almost sweet. "Nadia's not here." He had begun to sound desperate. "You can probably find her at school."

"I'm not here for Nadia." With that she raised her hand, two fingers touching his shoulder, and she unleashed a spell of desire no man could resist. . . .

Violet light flashed. Mr. Caldani blinked, straightened up, and was affected by her no longer. If he even remembered wanting her, there was no sign. "Elizabeth, I'm afraid I have to go. My son's in a school play. And besides, I think you should only come by when Nadia's invited you. Don't you agree?"

Elizabeth took a couple of steps backward. Her mind was now unfocused, her breathing fast, her cheeks flushed: arousal. Human arousal. She hadn't felt this so vividly in centuries. All the desire she had meant to inflict upon Nadia's father was now infecting her.

"Hey, what was that flash of light?" Mr. Caldani said as he firmly guided Elizabeth out onto the front stoop, then pulled the door shut behind them and locked it.

"Flash of light?" She felt as though she'd been awakened from a dream.

"The purple? Never mind. See you later." With that he hurried to his car. Simon Caldani was no longer affected by her in the slightest.

Whereas she—

Betrayer's Snare, Elizabeth thought as she staggered along the street that led toward Rodman High.

Only Betrayer's Snare could have protected that man from the enchantments she'd laid on him, and sent that enchantment rebounding back on her. She ought to have anticipated that Nadia would try this—but she hadn't, and now, just when her concentration was most necessary, her brain was fogged with crazed desire.

Elizabeth had not felt true physical arousal for centuries. There had been some minor excitement when she'd ensorcelled Mateo before the Halloween carnival, tricking him into kissing her when he believed her to be Nadia, but that was nothing compared to this. Longing infused her, made her bones ache and her flesh clench almost to the point of pain. All the desperation she'd put into the spell for Simon Caldani was now in her, driving her to madness.

Just get to the school, she told herself. *Asa will be there. He can be made to serve.*

But as she wandered into the school parking lot, she saw someone else first: the tall, dark one who kept company with Mateo sometimes. Was his name Gage?

"Elizabeth," he said, his face lighting up. He'd never made any secret of his attraction to her, not that she'd ever cared about it one way or another until now. "Hey. What's up? Just . . . forgot my psych book in my car . . . my car here—" He pointed at the car, then stopped himself. "I'm acting like an idiot around you again, aren't I? Mateo says I ought to . . ."

His voice trailed off as she raised her hand and cast the spell again. It was far weaker than the one she'd directed at Nadia's father, but given Gage's crush on her, it would more than answer.

Gage's eyes widened. His psychology book fell into the gravel beneath their feet. He pulled her to him, forgetting where they were.

"You'll do," she said.

It was like one of his bad dreams, except he was awake.

Cole and his friends all huddled on the floor beneath their desks, hands outstretched to keep back the birds. The windows had all broken, and there was glass all over the floor, and even the teachers couldn't do anything but scream.

But some of the parents came in, and once there were more of them, they could get the birds back a little—and then Daddy was there at last, scooping Cole into his arms and putting a coat over his head until they were way down the hall. For a while Cole just cried out loud, and he didn't even feel like a baby for doing it.

"It's okay, buddy." Dad ruffled his hair. "It's okay. It's all over."

"What happened?" Cole whispered.

"I don't know. The birds must have seen their reflections in the glass."

"But why were there so many?"

Abigail's mom came by them and said, "Something is wrong in this town. Really wrong. You see it, don't you?"

"Well, obviously," Dad said.

"I mean, *strange*." She leaned closer to both of them, and Cole felt weird, because he didn't like seeing a grown-up as scared as a little kid. "This isn't natural, what's happening here. Maybe it sounds like something out of—a bad movie, I don't know. But it's real. You know it as well as I do. And we have to put a stop to it." With that she stalked off, pulling Abigail behind her.

Cole watched Abigail go. "Are we not having the Thanksgiving pageant?"

"I don't think so, buddy."

"What did Abigail's mom mean? Was she talking about the birds?"

Dad didn't seem to be listening, but he said, very slowly, "About the birds, and other things."

Nadia started getting the texts first thing in the morning. First Mateo—but his messages were blank, or garbled nonsense. At first she'd assumed she was just receiving butt texts that would stop when Mateo took his phone out of his back pocket, but they kept coming, one after another. It was like he was genuinely trying to reach her but wasn't coherent enough to do it.

Just as she was trying to tell herself not to be stupid, a message came in from her father about the chaos at Cole's school. Nadia was trying to think of what Elizabeth might have to gain by taking away some little kids' Thanksgiving play when her dad texted: *BTW, Elizabeth dropped by again. Seems odd. Does she have problems @ home? Might want 2 talk w/ school counselor.*

At first all Nadia could feel was triumph. Elizabeth must have made her move on her father, and failed. The Betrayer's Snare had worked.

But then she realized that Elizabeth had attacked the school, too, which meant she was springing all her traps at once. Those garbled messages from Mateo went from merely odd to terrifying.

When the bell rang for third period, Nadia dashed into the hallway. Through the scanty group of students still attending full time, she caught a glimpse of a fuzzy, pink sweater over a wide, white circle skirt—pure 1950s. "Verlaine!"

Verlaine turned from her locker, at first merely blasé, but her expression shifted into concern as Nadia pushed toward her. "Oh, crap. What's happening now?"

"I'm not sure, but we have to get to Mateo, this instant."

"Sounds like a good excuse to skip." Verlaine shoved her books back in her locker and slammed it shut. "To the Batmobile."

That was when the ground began to shake.

Nadia gasped and put her arms out, the better to hang on to the wall of lockers—but they were squeaking wildly, shaking open, sending heavy textbooks and tons of crap flying. Verlaine took her hand and pulled her back toward the center of the hall.

"Earthquake!" someone yelled.

"Since when can Elizabeth make earthquakes?" Verlaine huddled on the floor next to Nadia, both of them putting their hands over their heads just like in those stupid drills.

"She can't." Some things were beyond even the power of witchcraft. "But the One Beneath can."

After only a few moments, though, the tremors stopped. The school still seemed to be in one piece, though people were crying and freaking out. "Forget about skipping," Nadia said as she and Verlaine rose slowly to their feet. Plaster dust had fogged the air. "I think school's out."

Verlaine coughed once. "Okay, even if you didn't know

about witchcraft? You'd have to know this whole situation is severely screwed up."

She was right, Nadia realized. It took very little to veil the world of witchcraft from everyday people simply because they were so quick to explain away deviations from the norm. To convince themselves they hadn't seen something that would make them question the reality they knew. But Elizabeth and the One Beneath were abandoning even that faint pretense. They meant to terrify. They meant to be known.

"Come on," Nadia said. "Whatever's going on, it's happening to Mateo."

Together they ran for the doors, but they swung open just before Nadia and Verlaine would have slammed through. Faye Walsh stood there, her once-pristine white sweater twin-set now grubby with dust and debris. "Excuse us," Verlaine said as she tried to duck past, but Ms. Walsh put out her hand, halting them in their tracks.

"We need to talk," Ms. Walsh said. "Nadia, I've been trying to talk to you for a long time."

Nadia forced herself not to scream with frustration. "Yes, ma'am, I know, and I'm sorry, but honestly—is this the time?"

"Oh, yes. It's time." Ms. Walsh crossed her arms. "When I see evidence of witchcraft, I want to talk to a witch."

24

AT FIRST NADIA COULD ONLY GAPE AT MS. WALSH. WHEN she could speak, she said the only thing she could think of: "You're not a witch."

"No, I'm not," Ms. Walsh said. "But my mother was, and my grandmother before her. They taught me the signs. Bound me close. Made me a Steadfast."

"You're a Steadfast?" Verlaine, who had been looking even more panicked than Nadia felt, brightened, but only for a moment. "Wait. If your mom and grandmother were witches, why aren't you one?"

Ms. Walsh stiffened slightly; this was a difficult subject. "I didn't have the gift. It happens that way sometimes."

Verlaine nodded. "Oh, so you're a Squib."

"No Harry Potter stuff," Nadia said hurriedly. "I keep telling you. Witches hate that." Her initial shock began to shake away; now she could only think of Mateo. "My

Steadfast is in trouble right now. Come with us. We'll talk on the way."

"She's not your Steadfast?" Ms. Walsh said, looking at Verlaine.

"Everyone thinks that," Verlaine said. "Understandable mistake. But wow, are you in for a surprise." She took Ms. Walsh's arm and began ushering them out of the school building. With the postquake chaos, nobody would notice their departure—and besides, Nadia thought, they were leaving with a faculty member.

"You know this isn't me," Nadia said as their steps quickened to a jog at the edge of the parking lot. "The sickness, the destruction, any of it."

Ms. Walsh replied, "That's Elizabeth Pike. Is she doing what I think she's doing?"

"If you think she's trying to turn Captive's Sound into the gateway to hell itself?" Nadia said. "Then yes."

It turned out Ms. Walsh could run fast enough to keep up with them at full speed, even in her high heels.

They found Mateo in the back alley behind La Catrina. He lay on the cold pavement, not unconscious but in a stupor; his cell phone had fallen from his hand. A stray cat watched from the far steps as they struggled to get him inside.

Nadia's hands shook as she sifted through the under-the-bar first-aid kit and found a shiny, silver emergency blanket; she wrapped it around Mateo, who now lay on one of the long, leather booths. Verlaine held his head, and Ms. Walsh his feet.

"A male Steadfast," Ms. Walsh said as she looked down at him. "Unbelievable."

"That word is almost meaningless to me now," Verlaine replied, almost absentmindedly. "I guess I used to think some things were unbelievable, but I can't remember any at the moment."

Now to help Mateo recover—but how? Nadia didn't know whether he was suffering from a new and more horrible aspect of his family's curse, or some other spell of Elizabeth's entirely. One of magic's great powers was its mystery; it could be difficult to tell precisely what spells had been cast. Great if you were the spellcaster—not so great when the guy you loved was suffering.

But Mateo stirred, as if the warmth and their voices had awakened him from a nap. He opened his eyes just a crack. "Nadia?"

"Mateo!" She clutched his hand and was relieved to feel him squeeze back. "What happened?"

"The dreams—the ones from my—" Then he caught sight of Ms. Walsh and immediately froze. "I mean, I think I got dizzy. I passed out."

"The dreams from your curse," Ms. Walsh said. She smiled. "It's okay. I'm a Steadfast, too."

"Really?" Mateo looked back at Nadia, who nodded.

Verlaine cut in. "Wait. You said you're Steadfast for your mother. But you said your mother was a witch, that she left you her Book of Shadows. Did you keep the powers after she died?"

Ms. Walsh kept smiling, but it was obviously a struggle now.

A deep sadness filled her eyes. "My mother has Alzheimer's. No spells overcome that, I'm afraid. She held on as long as she could, but a couple of years ago, she turned over her bracelet and spell book to me. Said she couldn't be trusted to use them any longer. Now she's in a home up in Boston. I go see her as often as I can. Sometimes she even knows me. But she's not a witch anymore, not in any meaningful sense. Still, the Steadfast bond—it endures. Through everything."

Nadia's eyes met Mateo's, and they each smiled. As terrifying as it was to remember they were bound together forever, their whole lives long—it was even more beautiful. In some ways, it was just proof of something they'd sensed the first time their eyes had met.

Sometimes Verlaine tried to write news stories in her head about her own life, just to get practice at summarizing quickly, and putting the most important information as the lede.

As near as she could tell, the front page for the *Verlaine's Life Gazette* would read something like this:

END SERIOUSLY NIGH
Area Sorceress Near Completion of Bridge to Underworld
Locals Feel Magical Effects: Earthquakes, Mysterious Illness, Demonic Incursion

Captive's Sound came even closer to apocalypse today when Sorceress Elizabeth Pike initiated the final steps of her plan to bring demonic overlord the One Beneath into the mortal world. Should she succeed in completing her bridge between the underworld and our town, only a thin seal will remain between the world we've always known and total destruction.

Local witch Nadia Caldani, along with Steadfast Mateo Perez and stylish sidekick Verlaine Laughton, has been working tirelessly to stop Elizabeth Pike, with only limited success. Now, however, the Gazette *has learned that Rodman High guidance counselor Faye Walsh is also a Steadfast and may have new insights about the magic being performed—perhaps enough to turn the tide.*

That about summed it up, Verlaine thought. All she had to do was add *Horoscopes, Page Five.* And the horoscopes would be easy enough to do: Every single sign's forecast would read *Pray Really Hard.*

"My dreams of the future aren't waiting for me to fall asleep any longer," Mateo explained. By now they were all seated around one of the big circular booths in the strange stillness of the closed restaurant. Nobody had even turned on the overhead lights, so the only illumination was the grayish excuse for sunlight that came through the windows. "It's okay right now, but earlier—the dreams were taking me over. I couldn't talk, couldn't think, could hardly even move."

Nadia never took her hand from his. "Elizabeth's deepened the curse. I'm not sure why she'd do that, though. Your dreams help us sometimes, even though they hurt you."

Ms. Walsh—no, Faye; she'd told them they could call her that off-campus—shook her head. "Elizabeth may not have a choice. The level of magic she's performing now goes beyond anything even she would have done before. Right now all her magic may be intensifying at once. She can't strengthen her influence in the world without strengthening every one of her curses, every one of her spells, at once."

So, are people going to be even meaner to me? Verlaine wondered, then felt bad about even thinking it. The fate of the world was slightly more important than her social life. Besides, if the world ended, it would kind of be a moot point.

"She needs these people to suffer," Nadia said. "All the ones she's put in the hospital. And I've learned—the One Beneath uses emotions, a lot. He steals them. He takes them in trade." She went silent for only a moment. "So maybe He uses them to build. Maybe those people's pain is exactly what He's using to build the bridge. I think pain is what the bridge is made of."

Faye nodded. She looked . . . well, *encouraged* was too strong a word, but like they might be getting somewhere. "I went through my mother's Book of Shadows, searching for something like a remedy for illness caused by witchcraft, something like that. I didn't see anything, but you might." From her leather satchel she pulled out a clothbound book. The cloth was plain, faded black, the kind of thing that generally didn't earn a second glance. But Verlaine reminded herself that Nadia had said every Book of Shadows was different. Every Book of Shadows had its own power.

Sure enough, as Nadia reached for it, the pages flipped open of their own accord. "Whoa," Mateo said. "Did it hear you?"

"Sometimes Books of Shadows do." Nadia smiled almost fondly at it, then glanced at Faye. "Your mom must have been really powerful."

For the first time since she'd come to them, Faye smiled. "She was something else. I wish you could've seen her in her prime."

Nadia looked down into the Book of Shadows. At first Verlaine wondered if a light had come on somewhere, then realized the spell book was glowing. The gentle golden illumination revealed Nadia's dawning excitement. "This isn't a cure for illness. But it's a way to ease pain, and end suffering. It's pretty serious magic, but I think—I think I could do it."

Wait. Had things suddenly gone from sucky to awesome? Verlaine brightened. "So you can stop Elizabeth from hurting Uncle Gary and all the others. When they stop hurting, she's not causing them any more pain. And if they're not in pain, she loses the building blocks she needs for the bridge. The bridge collapses, the One Beneath can't get here, Elizabeth's defeated, and it's the best Thanksgiving ever. Right?"

"That's the idea." But Nadia only looked about one-tenth as excited as she ought to. "Verlaine, it's dangerous."

Of course it couldn't be easy. Mateo leaned closer to Nadia. "You mean, you could be hurt?"

"Maybe, but that's just part of working high-level magic." Nadia didn't even glance at him; it was Verlaine she spoke to. "I'm not talking about it being dangerous for me. I meant for Uncle Gary."

"He's in the hospital with about a zillion tubes in him and a crazy, evil witch keeping him in pain," Verlaine said. "How much more dangerous could it get for him?"

Quietly Nadia replied, "If I do it wrong, he could die."

Verlaine sucked in a breath. Faye put one hand on her shoulder, temporarily back in school-counselor mode.

It wasn't like Verlaine hadn't been afraid of this before now. She'd hardly been able to think of anything else since Uncle Gary's collapse. But hearing it from the exact person she'd been counting on to save him—that made it much more real. She whispered, "Why would he die?"

"Right now the magic is holding him in this painful space between life and death." The amber light from the spell book still played across Nadia's face. "I'm going to ease his pain, which means easing the spell's hold on him. He should come back to the side of life. But—I don't see anything in this spell to guarantee that. I don't know what kind of condition he's in, or whether there's more to what Elizabeth has done. So I'd be cutting all her ties at once, and anything could happen."

"The spell is about easing suffering, right?" Verlaine demanded. "What kind of loser spell would only end suffering by killing people?"

"It's probably more about helping people who are sick or injured through normal means, rather than suffering because of magic," Faye suggested.

Mateo said, "Are we sure this is a good idea? There are a lot of people in the hospital. That's a lot of lives to take a risk with."

"I don't know." Nadia bit her lower lip. "Maybe—maybe I jumped to conclusions."

They were jumping to conclusions about something that could kill Uncle Gary? And yet what was the alternative? Her brain was doing the calculations her heart was too weary to handle.

"We should think about it," Mateo said.

"I know," Nadia agreed. "I know. We just don't have much time to think. And the spell has to be anchored— someone would have to be at the hospital, in the thick of it, wearing one of my own witching charms. The pearl. That person would bear the biggest part of the risk. Even if none of the patients died, this person might."

"I could do it," Faye offered. "If we decide to cast this spell."

Verlaine made up her mind. "You have to do it. You have to try. And I'll anchor the spell."

Everyone stared at her. Verlaine couldn't quite believe she'd said that herself. But she knew what she knew.

"I love Uncle Gary as much as I love anybody on Earth." Her breath didn't want to support her voice; it felt caught in her chest, waiting for tears she wouldn't let come. "But I don't just love him. I *know* him. And if we could tell him how much is at stake—that this could mean the deaths of thousands and thousands of people if we fail—then he'd say to take the chance. He'd do it himself if he could. I know that, for sure."

It felt beyond horrible to risk Uncle Gary's life like that. Just getting the words out seemed to have stolen the strength from her body.

But a life was more than a pulse, more than a breath. A life was also made up of what you believed and what you stood for. Of what you were willing to do—and who you loved. Protecting Uncle Gary's survival at the cost of so much pain and suffering would betray his life more surely than anything else, and Verlaine knew it.

"I'll take the chance with him," she said, holding out her hand for Nadia's pearl charm.

Mateo reached across the table and took her free hand. Verlaine was surprised how much it helped.

"I'm going to get it right," Nadia said . . . no, promised. Her dark eyes burned with intensity as she removed the pearl charm from her bracelet and put it into Verlaine's palm. This was the swearing of a solemn oath. "I can do it. I can and I will."

"I know," Verlaine replied, and for a moment she could really believe.

Mateo's hand tightened around hers. At first she thought he was still attempting to comfort her, but then his grip became even tighter, until the bones of her hand ached. She looked at him in alarm, but he was staring past her—through her—

Nadia shook his shoulder. "Mateo?"

He collapsed.

"I serve the One Beneath, and he will not be denied," Elizabeth said, storm winds whipping her chestnut hair, her eyes alight as if with an unearthly fire.

"Someone, help!" Verlaine ran along a corridor, pursued by pounding footsteps and the shouts of dozens of—people? Demons? In the shadows Mateo couldn't tell any difference. All he saw was fury and destruction, bearing down on her faster by the moment.

Nadia was attempting to stand amid rushing water, as though she were in the middle of a flooded river. And yet she was holding on to something like a door, or a pillar—like she was inside, even as the waves rose higher.

The storm winds whipped Nadia's blue-black hair, lightning brilliant in the sky, as she said, "I serve the One Beneath—"

"Mateo? *Mateo!*"

The dizzying swirl of potential future and present steadied, and he once again knew where he was: La Catrina, specifically lying on the floor. His head lay in Nadia's lap, Verlaine was patting one of his hands, and Faye seemed to be grabbing something from the bar, maybe a damp rag or some ice. Mateo shifted his weight, then winced. "Ow."

"You fell pretty hard," Nadia said. "The visions again? What did you see?"

"I can't tell. Sometimes the dreams aren't literal; you know that." He groaned and pushed himself to sit upright. "I saw you in trouble—as usual. Verlaine, too."

"Oh, yay," Verlaine muttered.

The front door jingled, and Mateo frowned; he thought he'd locked that door. But someone else had a copy of the key—Dad, who was staring at him in dawning horror.

"*Madre de Dios*, Mateo, are you all right?"

"I'm fine," Mateo said, but he didn't think it was too convincing, seeing as how he was sprawled out on the floor.

Sure enough, Dad ran to him, his face white. "Is this another one of the seizures? I was just starting to think maybe that was a one-time thing, but now—"

Last month, a spell gone wrong had landed Mateo in the hospital overnight; the doctors, having no other way of understanding what ailed him, assumed he must have had a seizure. Mateo had felt awful about panicking his father, but he'd thought they'd all get over it quickly enough. So much for that. "I don't think so."

Dad wasn't buying it. "We're taking you to the hospital, right now."

"You shouldn't do that," Faye said, stepping out from behind the bar, ice bag still in her hands. "Mr. Perez? I'm Faye Walsh from Rodman High. I understand your concern for your son, but given the illness sweeping through the community, not to mention the quake—the hospital's not going to have capacity for Mateo right now. These are emergency situations."

Wow, she was a good liar. And because she was an adult, Dad actually listened.

"I don't like it," his father said, but he sighed. "You're right, though. Mateo, have you been taking your antiseizure medication?"

"No," he admitted. This was because the stuff was useless, but at least Dad wouldn't look any harder for an explanation.

"I tell you, and I tell you! In one ear and out the other!" Dad rarely yelled unless he was really, really scared. He was yelling now. "Come on. I'm taking you home. You're going to take your medicine and lie down for a while."

Mateo turned to Nadia in dismay. He wanted to be with her now—to lend his Steadfast power to the spells she would cast. That had just become impossible.

She closed her eyes for a moment, as if concentrating, and suddenly they were suffused by an aquamarine light. He realized immediately that nobody else could see this besides him, and perhaps Faye: This was magic. Nadia had just cast a spell, and whatever it was, it made him feel steadier instantly. It was a little like being desperately seasick aboard a boat, then stepping onto solid ground.

"This should help you sort out the dreams," she murmured, low enough for Dad not to hear. "I don't know that it's going to stop them, but you should be able to tell the difference between dreams and reality."

Faye had engaged Dad in a conversation about how the school could accommodate Mateo's condition. He decided he liked her. Quickly Mateo whispered, "I can sneak out. Just give me ten minutes or so at the house."

To his surprise, Nadia shook her head. "If you're overcome—it's dangerous to both of us, Mateo. What I want you to do is to report the visions to me if you can. Text me, or call. If you start to see a more definite future, and there's something you can warn me about, then warn me, okay?"

"Or me," Verlaine piped up. He'd almost forgotten she was sitting near them. "Since I'm in danger, too. If the One Beneath is coming after me, I'd appreciate a heads-up."

"I want to be with you," he said to Nadia. "I want to help you."

"You do. Every hour. Every minute." She framed his face with her hands. "You're my strength, always."

It didn't matter if the others were watching. Mateo pulled her close and kissed her, and tried very hard to believe it wouldn't be for the last time.

"That was *amazing*," Gage said as he smiled dazedly at the ceiling.

Naked, Elizabeth rose from the pile of blankets that Gage believed to be a bed. His mind was now clouded by her magic. The worst effects of Betrayer's Snare had by now worn off; a couple hours' use of a male body had burned away the fever of her desire and left behind only sore muscles and a slightly elevated pulse.

"You always seemed so, I don't know—*shy*." He grinned over at her, utterly besotted. She stared back impassively; he would be incapable of recognizing her indifference. "Guess I got that wrong. Or maybe you just choose your moments to show that wild side."

"I choose my moments," she said, considering her options.

It would be easy enough to make Gage forget the entire encounter. However, she could do that at any point. With Betrayer's Snare no longer influencing her, she would have no more need of him in her bed, but that didn't mean he was useless.

Sex was a necessary ingredient in a spell she hadn't cast in a very long time. At this critical moment, couldn't she use more than one servant? Asa's loyalties were so cloudy, his obedience so grudging; to have a slave who obeyed from slavish adoration rather than fear might prove useful.

Once Gage became her thrall, she could use him to spy. To undermine. Even to kill. And he would never question it.

"Come here, my love." Elizabeth held out her hand. Gage rose to take it, just as willingly as he would soon give her his blood.

25

NADIA STOOD AGAIN AT THE BEACH. THE AREA WAS deserted. Everyone in Captive's Sound was probably either inspecting their homes for earthquake damage or running to their loved ones. That meant she had the wide expanse of pale sand and the dark, churning sound to herself.

At least, for now. She had no doubt Elizabeth would find her soon.

Her phone chimed with texts, one after the other. She held it up to look at the screen.

From Mateo: *Dad helicoptering. Feeling all right. No more dreams yet. You okay?*

I'm fine, she texted back. *Setting out any second. Love you.*

From Verlaine: *I'm at the hospital. All systems go!*

The phone chimed one more time. This time it was Faye. *In front of Elizabeth's house. There's light inside—she seems to be home, and I don't think she's alone. I'll let you know if she's on the move.*

Once again Nadia felt a quiver in her belly, both of astonishment and of doubt. The astonishment came from having finally found someone else who understood witchcraft and was willing to talk. No, Faye wasn't a witch herself, but her mother's Book of Shadows had already proved incredibly useful.

The sky overhead rumbled with thunder. Mateo had often told her about the horrible roiling he saw over Captive's Sound; it was evidence of Elizabeth's hold on this town, visible only to a Steadfast.

Or it had been. Now even Nadia thought she saw a movement in the clouds that was less like the wind, more like the slithering of something almost alive.

Could everyone see it now? With all the signs and portents—the way this town was literally coming apart—would others realize that something unnatural was at work?

It didn't matter. That was something for Nadia to deal with after this, if there was an after.

She walked toward the nearby pier, where a lone rowboat was tethered, bobbing up and down on the waves. For a moment she imagined herself as being just as alone, but that wasn't true.

Her friends were all doing their part—and Mateo was with her, no matter what.

Faye tried to make herself comfortable in her car. Like anyone could get comfortable when the sky was doing . . . that.

I'm glad you can't understand this any longer, Momma, she thought. *And yet I can't help wishing you still had your Craft and could come here to kick some Sorceress ass.*

Could her mother have overcome Elizabeth's power? No telling. But it wouldn't have hurt to have her on Nadia's side.

She'd known the minute she first drove into Captive's Sound that this place was serious trouble. To a Steadfast, every inch of this town looked like a nightmare come true. No wonder Mateo Perez had had trouble with it; even Faye, with her years of experience, had been terrified by her first sight of the many spells that wove along the streets and buildings and sea. Evil dwelled here: no question about that.

But she'd taken the job exactly because this town was so troubled—because, even if she'd never be a witch like her mother, she wanted to think she could do some good.

Well, now was her chance.

The front door of Elizabeth's house opened, and Faye tensed. But it wasn't Elizabeth who walked out. To her astonishment, it was Gage Calloway.

Gage? He was a good kid. What the hell would he be doing with Elizabeth Pike?

Faye grabbed her phone to text Nadia. Maybe this wasn't something she needed to know—but maybe it was, and Faye didn't intend to take any chances.

When she began typing, though, her car door swung open.

Startled, she turned to see Gage just as he grabbed her arm and towed her out of the car.

"What are you doing?" Faye struggled but couldn't pull free; he was strong. "Let me go!"

Gage didn't listen. No—he *couldn't* listen. His eyes stared at her vacantly, completely devoid of their usual intelligence and humor. And now that he was this close, she could see, hanging around him like an aura, the sickly, red light that could signify dark magic.

Elizabeth's controlling him. He's her thrall.

Faye stopped trying to escape and started fighting back. She tackled him, and apparently the element of surprise was enough to get him to stagger backward. That gave her a chance to yank her arm away and leap into her car.

Gage smashed at the door, but her shaking fingers were already turning the key in the ignition. Within seconds she'd sped off, panting as she glanced in the rearview mirror to see Gage staring after her impassively.

What was it her mother had taught her? *Thralls can't do anything complicated, not while they're being directly influenced. They love their creator, and only their creator. They can sense danger to the Sorceress. And they'll fight to protect her.*

Right now, all of them represented some danger to Elizabeth—Nadia, Mateo, Verlaine, everyone. The only question was which of them Gage would go after next.

Stop looking at it! If people see you staring, they'll wonder what you're staring at.

Verlaine curled into one of the plastic chairs at the hospital and tried very hard not to imagine that the pearl she now wore in the locket around her neck wasn't warm. Or glowing. Or tingling with energy. Because it wasn't—she'd

305

double-checked the glowing part in the mirror. That was just her imagination running away with her, reminding her of the power she would soon help to channel.

The power that might soon kill her—

Once again the ground trembled, and people cried out in alarm. The quake wasn't as bad as the one that morning, though; the shaking died down after only a few moments. For Verlaine it was a relief: *Probably just Nadia at work,* she thought.

But for everyone else in the waiting area, all the exhausted family members of mysteriously ill patients, the quake seemed to be the last straw.

"This isn't right!" one woman cried. "This isn't natural, and we all know it!"

People murmured in assent. Then the murmuring turned into anger. Verlaine kept her face turned away in an attempt to hide her astonishment. Were the residents of Captive's Sound finally catching on to the fact that their town was seriously messed up?

In one way, that would be cool, because it would prove that the people around Verlaine were marginally less stupid than she'd believed them to be. But if people suspected the truth, wouldn't Nadia's work suddenly get more complicated? Because then people would be looking for the signs of witchcraft, looking for the witches themselves—

"That one!" someone shouted. "She's always around when things go wrong, and look at her! She's pretending the quake didn't even happen!"

Verlaine glanced up to see who they were talking about, only to see the entire group staring directly at her.

Oh, crap, she thought.

"I—" What was she supposed to say? They seemed to expect her to say something. She went back on the best defense she could think of, which was a total lie: "Come on, people. There's no such thing as, uh, the supernatural."

"She's always sneaking in and out," someone else said. The group began to move closer to her, slowly, but the hairs on Verlaine's arms rose. "She's always poking her nose in where it doesn't belong."

Any other person might have been protected, Verlaine realized, just by the friendships and connections people made in a small town. This angry, upset crowd ought to remember that she was Gary and Dave's daughter, that she went to school with their kids, that they saw her in the same stores and on the same streets where they were themselves. They should have seen her as one of them.

But Verlaine was masked by black magic. Nobody loved her. Not many people even liked her. They couldn't.

That meant they were free to fear her. To hate her.

"You're not yourselves," she said as she rose to her feet. She closed her fingers around the locket on her neck, instinctively protecting the pearl charm. "You're not thinking straight. We're all upset. Everyone needs to calm down."

With that she turned and began to walk out of the hospital. If she didn't panic, they wouldn't, either. *Slow and steady, easy does it . . .*

"Stop her!" came the shout, and then the footsteps pounded behind her, and Verlaine could only run.

Her heart seemed to be pounding its way through her rib cage, as though it wanted to shatter her. Verlaine's first instinct was to run for her car, but already people were crowding the hallways all around her and blocking her way. Their eyes were wild, hardly even human. They'd been pushed to the limits of their endurance, beyond the point of rational thought. They blamed her for what was happening in Captive's Sound, and they intended to make her pay.

Uncle Gary! she thought. They wouldn't hurt her if she was with the patients; they'd calm down if only to protect their own loved ones. And if they remembered that someone she loved had been struck down, too, maybe that would snap them out of it.

But they were close on her now—shouts and footsteps an ever-increasing roar behind her—and Verlaine nearly gave way to panic.

She flung open the door that would lead her toward the elevator and dashed through, then skidded to a stop.

Asa stood there. Verlaine didn't even have to wonder why he'd come; Elizabeth had sensed some small part of their plan and sent her demon henchman to keep it from unfolding. And now Asa could trap her, right where the mob could tear her apart.

As the winds on the sound picked up, so did the waves. Nadia clung to the weather-beaten white stucco of the lighthouse as water crashed right at her feet. Sea spray soaked her clothes, heightened the chill.

Now or never, Nadia decided.

Hand on the garnet on her bracelet, she summoned the ingredients for the spell:

Soothing the nightmare of a child.
Healing a wound that struck deep.
Forgiving what could not be forgiven.

Once again the ground rumbled. Nadia glanced toward the dark, choppy ocean; even she could see hints of the bridge now. The One Beneath was so very close.

Holding Cole in her arms, rocking him back and forth, whispering that there were no monsters outside, no monsters at all, not while his big sister was here to protect him.

A morning about three weeks after Mom had left, when they were all eating cereal in the kitchen without saying a word, and then a stupid old disco song from when Dad was little came on the radio, and he started singing and Cole started laughing and before Nadia knew it, she and her dad were doing the stupidest dance they could think of, just because it felt so good to have fun again.

Crying quietly on the bus in Chicago, telling herself over and again that Mom had done what she'd done for love, and feeling a terrible weight finally lift from her after far too long.

The power of it rippled through Nadia, shaking her even more savagely than the quakes had. And yet it didn't scare her; it didn't hurt. This was white magic—stronger and more transformative than she'd ever worked before. It felt like celebration, like sunlight. It felt sweeter than anything she'd ever known except love.

Nadia opened her eyes. Had it worked?

Before she could even cast one of the spells that would allow her to learn the truth, her phone chimed with a text. With cold, numb hands, she fished her phone from her pocket, hoping for a message from Verlaine that everyone at the hospital had already begun to heal.

Instead the text was from Faye. *Gage is in Elizabeth's thrall. He's dangerous & can't help it. He could be coming after any of us. I'm going to warn Mateo.*

Elizabeth had created a thrall? She'd done that to Gage? Nadia was torn between horror for Gage's plight and an even greater fear for Mateo's safety. And Verlaine—Gage might go after her, too. She had to get to them as fast as possible.

Was it safe to take the rowboat back to shore? The storm hadn't let up, but it might not right away. Yet the waters seemed to churn even stronger—the foam splashing up toward her feet—

—no, not splashing, *crawling*—

She cried out as the water swirled up into a column so dark it glinted like obsidian, until it splash-shattered into a human form. Elizabeth stood in front of her, chin high, expression mocking.

Before it had seemed as though Elizabeth was getting more bedraggled and weak by the day. Now she was glorious. Light almost seemed to shine from her skin, and the scars and dirt of the world couldn't even touch her.

"Your interference is no longer amusing," Elizabeth said.

Nadia could hardly speak or think. "How did you do that?" Surely Elizabeth hadn't always possessed that kind of power, the ability to move herself in supernatural ways. How had she broken the bonds of physical reality?

"I grow stronger as my love comes closer. When He arrives, I will share in His power. And He is very close to arriving, try though you will to stop Him." The wind caught Elizabeth's curls, twisting them behind her like snakes. "Let us reckon, you and I."

26

MATEO LAY IN HIS BED, TWISTING AND TURNING, HANDS clenched into fists hard enough to hurt. That helped keep him focused, but not enough.

He pushed himself off the mattress—*or was that a boat? A boat carrying him and Nadia, bobbing treacherously on the waves growing higher by the moment*—and fell in a crouch on the floor. Breathing hard, he tried not to look at the visions in front of him. (*Nadia by the lighthouse, falling to her knees in front of the triumphant Elizabeth.*) Instead he tried to concentrate only on the feel of the floor beneath his hands and knees as he crawled toward the place where he knew his dresser must be.

With one sweaty hand, he reached out and found the sharp corner of the wood. Mateo drew his arm back, then swung it as hard as he could.

Crack! He sucked in a sharp breath, but with pain came clarity. By smashing his forearm against the dresser, he'd earned himself a throbbing, red mark that would soon be an ugly bruise, but that didn't matter. The only important thing was making sense of the visions he was seeing, so that he could help protect Nadia.

Panting, Mateo leaned back against the wall. Another dream surrounded him already, but the combination of Nadia's spell and the ache from his arm allowed him to watch it as if from the outside—like he was watching a movie.

Elizabeth lifted her hands high, and it was as though the enormous waves behind her rippled and crashed at her command. Yet he could sense the energy emanating from her, feel it curling and growing like the tendrils of vines, until they snaked around the throats of every sick person, stealing breath and life—

And Nadia was there, powerless to stop her.

Mateo emerged from the dream with a gasp. The storm, Nadia's presence at the lighthouse: His dreams might be showing him the future, but it was the very near future. Maybe not even hours ahead—maybe only minutes.

If he could reach Nadia before Elizabeth cast that spell, maybe it would give her a chance to prepare and save the people at the hospital. It might save Nadia, too.

Where was his stupid phone? He swore as he realized his father had moved it, trying only to help his son to rest while he went to inspect the restaurant for quake-related damage. Mateo managed to get to his feet and start going through the house. Chances were Dad had put it in the kitchen, right by the door. . . .

As he walked into the kitchen, someone rang the bell.

Mateo went to answer it, figuring the only person who would come here now had to be Verlaine.

Instead he opened the door to see Gage.

In that first second, Mateo thought the strange reddish haze around Gage was only a remnant of the dream visions. After that, though, it hit him: that was his Steadfast power revealing magic at work.

But that first second was all it took.

Gage's amiable expression melted from his face, and the guy who tackled Mateo to the floor—he wasn't Gage any longer. Mateo landed hard on his back, but he managed to get his arms up just in time to keep Gage from wrapping his hands around Mateo's throat.

They fought there on the kitchen floor. Gage never spoke; Mateo never bothered. In movies, fights always had guys on their feet, trading ninja kicks and manful blows. In reality, it usually came down to this: wrestling, gouging, shoving, never quite knowing what was going on. He pulled his punches as much as he could, because he knew Gage wasn't himself and he didn't want to mess the guy up. But whatever had Gage in its grip wasn't playing by the same rules.

Mateo could think only of Nadia, in so much more danger, and he couldn't even get to his damned phone to warn her.

Then Gage slammed him down so hard that Mateo couldn't breathe. It felt like his ribs might have cracked, or broken.

He didn't want to hurt Gage—but what if that was the only way he could get out of this alive?

Gage grabbed the toaster and held it over Mateo's head, obviously preparing to use it to bash Mateo's head in. He tried to roll out of the way, holding one hand up to block as he thought, *No, no, no—*

The red light around Gage pulsed, flickered, went out. And Mateo knew—just knew—that something from within him, something about his outstretched hand, had done this.

Gage froze. For a long moment he just stood there. At first Mateo could only stare up at him, and then he thought, *This might be a good time to dodge.*

As he scrambled back, Gage said, "What were we just doing?"

"Uh—I—" Mateo couldn't find words. Had he actually broken the spell on Gage by himself? Had he performed some kind of magic?

Shaking his head as though to clear it, Gage stared down at the toaster in his hands. "Were we making toast?"

"Yeah. You came by to check on me, and we wanted some toast. That's it." Mateo scrambled to his feet. To hell with the phone: He was getting in the boat and going to Nadia, now. If he had even a fraction of magical power, he was going to use it to help her. "Hey, can you hold down the fort here for a second? If my dad comes back home, tell him I'm fine. I'll be right back. Okay?"

Gage, clearly somewhat confused but determined to get through it, put down the toaster and went to get the bread. "Sure thing."

Mateo ran from the house, desperate to reach Nadia in time.

Nadia shouted so that her voice would carry over the howling wind: "You can't hurt them any longer! You've lost your pain, so you've lost your bridge."

Elizabeth only shook her head in what looked like fond exasperation. "You never understood the magic to begin with."

"The bridge is built on pain. I know that's why you hurt all those people and put them in the hospital." *It worked; it has to have worked; Elizabeth just hasn't realized it yet—*

"Yes, the bridge for the One Beneath is built on pain," Elizabeth said. She stepped closer, so that they were nearly within arm's reach of each other. "The better the pain, the better the bridge. Physical pain is nothing, really. Just a habit of the body."

Hearing her say that so carelessly after seeing the torment Uncle Gary and Riley and Mrs. Purdhy had been put through enraged Nadia almost past endurance. But then her mind focused in more sharply on what Elizabeth had said. Realization began to dawn, and Nadia saw it reflected in Elizabeth's knowing smile.

"To build a true bridge—a strong bridge, one capable of carrying the One Beneath to our world—I needed an agony far greater than the suffering of a thousand tormented bodies. I needed the pain of the soul, of so many souls."

"You didn't build the bridge on the people in the hospital," Nadia said. "You built it on their families. Their friends. You built it on the pain of every person who went through all this time not knowing if the people they loved would live or die."

On Mrs. Purdhy's family. On Kendall. On Verlaine.

Elizabeth said, "I knew you would see eventually. You're bright enough for that. But I also knew you would see it too late."

Failing to understand Elizabeth's magic was humiliating—but what did it matter now? Nadia lifted her chin. "The bridge isn't complete, and those people are free. They'll wake up any minute now, if they haven't already. So all the families are going to be happy again."

"The bridge is almost complete," Elizabeth replied, "and I need so little to finish it. Really, if you'd left me one more hour, I could have left it at that."

It sounded like an admission of defeat, but it clearly wasn't. Nadia felt a new, dawning wave of fear. "You won't get one more hour."

"No, I won't. But I remain tied to the patients, still; a few threads linger. I'll have to give the threads a pull. You've blunted my original spell, so this time I'll have to act more decisively." Elizabeth lifted her hands. "I'll have to kill them all."

Verlaine tried to run past Asa, thinking that if she could just get to the stairwell, she might make it—but he grabbed her arm. She fell, swinging down to the ground at his feet, his hand still wrapped around her elbow too tightly for her to pull free.

The betrayal stung even more than the fear. Even though the mob was closing in, she could only look up at him in utter despair.

Then Asa straightened and shouted, "Get away from her!"

Everyone stopped. They still looked angry, but the shock of seeing someone defend Verlaine had been enough to make them hesitate.

"You idiots," he snarled. "Every horrible thing that's happening around you, and you blame one of the only people who cares enough to try to help. You go after someone you think doesn't have anyone to defend her. Well, you thought wrong." Asa let go of Verlaine's arm so that he could step in front of her, between her and her would-be attackers. "Get back before I make you get back."

Verlaine felt a shiver go through her then, and knew the rest had felt it, too. Although there was no overt sign that Asa was someone besides Jeremy Prasad, something other than human, it had somehow become completely clear that he could stop them all if he had to—and make them sorry they'd even tried to get past him.

"Later," one man said, shooting a venomous look at Verlaine. But people shuffled out begrudgingly; their anger still simmered, but it was in check for now.

The moment the last of them left the elevator bank, Asa towed her up to stand by his side. Verlaine's legs trembled from adrenaline and exhaustion, but she managed to stay upright. His hands on her shoulders were comfortingly warm. "We have to get out of here," he said. "As far from this place as possible. Now."

She shook her head. "I'm part of Nadia's spell. That means I have to stay here."

"Of course," Asa breathed. He understood now, and his expression shifted into horror. "You could die."

"Then I die."

"Don't do this."

"Take me to Uncle Gary's room." The CDC people had shooed her out earlier, but by now maybe she could get back in. "I want to be with him, no matter what happens."

Asa's dark eyes flashed with emotion she could no longer read. "I'll come with you as far as I can."

Mateo dashed out onto the beach to see—a hellscape. That was the only word for it. He could hardly tell the smoky, snarled clouds overhead from the writhing ocean that stretched out to a dark horizon.

And you're going to go out on that in a boat? said the part of his brain that still wanted to think he lived in a normal world.

But he ran for the nearest boat, untied the moorings, revved the motor.

Together Verlaine and Asa ran up the stairs, which was faster by far than waiting for the glacially slow hospital elevators. As Verlaine's Converse pounded the concrete steps, she noticed how lightly Asa ran, as though he had no weight at all. As if he could almost fly.

She felt as if she had never understood Asa before this . . .

no. That wasn't right. She had always understood him, from the first moment she learned what a demon was and saw the desperate resignation within Asa. But she hadn't dared to trust what she knew until now.

They emerged onto the fourth floor, Verlaine breathless, Asa not even beginning to tire. When they burst through the doors, though, a small group of CDC doctors down the hall whirled around to look at them. "Hey," one woman called. "You're not allowed in here."

Asa brought his hands together—and like that, time stopped. She turned to him and smiled, and he smiled back tentatively, as if he still couldn't believe she trusted him. "Come on," he said, and they hurried down the hall.

Uncle Gary lay in his hospital bed. For a split second the stillness of the heart monitor gave her pause, but of course, time remained frozen. He was caught between heartbeats.

Suddenly titanic, consuming pain lanced through her, coring her out, as surely as though she'd been impaled. Verlaine clutched at the locket around her neck—that was where the pain came from, and it had to stop, *it had to stop!*—but then she remembered and grabbed her hair instead.

Warm arms closed around Verlaine, held her tightly. "Be strong, my beautiful girl," Asa whispered. "It's terrible but it won't last long; I promise you it won't last long."

It had to be a lie. There could be no living through pain like this, no surviving, no after. And yet she was Uncle Gary's only chance, and Asa was here with her, helping her be strong. She just had to breathe—and again—and again—

The pain ended as swiftly as it had begun. She gasped, almost unable to believe she was still in the world.

"You did it," Asa said. "Elizabeth's spell will shatter my own small power soon. But at least—at least I was here for this."

"Thank you," she said. Their eyes met—and he let go of her even as she stepped away.

Quickly Verlaine pulled a chair next to Uncle Gary's bed and took one of his hands in hers. Just being with him made her feel steadier. Then she glanced over her shoulder at Asa and repeated, "Thank you."

"It's no less than you deserve," he said. "About time you finally got some shred of what the world owes you."

"Will you stay with me? After time starts again?"

He shook his head very slightly; already his gaze had turned inward, as if he were trying to listen for a distant sound. "Not for very long. I won't be able to. You see, I can defy Elizabeth—but not the One Beneath. There's a price to be paid now. I shall have to pay it."

Verlaine realized that Asa had defied the One Beneath by saving her. "What happens now?"

"That's not up to us. It never has been. One thing we have in common, you and I—the great and mighty plot their wars, and we shiver down in the trenches. We fight for others' glory, or at best our own survival. Ours is not to question why."

Verlaine wanted to protest. She fought alongside Nadia and Mateo because she trusted them, and knew that their goals were worth fighting for. But she realized that wasn't a justification she could throw in Asa's face. It was a luxury he had never been allowed, as a slave to the One Beneath.

Asa brought his hands together again. The room remained still, but the heart monitors began beeping again. Verlaine sighed, reassured by the sound. "What about the doctors?" She gave the door to the room a meaningful glance. "They saw us in the hallway."

He backed a few halting steps away. "They'll think they imagined it—or that you left—not that you magically— magically went right past them—"

"Are you all right?" Verlaine stared; Asa had begun to shake. The lamp by Uncle Gary's bedside shone toward him, highlighting his strained face, casting his shadows even blacker. "What's happening?"

"Time for me to pay."

Then his shadow changed.

It *tore*.

Asa winced as one sliver of his shadow, then another, was ripped away. The darkness didn't just disappear; instead it fluttered away, as though it had turned into one of Elizabeth's menacing crows. The slivers ripped from him faster and faster, until he cried out in pain.

Verlaine dropped Uncle Gary's hand and ran to Asa. In the moment before she would have reached him, he cried out and vanished.

For a moment the remnants of his shadow fluttered in the corners, making soft, raspy sounds like wings, and then they, too, were gone. Nothing of Asa remained.

"No!" Nadia cried, but Elizabeth didn't listen. Her rings glinted on her fingers; her minerals were with her, and even now she must be summoning the ingredients for her murderous spell.

A few protective spells flashed through Nadia's mind, but none of them was strong enough. None of them was right. *To hell with it,* she thought, and threw herself bodily at Elizabeth.

They fell together on the scrabble of seashells, and for a moment they grappled with each other. But then a hook seemed to arch around Nadia's body and yank her away so sharply that she tumbled onto the steep slope that led to the water. She was only just able to grab at the gravel and shells enough to stop herself from falling in. A wave crashed high enough to soak her jeans with near-freezing water, and drag her another couple of inches down.

The hook she'd felt so clearly didn't exist. It was, of course, just another of Elizabeth's spells.

Elizabeth knew too much. She was too strong. Nadia was outclassed, and all the help she'd gotten—everything she and Mateo and Verlaine had tried to do, every spell she'd read in the Books of Shadows—it wasn't enough.

"You've lost," Elizabeth said. "The only question is whether you'll make the others die along with your hopes."

"I can keep you from killing them." But how? Nadia's defiance was empty, and she knew it. Still, she kept scrambling up toward Elizabeth, determined to at least meet her again on her feet.

Then she heard Mateo's voice: "Nadia!"

She whirled around to see the boat he sometimes borrowed. Despite all her warnings, Mateo had sped across this dark, stormy sea to her side. Because he was willing to die with her.

As she stood, waiting for him to join her, Elizabeth said, very calmly, "You can save them."

"What?"

If Elizabeth had even noticed Mateo's approach, she didn't seem to care. "You can keep me from killing them."

Nadia hesitated. Whipping winds thrashed her hair; a few damp strands stuck to her cheek. The cold made her shake, and by now the sky seemed far too low. This was where Elizabeth had wished to lead her. This was the trap. Yet she had to ask, "How?"

"You give me enough power to finish the bridge without killing them," Elizabeth said. "It's simple, really."

Her meaning sank in, biting at her bones as sharply as the chill. There was only one way Nadia could make Elizabeth more powerful now—by giving her an apprentice.

Mateo's skiff hit the shore of the small lighthouse island, and he ran as fast as he could up the steep bank. As he approached, Elizabeth never turned toward him—but then she held out her hand, and suddenly he couldn't move. It was as though he'd been shackled in place; it was as if he could feel the iron cutting through his flesh around his wrists, his waist, his feet, everywhere.

324

Once again he tried to call on whatever power it was that he'd discovered deep within, the power that had broken the spell on Gage . . . but Mateo couldn't find it. Whatever Elizabeth was doing was far too strong.

Yet his own fate bothered him less than the way Nadia was looking at Elizabeth. She looked worse than afraid.

She looked defeated.

Nadia tried to think of another way to stop Elizabeth, but she couldn't.

The bridge for the One Beneath would be completed no matter what. From now on, only one thin seal would keep Him from reclaiming the mortal realm—and Elizabeth would be doing her best to break that seal and bring Him here.

Nadia could keep her freedom, but only by sacrificing the lives of innocent people.

Only then did she think, *If I join Elizabeth, I know what she's doing. I learn her magic. I learn exactly how the One Beneath plans to enter our world.*

That might be the only way I learn enough to stop Him.

But taking this vow—breaking this most vital of the First Laws—becoming a Sorceress like Elizabeth—that would have its own power. Twist her magic. Change her world in ways she couldn't guess.

Nadia had only one chance. She took it.

"I'll join you," she said.

Mateo cried out, "No!" But Nadia didn't look at him; she

couldn't afford to now. She would face his betrayal and anger later. For now, this had to be done.

Elizabeth straightened, a gleeful smile dawning on her face. "You have to swear it, you know. And there are penalties for oath-breakers."

"I know." She'd pay when the time came. "I know."

"Then swear him your obedience now."

She dropped to her knees on the seashells, bowing to the last thing she had ever wanted to bow to. Voice trembling, she said, "I am sworn." The winds pitched even higher, so much it was hard for Nadia to remain upright. But she got out the words again: "I am sworn."

Thunder rumbled, and Elizabeth cried, "Once more! Once more and be His. Be mine."

Mateo's voice was almost lost in the wind. "Nadia, don't—"

I'm sorry, Mateo.

I'm sorry, Mom.

Nadia whispered, "I am sworn," and it was done.

27

ELIZABETH STRETCHED WIDE HER ARMS AND SURREN-
dered to the storm. Instead of controlling it, she let the
winds and wildness own her. Her power became part of the
storm as the storm became a part of her. The waters circled
as though caught in a whirlpool, until suddenly they went
still—more motionless than the ocean would ever be.

To her it was as though everything uncertain had just been
made solid. As if a bone out of joint had popped into place,
or a fire had been lit in a cold room. Whatever it was, this
sudden sense of order imposed on the chaotic mortal world,
Elizabeth knew what it meant: The bridge was built. The
One Beneath would come. Nadia's capitulation had completed the great work, at least for now.

As an afterthought, she let Mateo go; he sagged to his
knees. His Steadfast powers had made Nadia stronger, just at
the moment when that strength could be used to tie her to

the One Beneath irrevocably. Perhaps there was something to be said for young love. Without Mateo, Nadia could never have been so unbreakably damned.

"It is done," she said, and Nadia hung her head, unwilling to look Elizabeth in the face. "We now have but to break the final seal. That is the hardest of all—but not hard, not truly. Not when His power mingles with our own."

Still Nadia would not lift her eyes. It was only natural that she would find this a defeat instead of a victory, new to service as she was. Given time, Nadia Caldani would embrace her new role and even glory in it.

Perhaps the girl also suffered from wounded pride. She had, of course, been beaten; no doubt the fact of it shamed her. But servants of the One Beneath learned to do without such luxuries as pride. To humble oneself, to give oneself over to his unhallowed love completely—that was the only joy remaining, after a while.

"The people in the hospital," Nadia said, voice ragged. "They're okay?"

What did they matter any longer? Elizabeth shrugged. "I would assume. I do very little for spite. Cruelty should serve a purpose, and it serves many purposes very well. You'll see."

Nadia shivered, and for a few moments neither of them spoke.

By now the storm was smoothing into soft rain, which would soon turn into snow. Elizabeth held out her hand. "Return with me to the shore, and our lessons can begin."

"But—" Nadia looked back at Mateo, who was staring at

her as though he had never seen her before.

Such distractions ill-suited a Sorceress, but this lesson was one better taught by experience. Elizabeth smiled thinly. "As you will. Say farewell to your former love. See your friends and your family. But tomorrow night, you present yourself to me, and your instruction can resume."

"All right." Then Nadia blinked and said, more formally, "I have sworn."

Elizabeth flung her arms out, hands reaching downward, fingers splayed. Once again, the water swirled up to cocoon her and carry her across the waves. As it shatter-splashed onto the beach, Elizabeth smiled. The new powers she had gained would be interesting to explore.

Now the One Beneath was close. Now He could give her strength. Now He could reward his servants—

—including Nadia.

How badly He had wanted Nadia to join them. How eager He had been for the child of two witching bloodlines to take up magic in his service. Already He valued Nadia.

Soon He would treasure her beyond any of His other possessions.

Even though Elizabeth was the one who had served Him for centuries, the one who would make his final triumph possible . . .

A thought flickered in her mind: *It is unfair.*

Elizabeth banished that thought immediately. It was not given to her to question the One Beneath. She was to love and serve Him with no thought of reward.

And yet the hot ember of new jealousy burned down deep within her heart.

Mateo felt numb. He pushed himself to his feet to walk toward Nadia.

She stood before him, trembling. "I had to do it," she said, and her voice broke. "I know you don't understand. I know you can't forgive me for it. But it was the only way, Mateo. Please believe me."

Very slowly he said, "Of course I believe you."

Nadia sobbed once, but she shook her head, like it couldn't be true.

Mateo grabbed her into his embrace. "Don't you think I know you'd never do that unless—that you just gave yourself up for all of us? Nadia. Oh, Jesus, Nadia. I know you. I love you. You did what you had to do." He kissed her hair, clutched her close, and let her cry her heartbreak into his chest, so that the sound was lost in the rolling of the sea.

Verlaine sat in the hospital room, her head on the same pillow as Uncle Gary. She'd already cried all of her tears for Asa. If the worst happened now, she didn't think she could cry anymore. Maybe she couldn't feel anything anymore. All the emotion that had been drained out of everybody else when they looked at her—she was starting to think it had been drained from her, too. By the end of this there wouldn't be anything left of her but resignation.

She wondered where Asa was now, whether she'd ever

find out what had become of him. Could she even ask Nadia? Nobody else cared about demons.

That's the one thing we had in common, she realized.

If only she could have given him something in return . . .

Uncle Gary's monitors started making different sounds. It was all just so much beeping and blinking to Verlaine, but she knew same from different, and this was definitely new. She jerked upright, terrified that at any moment he would flatline.

Instead she saw Uncle Gary open his eyes.

"Hey," she whispered, squeezing his hand tightly. "Can you hear me?"

He nodded, then made a face. "Are there tubes in my nose? Oh, gross."

"Lie still." Doctors—they needed doctors! "Hang on, okay? I'll be right back, I swear."

In the next bed over, Mrs. Purdhy turned her head as she, too, began to awaken; Riley Bender started to stretch. They were okay, too. Everyone was waking up—everyone at once: Nadia must have won.

Verlaine had thought she'd never be able to feel anything again, but she'd been so wrong. Her heart still had room for joy.

By the time Nadia and Mateo returned to shore, Mateo had told her about what Gage had done. But she shook her head when he claimed he'd broken the spell. "Not possible," she said. "You don't possess magic."

331

"Men being Steadfasts isn't supposed to be possible, either," Mateo pointed out. His arm supported her as they walked along the beach. Her entire body shook with exhaustion, and with the enormity of what she'd done. If Mateo hadn't stood by her, she wasn't sure she could have borne it.

When they went into Mateo's home, Gage was gone—but Verlaine and Faye were sitting in the living room, munching on a large plate of toast Gage had apparently left behind. Verlaine was listening to Faye raptly as they sat by the fire.

"A thrall?" Verlaine said through a mouthful of toast. "What's that?"

"A servant to a Sorceress," Faye said.

Verlaine went very still. "You mean, like a demon?"

"No," Faye explained. "Demons are supernatural beings, with motives and powers of their own. Thralls are humans who fall under a Sorceress's control. Usually it begins with love—the thrall falling for the Sorceress, then going to bed with her. Once they're bound by sex, then the Sorceress can take over his will as absolutely and often as she wants." Then Faye saw them and smiled. "You made it."

"Yeah." Mateo's eyes met Nadia's, but only for a second. He tried to make a joke. "So, Gage finally got with the girl of his dreams without realizing she was the girl of his nightmares."

"Before we bury the lede here—Nadia, you did it!" Verlaine flung her arms around them both. "Oh, Nadia, you did it! Uncle Gary's just fine."

"Momma's spell worked?" Faye grinned at the group of

them; Nadia suspected she would have liked to join in. "I'm so glad."

"The spell worked." Nadia's words were muffled until she pulled back from Verlaine. "But it didn't stop Elizabeth."

And as she told them the rest—the price she'd had to pay—she could only watch as Faye's and Verlaine's faces fell. Even Mateo winced as he heard Nadia finish: "As of my oath, I'm the same as Elizabeth. I'm a Sorceress."

Verlaine found her voice first. "Does this mean you're here to kill us?"

"No! God, no. Never. I would never do that." Nadia ran one hand through her damp hair, trying not to give in to tears. "But I took a binding oath. From now on, I'm tied to Elizabeth. I just hope I can use the connection. Turn it to our advantage."

"You're a fool." Faye's words hit Nadia like a slap. "You think you can use darkness? Trust me, it always winds up using you."

"I didn't have any other choice," Nadia said. "Everyone would have died."

"Then you should have let them die." Faye grabbed her satchel and walked up to them, clearly heading for the door. She said, "My mother's Book of Shadows is still at La Catrina. I'm taking it back. Don't try to stop me. I may not be a witch, but I have a few tricks up my sleeve. Test me and you'll find out."

Nadia protested, "We're not enemies."

Faye shook her head. "If you're sworn to the One Beneath?

We most certainly are." With that she stalked outside.

Verlaine twisted the length of her silvery hair, a gesture that by now Nadia knew meant she was nervous. "We're not enemies," she said, "but I have to admit I'm kind of freaked out at the moment."

"Me too," Nadia confessed.

"I'm gonna—I need to collapse for about two days straight right now," Verlaine said. "And I'll think about the rest later."

Nadia nodded. "Okay."

"So I'll see you at school. I guess we'll have school again, now that everybody's gotten better." Verlaine went for the door, then paused. "Do you still get to go to school, and live at home, and do, uh, normal human stuff?"

After a moment's hesitation, Nadia nodded. "At least, as far as I know."

"Then I'll see you at school," Verlaine repeated more steadily, and then she went out and left them alone.

They stayed together as long as they could that night, until Mr. Perez texted that he was on his way home. Nadia hated to leave Mateo—hated the thought of being separated from him for even a moment. She needed the people she loved more than ever now. They were her best defense against the darkness. Maybe her only defense. Whatever hope she had of ultimately defeating Elizabeth lay with them.

She remembered her mother's voice in her head: *Love is the only thing that makes life worth living.*

And yet a price had to be paid.

Mateo walked with her out on the beach. Already the

sky was almost clear; many of the stars shone through the scanty clouds. Neither of them spoke for a long time, until Mateo finally said, "We have to break the Steadfast bond, don't we?"

He'd glimpsed part of this, at least, but it didn't make what Nadia had to say any easier. "No. We can't. It's like I told you—at this point, for us to break that bond, I would have to sever my connection to magic, completely and forever."

"I thought maybe—maybe you felt like you had to do that."

She wrapped her hand around his. "I don't have the right to do that anymore. I'm sworn to the One Beneath. If I even tried it, I'd die."

It might come to that, in the end. But Nadia knew better than to say so to Mateo. That knowledge was too terrible to burden him with, at least until there was no other choice.

"But I make you stronger," Mateo said. "Just by being near you. And now, if you have to do things for the One Beneath, I'll be making him stronger."

She nodded. "Just by being near me."

He understood then. His steps faltered, but he didn't let go of her hand. The pain she saw in Mateo's eyes cut her to the quick—but worse by far was the compassion she saw there. The total commitment. Mateo knew why she had to do this, and he was strong enough not to hate her for it.

Nadia only hoped she was strong enough not to hate herself.

"If we're together, you'll make me too strong," she said.

"You'll make me too useful to the One Beneath. I always draw power from you—you always make me stronger, always. But we have to minimize that as much as we can. That means staying apart as much as possible. Besides—" By now her voice shook, and her throat ached with unshed tears. "From now on, every moment is dangerous. Every step I take could go wrong. I need to know you're safe, Mateo. Otherwise I don't think I can do this. I can only do it without you."

She could see the anguish in his eyes, but when he spoke, none of the pain came through. Only the love. "You're going to come back to me, Nadia. You will. You're going to take them down from the inside, Elizabeth and the One Beneath. And then you're coming back to me." Mateo pulled her into his arms. "Promise me."

How could she promise what might not be possible? But that was exactly why she had to promise, Nadia realized. She had to promise it before she could believe it, and if she couldn't believe it, she couldn't make it real. "I promise, Mateo. I promise."

They kissed each other, a kiss almost terrible in its desperation. Nadia closed her eyes tightly and tried to believe this kiss wasn't their last.

EPILOGUE

TWO DAYS LATER, ON THANKSGIVING, VERLAINE FELT halfway normal again.

Only halfway. Her heart still ached every time she thought about Asa. The more she thought about what Nadia had done, the more she believed it was both the bravest and stupidest thing she'd ever heard of. Uncle Gary was still in the hospital, just for observation, so as cute as it was to see him and Uncle Dave being sweet to each other, her house was still empty most of the time. (Well, except for Smuckers, but even the snuggliest cat in the whole world couldn't make up for everything.)

More than that, Captive's Sound was clearly not exactly what it had been. Although the quarantine was due to be lifted tomorrow, people were still penned in. Most Thanksgiving dinners in town this year would come out of cans: yuck. But the bigger worry was how suspicious people were.

337

How they whispered among one another.

Everyone in town had seen just how strange things could get. How much longer could they deny the truth? How much longer would Elizabeth—and Nadia—remain hidden?

In midmorning, Verlaine put on her leopard-print coat and wrapped her white silk scarf around her head. Red lipstick, cat-eye sunglasses: perfect. She'd be overly chic for a Thanksgiving meal at the hospital cafeteria, but hey, at least that way it would feel like an occasion.

The land yacht was running on fumes, and Verlaine wasn't due to get her gasoline ration until tomorrow, when the stupid rationing would be over anyway, but rules were rules. It was about a half-hour walk to the hospital; she could manage.

But the day was the coldest they'd had yet, the first one that really felt like winter. The low clouds overhead were ominously gray, and sure enough, just as Verlaine closed her front door, she saw a snowflake land on her sleeve, bright against the leopard print.

"Oh, sure. Send the first snow just when I have a long walk outside." She scowled up at the sky—but really, she loved snow. The only question was whether she needed to trade in her beloved red Converse for snow boots. Not today, she figured, and she got started on her way.

As she walked along, she watched the soft fall of snow begin turning the town from its usual dingy, dilapidated state to the beautiful New England village it ought to have been. It was as though the snow erased the scars Elizabeth's magic had left behind and made the world new.

If only it were that easy, she thought.

The flakes wheeling slowly down were big and fat, large enough that when one landed on her sunglasses, she had to stop and wipe the lenses with the end of her scarf. Verlaine glanced up as she moved to put them back on—and saw Asa standing in front of her.

"Oh, my God," she whispered. Quickly she stashed her sunglasses in her coat pocket. "You're alive?"

"As alive as I ever was." His cynical smile was a shadow of its former self, but she was glad to see it nonetheless. "Which is to say, not all that much. But I'm back. Will that do?"

Verlaine took a couple of steps toward him, then stopped short. "What happened to you?"

Asa shrugged. His sleek, black jacket should have been too thin for the cold, but his unearthly warmth must have protected him. The snowflakes seemed to melt as soon as they touched him. "The One Beneath doubted my loyalty. So he showed me the price of disobedience."

She bit her lower lip. "The price?"

"Pain beyond imagining," he said, so simply that it made her shudder. "For days on end. The agony is meant to blot out any memories of the mortal world, or any bonds we might have created there. It's supposed to make us forget."

"But you didn't forget." Verlaine stepped toward him. "You didn't, or you wouldn't be here now."

Asa stepped closer to her. The snow beneath his feet melted instantly, leaving clear patches everywhere he'd stepped, and he seemed to be wreathed with wisps of fog. "No. I didn't forget."

Snowflakes caught on Verlaine's eyelashes and kissed her cheeks with cold. She felt as though she could hardly breathe. "I'm sorry you had to suffer for me."

"I'm not. Feeling all the pain was worth it, if it means I get to feel—everything else."

Yet again she swayed toward him, but stopped herself. "Are you free? Can you ever be free?"

He shook his head. "The battle's on now. The time draws near. As they command, I must obey. If they ask me to kill you, I'll have to do it." His voice choked off; it was the first moment that Verlaine realized he was as overwhelmed as she. "After that they wouldn't have to send me to hell. Every single second would be hell to me."

". . . As touching as that is, in that scenario, I'm actually more worried about me."

Asa laughed in what seemed to be genuine delight. "That's the greatest thing about you. No matter how the world tries to beat you down, you always stay focused on what matters most." The wind tugged at the edges of his black scarf; the way it rippled reminded her of his shadow being torn apart. "Forget me, Verlaine. It's the only way. And if I ever have to come for you, kill me with my blessing. I can't think of a better way to die."

"So, that's it." Verlaine's astonishment had been electrified into anger, and into something else she could hardly define, but it quickened her pulse, burned along her skin, shrank the entire world down to her and Asa in the middle of the swirling whiteness. "That's all we get. The little time we've had is all we'll ever have."

"Afraid so." He studied her so intently that she could no longer feel the cold. "But—if I might beg one favor—would you allow me one moment out of time?"

Verlaine took a deep breath, then nodded.

Asa clapped his hands together, and time came to a stop. Snowflakes hovered in all around them, frozen in place, making the whole world sparkle softly. He walked toward her, feet crunching on the snow now, because it couldn't melt without time, even though she could feel the heat of him coming closer. Then Asa took her in his arms.

The kiss was her first. Her only. Verlaine hadn't expected to react like this—going hot and cold at once, forgetting everything else, allowing every thought in her mind to slip away until she didn't know anyone or anything besides Asa. His mouth opened against hers, and she would have cried out, except that the sound was muffled by his kiss. Her arms slid around his waist as his hands came up to cradle her face.

So warm, she thought in a daze. *Like we're in the heart of a fire.*

Even though she knew this could never be, she couldn't be sad. Couldn't be angry. Verlaine's entire heart sang with happiness, and that happiness felt like the only thing that had ever been true.

They broke apart. She gasped for breath. Asa looked nearly as shaken as she felt. For a long moment neither of them could speak. Then he pulled back his hands and brought them together; time began again, and the snow resumed its gentle, swirling descent.

Asa's thumb brushed against her cheek, drawing a soft arc of heat. He whispered, "Kill me if you can."

And then he was gone—almost faster than the eye could see.

Once again she stood alone, the hospital still several minutes' walk away. She stared down at the bare places where he'd melted the snow, but the fresh flakes were already erasing those traces as though they'd never been.

Mateo's dad was still too nervous about the "seizure" to let Mateo mop the floors; that was pretty much it for a silver lining. But he still had to help out as La Catrina prepared to reopen. Today he was more or less alone in front, replacing the fall menu inserts with the ones for winter.

As he sat in one of the booths, patiently getting through the tedious job, he heard the front-door bells jingle. "Sorry, still closed," he called out—then saw that it was Faye Walsh standing at the door.

"Bad time?" she said.

"Uh, no." Though he was caught off-guard, Mateo decided to seize the moment. "Listen, you know Nadia only turned to Elizabeth because she had to."

"Yes." Faye walked closer. "But I also know she turned to Elizabeth, and that's not a path you turn back from."

"Don't doubt her. Nadia's stronger than you realize."

"Evil is stronger than *you* realize. But we're lucky, Mateo.

There's more to being a Steadfast than seeing magic, or helping our witches. More to it than even most witches know."

Hope sprang up inside him. "Do we have magic of our
own?" That would explain what had happened with Gage,
surely.

But Faye shook her head. "That's not how it works. We
have one power more valuable than any other, Mateo. We
can make our witches stronger. But we also can be the only
check on a witch's power. A witch's Steadfast can be the only
thing between her and ultimate darkness."

He remembered the powerful spells in her mother's Book
of Shadows. "Is that what you had to do?"

Faye didn't answer. "If I teach you the way to weaken
Nadia's powers—to destroy them—will you do it?"

A Steadfast could do that? Mateo had never dreamed that
could even be possible. To destroy Nadia's power . . .

"No," he said. "I won't."

Faye smiled then, and somehow the expression was kind.
"There might come a point when she'd wish you had."

"I trust Nadia. I believe in her."

"I know you do." She patted his shoulder before heading
back to the door. "But if you change your mind—"

The bells jingled, and she was gone. Mateo sat there for a
long moment. He knew he would never turn on Nadia, no
matter what.

But if he had to kill Elizabeth to save Nadia—if he had
to become a murderer, risk his own soul the way Nadia was
risking hers—he could do it.

❧ ❦

Across town, a few hours later, Nadia made her own journey on foot.

Her family had done their Thanksgiving meal at lunchtime. Since the elementary-school pageant had never occurred due to bird interference, Cole had given his mashed-potato speech to her and Dad; they'd applauded while he took his bows. Since the quarantine hadn't lifted in time to get makings for the traditional turkey and stuffing, they'd improvised based on what she'd been able to find in the back corners of the pantry. If pad thai wasn't a proper Thanksgiving meal, well, it ought to be.

In every way, her day had seemed totally normal. Everyone was in a better mood now that the sick had gotten well, and now that people could go in and out of town freely. Cole would have nightmares about birds for a long time to come, but he was doing okay, she thought, and Dad was in better spirits than he'd been all month. Nadia had smiled and pretended to celebrate along with them, but inside her heart was dying.

Every moment, she longed for Mateo. Every hour, she wanted to be with him. They still texted each other and spoke on the phone—that much was okay—but Nadia knew she had to stay away as much as possible. Just a few days in, and already that burden seemed unbearable.

But she would bear it. The only alternative was to give up any hope of seeing Mateo again, and that was something she'd never do.

Even worse was the knowledge of what waited for her

now. Yet Nadia walked on, trudging through the deepening snow, until she reached Elizabeth's house.

While so many of the other windows of homes in town glowed almost golden, hinting at the family celebrations going on inside, Elizabeth's house remained gray and cold. Nadia walked up the steps, feeling vaguely sick, and forced herself to knock on the door.

It swung open of its own accord. Nadia stepped inside cautiously, remembering the last time she'd been in this house—when Elizabeth's Book of Shadows had tried to kill her. But nothing attacked this time. Even the spiders seemed to have skittered off. The house remained utterly derelict inside, though some of the broken glass had been kicked aside.

Elizabeth sat in the middle of the floor, her Book of Shadows open in front of her. She didn't look up. "I had expected you before."

"You didn't say when to come."

"The One Beneath needs us," Elizabeth said. She glanced up, only her eyes moving. "You will learn to divine His purpose. You'll learn a great deal these next few weeks."

Nadia hesitated. "Why do you say 'these next few weeks'?"

"That's all the time this world has left. What comes after, during His glorious reign—we'll discover that together, you and I."

Despair clawed at Nadia's heart, but she refused to give way to it. Everything she learned now could turn into something she might use against Elizabeth later. Until the bitter end, there could always, always be hope.

Yes, she'd given up so much to be here—but her mother's words echoed in her mind, giving her comfort: *Sacrifices have their own power.*

She could only hope her sacrifices would be enough.

Nadia sat beside Elizabeth, who smiled in satisfaction and said, "Let us begin."